TARGET: NEW YORK

LEE JACKSON

SEVERN RIVER
PUBLISHING

Severn River Publishing
www.SevernRiverBooks.com

This is a work of fiction. Names, characters, businesses, places, events and incidents are either the products of the author's imagination or used in a fictitious manner. Any resemblance to actual persons, living or dead, or actual events is purely coincidental.

ISBN: 978-1-64875-573-6 (Paperback)

ALSO BY LEE JACKSON

The Reluctant Assassin Series

The Reluctant Assassin

Rasputin's Legacy

Vortex: Berlin

Fahrenheit Kuwait

Target: New York

The After Dunkirk Series

After Dunkirk

Eagles Over Britain

Turning the Storm

The Giant Awakens

Riding the Tempest

Driving the Tide

Never miss a new release! Sign up to receive exclusive updates from author Lee Jackson.

severnriverbooks.com/authors/lee-jackson

Dedicated to the Victims of Terror

PROLOGUE

Austin, Texas
March 1991

Klaus crashed through the bushes, searching for shelter from the epic blast that would seal his real name, Sahab Kadyrov, among those of the martyred heroes in the annals of Islam. He thrilled at the thought, although he regretted leaving this life. He found exhilarating the feel of breathing, the pulse of blood through his beating heart, and the strain of running through the forest. His life had been difficult, but he had relished much of the challenge. *They'll write songs about me in Mecca.*

He stumbled in his flight. He had lost his night goggles during the melee with Atcho, so he only saw silhouettes where occasional shafts of bright moonlight filtered below the canopy of trees. He tripped over a log. On recovering, he sensed that it might be large enough to provide at least a modicum of protection from the flash flame and searing heat of thousands of degrees that would be the least of what he could expect upon detonation.

He had heard Atcho calling to a search party and police to seek shelter, and as he lay down alongside the log, he grinned. *There will be many dead infidels tonight.*

He guessed that Atcho might have taken the suitcase bomb and tossed it over the cliffs. If that happened, Austin would be smothered in radioactive dirt from the mother of all shaped charges, and the notion of surviving behind the log would not be farfetched, although the after-effects of burns and radiation exposure were not pleasant to imagine. *Either way, I'll be a martyr.*

He looked at his watch. *Should be any second.* He took a deep breath and buried his face in his arms. A minute went by. Then another.

In the distance, he heard the wail of sirens and realized that there would be no martyrdom for him this night. More minutes passed, and a new sensation emerged—burning on his left buttock. He remembered screaming when Atcho had fired his pistol and struggling to keep Atcho's wrist from turning for an effective shot. And then Atcho had pulled the trigger.

Klaus sat up in disgust. Obviously, the bomb had not detonated. His brother's death would not yet be avenged. He would have no seventy-two virgins waiting, no celebrations among the faithful of Islam around the world for the mass of dead and maimed infidels in the greatest strike ever against the Great Satan. All he had to show for his efforts was a seared butt—barely a crease. Worse yet, Atcho and his wife still lived and were expecting a baby. He climbed to his feet and headed deeper into the forest.

Atcho ignored the pain in his badly burned hand, the result of grasping a hot metallic object for too long. He faced the fighters gathered around the conference table at his corporate headquarters. They stank from their search for Klaus and his bomb along the cliffs below Atcho's house last night.

"We can't wait for Klaus to surface again," he said. "He detonated a nuclear bomb. He penetrated the United States. And he hates that I'm still alive. He'll try again."

"What's your plan?" someone asked.

"To hunt him down."

1

Buenos Aires, Argentina
March 17, 1992

A red Ford F-100 pickup truck with a white camper shell rolled east behind a yellow and black Ford Falcon on tree-lined Arroyo in a tranquil neighborhood, heading toward the intersection with Suipacha. The vehicle cut close to the street's edge and parked a few feet from the side entrance of the stately three-story Israeli Embassy. Its tires squealed against the curb, casting off an odor of burnt rubber.

Across the street, those were the last sounds that Father Juan Carlos Brumana heard as he strolled in front of Mater Admirabilis Cathedral toward the adjoining children's school. The blast of two hundred and twenty pounds of high explosives and shrapnel in the back of the pickup hurled a chunk of debris from the church, striking the priest and killing him instantly. It ripped the façade off the embassy and blew through the concrete and marble structure, sending it skyward in a cloud of dust.

The concussive force caught the Ford, heaved it into the air, and shredded it into thousands of unrecognizable pieces that rained to the ground, along with dust and rubble, revealing a gaping emptiness that formerly housed the embassy. The building's rear wall remained upright, still supporting sagging fragments of its corrugated roof. Remnants of the second floor spilled onto the first, bright red splotches identifying where human remains and body parts lay.

The roar of the explosion and its aftermath gave way to moans and cries of agony. Seconds later, wailing sirens joined them as emergency vehicles rushed to the scene. Good Samaritans waded in to rescue those they could, while onlookers formed a wary half-ring at the edge of the debris field.

Among the growing crowd, Klaus watched. He had known the time and place of the attack and had exulted on seeing the truck approach, pull alongside the ceremonial entrance, and disappear in a shock wave of dust and rubble. Now he allowed himself to be jostled aside as police moved in to clear the crowd and make way for rescue teams.

He moved aside to watch for a few minutes and then returned to his hotel to make a call. "It's done," he said. "Where should I go next?"

"Come back here," the deep voice replied. "I'll see you in a couple of days."

Two days later, Klaus climbed the wide stairs into a palatial home on the outskirts of Riyadh, Saudi Arabia. It belonged to Yousef, his *hawaladar,* the man who moved Klaus' money to wherever he needed it on short notice.

"Welcome, *Habibi.*" Yousef greeted him with the traditional exchange of kisses on the cheeks and led him to a seating area in a courtyard amidst swaying palms and tinkling fountains. A boy brought out a brass tray with small, clear glasses and a pot of tea.

"Tell me about the bomb in Buenos Aires," Yousef said, tugging at his traditional white Saudi garb and settling his portly form onto an ornate couch. He tossed his head to move aside the red and white headdress.

"Not much to tell. The operation went like clockwork. The embassy was completely destroyed. Twenty-nine people were killed, including the wives of two Israeli diplomats and two other staff members. Two hundred and forty-two were wounded. I'd call that a success. Thank you for arranging so that I could observe."

Yousef acknowledged his words with a slight head bow. "Let's talk about your next active mission."

Klaus gestured impatiently. "I'm glad to be with Al-Qaeda, but I have my own targets. That was the deal Osama bin Laden promised. I spent most of the last year training his recruits at the camps in Sudan. I'm tired of that. I want to return to action. I have my own money and three nuclear bombs. My name is still Sahab Kadyrov, and I want to strike for Chechnya."

"I know." Yousef nodded despite the slight edge to his voice. "But let's review the deal with Al-Qaeda." He settled his eyes directly on Klaus. "We offered to buy one of your bombs for a particular operation. The agreement included you going to our camps in Sudan to train a team there—and instructing our recruits in advanced military tactics."

Klaus could barely conceal his vehemence. "But that part of the bargain was so I could hand-pick and train my own team for wherever I wanted to use it—and I choose Moscow."

Yousef stirred with a hint of impatience. "I'm your friend. Don't be angry with me. The Soviet Union is history, gone, voted out of existence three months ago. Detonating one of your bombs there would be a waste, and anyway, there is talk that Chechnya will declare its independence from Russia soon."

"Russia." Klaus smirked. "The great northern bear will take only enough time in its cave to lick its wounds. Whoever emerges in the Kremlin as the strong man will not let Chechnya go—it's at the center of too much economic activity that benefits Moscow. We need to strike before anyone there consolidates power."

Yousef took a sip of tea while watching Klaus' face. "I understand, but a bomb in Russia would be wasted. Your goal was to destroy the Soviet Union, but it came down under its own pressure." He reached over and nudged Klaus. "Your higher objective is to spread Islam, is that not so?"

Klaus nodded.

"Let Al-Qaeda help you. Only one superpower remains. After it is brought down, the way will be clear to bring shariah everywhere and mold the Chechnya of your dreams."

Klaus regarded Yousef skeptically. He sat up and leaned forward, and when he spoke, his voice quivered with urgency. "I want to strike for Chechnya now."

Yousef shot him a cryptic smile. "Think of the US nuclear weapons at our disposal. You'll just order Russia to let Chechnya go, and it will have to comply. Can you wait nine months?"

Klaus stared at him in annoyance. "The things I do for Islam," he growled. "What's going on?"

"We're sending you to observe another operation—actually, two of them."

Startled, Klaus nudged Yousef's elbow. "Why? I know how to deliver bombs." He shrugged. "Look, I don't mean to be disrespectful, but I'm a *jihadist*, a son of Islam who proved his worth. I don't have patience for small talk or touring the world. Would you please tell me what you want me to do?"

Yousef cast a somber glance his way and then took a sip of tea. "You are certainly a worthy fighter," he said, "but let's face facts. You have not hit a target successfully. The coup in Moscow failed. The strike in Berlin failed. In Kuwait—"

"I get it." Klaus scowled. "We don't need to go through the history, although, for the record, I was not a principal in the Moscow operation. And you forget that I captured a plutonium bomb complete with fuel, then learned how to make them and get more fuel."

"Granted"—Yousef nodded—"and you're doing an excellent job with our recruits in Sudan. You bring expertise we didn't have." He took another sip of tea. "But that's not your greatest value, and that's not why you joined the *jihad*."

"Exactly." Klaus sipped from his own small glass while gathering his thoughts and then leaned forward again. "Allah put in my hands the means to bring down infidel nations. That's fact, not arrogance. I must live up to the faith bestowed on me."

"I understand and agree." Yousef spoke quietly, firmly. "On the other hand, victory has not yet been yours. We want to determine why. When you strike again, you must succeed."

Klaus leaned back into the couch. "Is Al-Qaeda doubting me?" His eyes burned with frustration.

Yousef waved his hands in a declining motion, then grasped Kraus' elbow. "Not at all. We're trying to help you, and by helping you, we help Islam." He pursed his lips in thought. "What do you think caused your missions to fail?"

Klaus grimaced. "That's easy. Atcho interfered."

Yousef studied Klaus. "He's not a superman. Resourceful, yes. Tenacious, absolutely. But he has no more ability to move about this planet and affect things than you do. He is a private citizen?" He waited for Klaus' nod. "Then how has Atcho managed to be out front each time? If we can determine that, we can limit your exposure so that you reach the target undetected. Does that make sense?"

Reluctantly, Klaus nodded, though his irritation was still evident. "But why did you have me travel all the way to Buenos Aires? That was a Hezbollah operation, and we're Sunni."

Yousef's bulky stomach jiggled under his robes as he chuckled. He shook Klaus' shoulder. "Patience, my brother. We won't win our *jihad* in a day. Hezbollah is not our friend, but it is the enemy of our enemy and will help us destroy the infidel. When that is done, we can settle disputes among Muslims. Meanwhile, Hezbollah will sell us their experience, and they have fought the Jews and their allies for a long time."

Klaus' head jerked up. "You don't call them filthy Jews and godless infidels?"

"Filthy Jews, then, but I don't like to be redundant or get off subject. The point is, we sent you to observe the bombing in Buenos Aires so you could see the operation's successes and failures. We thought maybe you could offer advice or learn something useful from it."

"What's to learn? A guy drives up in a truck and pushes a button."

Yousef frowned. "You're making my point. Planning and executing a mission like that is not so easy. The bombing was revenge for the assassination of Hezbollah Secretary General Sayed Abbas al-Musawi in southern Lebanon by the Israelis back in February. In only a month, Hezbollah conceived, planned, and executed.

"You saw how careful the team was in the South American Tri-Border Region. Hezbollah already has a significant presence there. They have men, equipment, money—they can obtain anything and move it with ease. They knew the embassy's location and the traffic patterns. To this day, the authorities don't know if the driver escaped or was blown up." Yousef paused momentarily, cocking his head to one side. "Let me ask the question again. How did Atcho get ahead of you each time?"

Klaus shook his head. "He's smart, I'll give him that."

"Didn't you tell me that he and his wife were connected to the CIA?"

Klaus nodded.

"Then he had an organization behind him with intelligence capabilities that extended into the army and the FBI. That's why you can't act like a lone wolf. He stopped you in Berlin, Kuwait, and Texas. Walk me through each. We need to figure out how he anticipated your moves."

For the next hour, they pored over the details of the three operations, looking for mistakes Klaus might have made, errant signals he could have broadcast—anything that might have led Atcho and his team to the conclusions that had resulted in Klaus' failures. Finally, Yousef held up a hand.

"Three conclusions stand out to me. In all three places, he knew your objectives and how you intended to achieve them—not down to the fine detail, but enough to guess how you could accomplish them. In Berlin, he knew you wanted to stop the Wall from coming down. In Kuwait, since you were not active during US combat operations, he knew you had moved the bombs to the Middle East and figured out your plan to blow up the oilfields. And in Austin"—he arched his eyebrows—"well, guessing you would come after him at home was not difficult. He knew the nuclear threat you carried in your briefcase, and with that he could get intelligence and logistical support all the way to the president, which he probably did.

"And finally, Atcho knows you—your strengths and weaknesses, your capabilities and habits. Fortunately, you've been out of sight for the last fourteen months, so he must have lost track of you. But if you become visible again..." Yousef leaned forward to emphasize his point. "It is better that you learn new habits and stay invisible."

Klaus, listening quietly while Yousef spoke, now reacted angrily. "He killed my brother. I will have my revenge."

Yousef raised his hands in a placating gesture. "And you will have it. No one will take that away from you. Al-Qaeda promised assistance. But would it not be better to exact your vengeance while killing millions of infidels?"

Stunned, Klaus caught his breath. "Millions? How?"

Yousef leaned in closer. "Listen to me carefully, brother. We have a mission coming up early next year that suits you to perfection. However, it *must* succeed. Since your underground nuclear test in Afghanistan last year, the price of black-market plutonium has skyrocketed. We cannot afford to waste your bombs."

Klaus nodded.

"We want you to observe two more planned bombings." Seeing Klaus react with irritation, Yousef continued, "The emphasis is working in a team, learning new ways to communicate, and keeping operational security. We want you to observe how it's working in other operations." He nudged Klaus. "We are hitting bigger and bigger targets."

Klaus let out a long breath. "If I agree, what then?"

"As I recall, you have three plutonium devices remaining?"

Klaus nodded again.

"We will provide the intelligence, logistics, personnel support, and funds. We have the target. You will place your bombs."

2

Austin, Texas
One week later

"Terrorists have attacked seven times so far this year—and it's only March," Atcho said. "That number doesn't include the attacks Klaus tried to pull off in Kuwait and here in Austin. We know he wasn't involved in the others because he was busy with his own targets. We have to track his location. His bombs make him the most dangerous terrorist on the planet."

"So far he hasn't had a successful attack," Ivan Chekov interjected, "and he's made three attempts."

"That's because Atcho beat him each time," Burly said. "But we can only close him down permanently by getting in front of him—anticipate where he's going next."

The three men sat around a conference room table inside headquarters at Atcho's company, Advance Power-Source Technologies. The company manufactured a battery substitute that was stronger, lighter, and more durable. The product had proven itself in the recent Gulf War in Kuwait to expel Saddam Hussein. As a result, the defense department had doubled its orders and foreign armies were clamoring to purchase it.

A little-known by-product the company produced, the NUKEX, was designed to neutralize briefcase-sized nuclear bombs. The device had low demand but was employed twice.

Atcho's company had developed the NUKEX prior to him purchasing the firm. It worked by generating and projecting intense heat through proprietary alloys to a point several inches below the device itself. The object was to melt the trigger mechanism on small bombs before the radioactive fuel had reached critical mass.

The device's effectiveness was proven, but its operational limitations required it to be applied by hand. Atcho's wife, Sofia, had been the first to use the NUKEX in an operational setting, melting the trigger on a plutonium bomb planted on a cargo plane flying from Novosibirsk, Siberia, to Moscow. Atcho had used a NUKEX to douse a nuclear device planted outside his home, resulting in his badly burned hand.

As he listened to the discussion, Atcho massaged his injured hand. It was healing nicely but still hurt.

He had bought majority ownership of the company two years earlier when its founders had sought second-round financing, selling many of his real estate holdings in Washington, DC, to secure funding. By then, his background was legendary: West Point graduate, native of Cuba, airborne ranger, resistance fighter against Fidel Castro, freed political prisoner, successful entrepreneur, honored by Ronald Reagan... The passage of years had creased the corners of his eyes and mouth and added lines to the strong features of his face. Silver strands streaked his hair. He leaned his muscular frame across the table.

"How do we track Klaus?"

The door opened, and Atcho's wife, Sofia, entered. She moved lithely across the room, her hair falling in dark, lustrous locks that framed sparkling green eyes over a delicate nose and full lips parted in a smile.

"How's the baby?" Atcho asked. *I still catch my breath every time I see her.*

"He's fine." She grinned. "Isabel is watching him, along with your granddaughter." She laughed as she spoke, and her eyes sparkled.

Isabel was Atcho's daughter from his late wife who had died in childbirth. Kidnapped at the age of four and returned while Fidel Castro had held Atcho in prison, she had not known her father again until ten years ago—by then a fully grown woman. She was now visiting Austin with her small daughter while her husband, a US Army officer, traveled to Europe and the Far East on military business.

Atcho laughed. "My six-month-old son and three-year-old grand-daughter playing together. That should be interesting."

"It's fun to watch." Sofia chuckled, then turned to greet the others in the room. "What have I missed?"

"We started discussing how to track Klaus," Burly said, arching his eyebrows as he addressed the group. "Let me point out that because both Sofia and I are officially retired and neither of us is currently contracted with either the CIA or the State Department, our access to classified information is limited to nonexistent. That won't change unless we get one or more of the intelligence agencies on board, and that won't happen unless we come up with something solid."

"I still have my clearances through the company," Atcho said.

"You don't have the designation for sensitive compartmented information that would keep you current on this case," Burly replied.

"Got it." Atcho had known Burly since they had fought together at the Bay of Pigs in Cuba thirty years ago. In the last two years, they had worked jointly on four black ops in concert with covert agencies. Burly was a big, balding man, proud of his Irish ancestry and his years at the CIA. He had been Atcho's case officer.

Atcho turned to Sofia. "What do you think?"

She had been a covert CIA field officer, her cover being a senior intelligence supervisor at the State Department, and she had participated in all four of Atcho's operations with Burly. During a recent cutback in CIA personnel, she had taken an early retirement package in order to raise her baby boy.

She rubbed her forehead. "This one is going to be tough. We might get cooperation from the agencies on an informal basis, but without clearances or a need-to-know, any of their employees giving us classified information would be breaking the law. That could mean prison time for them. Let me think about how to do this."

"While you're thinking, let me add something," Ivan broke in. As a former KGB officer who had defected to the US two years ago, he had risked his life to save his family during a coup attempt in Moscow before the fall of the Soviet Union. Because Ivan was instrumental in averting the conspiracy, the Chairman of the Soviet Communist Party, Mikhail Gorbachev, had allowed him to emigrate with his wife and son to the US. He had worked with Atcho, Burly, and Sofia in their joint operations and won their friendship, loyalty, and respect. When Atcho had bought the company, he had helped Ivan form a security firm and contracted with him for those services.

Watching him, Atcho smiled. Ivan reminded him of a tough, physically fit version of the comedian Bob Newhart. "Go ahead."

Ivan glanced up. He had always been intrigued with and loved American Western lore. To him, Atcho brought to mind Gary Cooper's character in *High Noon*, a man with the cares of the world on his shoulders who could wreak untold destruction at any second. He pursed his lips.

"When the Berlin Wall fell and East Germany opened up, thousands of Stasi officers headed west." He spoke with a perfect Midwestern American accent, courtesy of extensive training. "The Soviet Union is winding down, and the same thing could happen with KGB officers." He shook his head. "Much as I hate to admit it, many of my former colleagues are known for low ethical standards. Between ex-Stasi and ex-KGB, that could mean selling off state secrets and assets to criminals—including nuclear technology and fuel."

"He's right," Sofia added. "With the Soviet breakup, we have high concern about safeguarding nuclear stockpiles. If black-market guys want to buy some, now's the time to put out feelers and bids."

Atcho grimaced. "And Klaus already knows how to get it."

They sat in silence for a few minutes. "Let's start with what we know," Sofia broke in. "Klaus' real name is Sahab Kadyrov. He became known as Klaus after he deserted the KGB and went to East Berlin before the Wall fell. He's a Chechen Muslim who hates the Russians and the Americans as much as he hates Israel." Her gaze bored into Atcho. "He hates you most of all."

Atcho nodded grimly. "That's what I get for killing his brother."

"He managed to get to the Middle East and hook up with Al-Qaeda,"

Sofia went on. "He brought along five nuclear suitcase bombs and several million dollars he stole from the East German government just before the Wall fell. We think he ran an underground test with one bomb, and we believe he can replicate them. Our best guess is that he still has three of them."

"He escaped both the local police and the FBI here in Austin," Burly chimed in. "We assume either he slipped out of the US or is lying low."

"I think he left the country," Ivan said. "He only brought one bomb into the US. He wants to secure the others and re-set for another target."

The other three nodded.

"How do we find him?" Atcho asked.

"We know he got his bombs into Saudi Arabia," Sofia replied. "That's probably where he hid them. That's a starting point."

"Agreed, but I had another thought," Atcho said. "I'm sure you all heard the report about a car-bomb attack on the Israeli Embassy in Buenos Aires last week. The driver wasn't found, and authorities don't know if he escaped or blew up in the vehicle. The street was empty except for one priest who was killed by flying debris, so there were no eyewitnesses. Israel is the main target of *jihadists*. Maybe we should take a look there."

Burly listened attentively. "I have a few contacts in the Mossad. I'll call. If they don't know about Klaus yet, we should clue them in."

"That's a long shot," Sofia cut in. "Hezbollah claimed credit for the Buenos Aires attack. It's a Shia organization. We think Klaus is Sunni; Al-Qaeda is too. They would compete with Hezbollah."

Burly arched his eyebrows. "Hold on. We can hope things stay that way, but Al-Qaeda is a new organization, while Hezbollah has been around awhile. That guy, Osama bin Laden, brings a lot of cash, and Hezbollah has built up experience and technical skill in their strikes against Israel in Lebanon. If those two groups can agree on who the enemy is, they might help each other. Klaus proved that he can penetrate the US and bring a nuclear bomb with him."

The others eyed Burly grimly.

"Make the call," Atcho said.

3

Tel Aviv, Israel
April 1992

Eitan Chasin hurried down the hall into his boss' office at Mossad headquarters. Tall, slender, and in his early thirties, he was younger than his fresh face and dark hair suggested. He carried a dust covered open cardboard box with electronic devices and dangling wires protruding from the top, and he scrunched a thin file between the side of his chest and arm.

"Sir, you should look at these."

The head of operations, Jaron Bryk, glanced up from documents he had already been reading, clearly annoyed. "You're new here. I get that. And you came over from the Kidon department. We're impressed. That doesn't mean you can barge into my office at will. I spent time there too."

Eitan fought down an urge to retort. Kidon was the most secret of Mossad's numerous departments. Often characterized in the media as a band of assassins, its operators were posted worldwide to combat terrorism and anyone posing a threat to Israel. Only the best operatives from Israeli special forces were recruited into Kidon.

"You're right. I apologize," he retorted. "You can see these later." He started toward the door. "Don't wait too long."

Bryk caught Eitan's irritation. "Wait." He leaned forward in his seat and waved Eitan to a chair in front of his desk. "I haven't been out of the field long myself. Sorry. This must be urgent."

Eitan crossed the room but remained standing. "It's about last week's bombing in Buenos Aires. I've gone through some of the rubble brought here for analysis. I might have found something." He set the box down on the desk.

Bryk peered at the jumble of electronics and then looked up at Eitan. "That's a little below your pay grade, isn't it? We've already had people take a look at this material."

Eitan sat down. "Have you heard of a terrorist the Americans refer to as Klaus?"

Bryk leaned back, searching his memory. He was approaching middle age as if the concept did not apply to him—full of energy and always ready for the next turn of the screw. His trim build and toned muscles were at odds with the headquarters' collegial air. Despite his current billet, he dressed for the field, ready to hit the streets at any moment. He understood the concept of having experienced operators in leadership positions and the existential need to gather intelligence accurately and analyze effectively. Knowing that, however, did not make coming into the sedate atmosphere any easier.

"Show me what you've got."

Eitan set the box on the desk and took the file from under his arm. "These are the remnants of the embassy's video surveillance machines." He gestured at the wreckage of electronics. "As you can see, they were pretty much destroyed, including the storage cards and backup units. I sent them to our technical geniuses for analysis anyway, and they managed to extract these." He opened the file and spread three blurry photos across the desk. "You can't make out any detail on these, but you can see down the inter-secting streets, and we captured the timestamps. Look at this dark blotch. It's located catty-corner from the embassy and down a little way. From there, a person could easily observe the side entrance without being threat-ened by the bomb, and that blotch looks like it could be a man."

Bryk peered at it. "So?"

"I sent a message to the embassy security personnel—obviously, they're working from a different location. I asked them to check with authorities to see if any other surveillance picked up an image at that time and place. They sent back this."

He moved the spread-out photos aside and showed Bryk an image of a man in profile.

"That's a close-up of the blotch. Look at how he stands backed against the wall and the direction of his view. He's watching the embassy."

Bryk picked up the photo and brought it closer to his eyes. "Light complexion. Curly hair. Heavy mustache. It's not very clear, though. What time was it captured?"

"Two minutes before the blast. He stays there the entire time, and that is not a sightseeing area."

"Maybe he was waiting to be picked up."

Eitan nodded. "Maybe, but look at this." He slid another photo forward. "Here he is among onlookers. He's an able-bodied man, on site at the moment of impact, and he does nothing to help. On the contrary"—he showed Bryk another image—"he walks away."

Bryk studied the photographs a while longer. "Who is Klaus, and what makes you think that's him in the pictures?"

Eitan exposed one more image, this time showing a man whose facial features undeniably resembled those of the subject in the other photos. "This is Klaus. He is a terrorist known to German intelligence and the CIA —a deserter from the old Soviet KGB who trained with the Spetsnaz. He escaped from the East when the Berlin Wall fell. He is confirmed to have participated in three failed bomb attacks."

Bryk shrugged and tossed the photos he was holding back on the desk. "Do you think he triggered the bomb in Buenos Aires?"

Eitan shook his head. "He doesn't come up in any of our monitoring before that event. I think he was there to observe the attack and its effects."

"Trying to improve his craft," Bryk mused. "Pray that he doesn't. If he keeps failing, he can't present much of a threat to us. What's our interest?"

Eitan took a deep breath and let it out slowly. "He's a Chechen and an avowed Muslim. He hates the US and Russia equally, and of course he hates Israel too. His bombs failed because the Americans stopped him before he could detonate—but they were never able to catch him. They put concerted effort on him because"—he took another deep breath—"his bombs are nuclear."

Bryk sat upright in his chair, his attention now fully engaged. He picked up the pictures and studied them again, one by one. "Where is he now?"

"We don't know for sure. We have sightings of someone who looks like him in the Sudan training camps, but no confirmation that he's there."

"How did you come across him?"

"A retired CIA friend was brought in twice to stop this guy. He contacted me about Klaus, who disappeared after each attempt and stayed hidden until the next attack. Klaus almost detonated one in the oil well fires in Kuwait last year, and then in Texas a few weeks later."

Bryk's eyes narrowed. "I heard about that one in Kuwait. Is he part of Hezbollah? They claimed bragging rights for the embassy job."

Eitan sucked in his breath and blew it out. "Well, no. He's Sunni." He watched Bryk's reaction. "We think Klaus is closer to Al-Qaeda, but in fact, he's somewhat of a lone operator. He could be a catalyst for more cooperative action between Hezbollah and Al-Qaeda."

"Hmm." Bryk examined the clearest photo. "The CIA thinks he's the guy in those pictures in Buenos Aires?"

"That's jumping a little ahead. Since the Texas event, the Americans kept up an active search for him, but until this came in, they didn't know where to look, and we didn't know about him." Eitan indicated a few pages stapled together in the file folder. "I've summarized the situation for you in this report."

Bryk scanned the first page. "What do you want us to do?"

"Assign me to the case. Let me meet with my CIA contact. I'll suggest to him that we go together to Buenos Aires to see what we can figure out."

"What specifically are you looking for?"

"We need to understand the tie-ins. The Buenos Aires operation belonged to Hezbollah. If that was Klaus, then he links Al-Qaeda to Hezbollah. Hezbollah's focus is Lebanon, but now they're hitting us in Argentina. That means two things: Hezbollah is going for a global strike capability, and they are moving toward cooperation with Al-Qaeda. That should be worrisome. The two organizations are fierce enemies on opposite sides of the Sunni-Shia split. If they start collaborating..."

Bryk sat forward, disturbed. "What do they bring to each other?"

"As the old saying goes," Eitan said, "'the enemy of my enemy is my friend.' They both seek the destruction of Israel and the US. Al-Qaeda brings lots of money. Hezbollah contributes training and technical experience. They might revert to fighting each other at some point, but between now and then, they can wreak havoc on us and our allies."

"Any chance that Klaus was in Buenos Aires on his own? He seems to offer know-how."

Eitan pursed his lips and shook his head. "I don't see it. For him to be there at the precise moment of the bombing, he had to be informed by Hezbollah. Despite his technical skill, he's a newcomer on the terror scene. He wouldn't have the contacts to know about that hit on his own. A Chechen wouldn't gravitate to Hezbollah because of his Sunni background. Regardless, he has suitcase nukes, and that should worry us."

"Because you think Klaus will eventually make his way to Israel with his bombs?"

"That's a given. My CIA friend thinks he's Al-Qaeda, and he has the ability to devastate us in our homeland."

"If he can get through our defenses."

"Many have."

Bryk eyed Eitan. "I thought your CIA friend was retired. What's he doing in the middle of this?"

"He *is* retired. He was a senior officer and goes active on a contract basis for specific missions. He was on the case for each of Klaus' previous attempts and helped thwart him. This tie-in to Buenos Aires was generated by his own initiative. He knew about the bombing and got curious—a 'leaving no stone unturned' inquiry. He pointed me in the direction of what to look for."

"Why not let the Mossad teams down there handle it?"

"Because they're concentrating on Argentina and the Muslim population in the Brazil/Argentina/Paraguay border region. This looks like a global thrust, and we're still gathering information. There's no operation on the table yet, and I know the background and parties. Faster ramp-up."

"What about the Sudan connection? Who found Klaus in the training camps?"

"We did, but we haven't confirmed the ID yet. My CIA friend doesn't know about that detail. Since the US is moving toward electronic snooping, with less reliance on boots on the ground, we have more access into Sudan. I sent several of these images to operatives in Kabul, and they located the man we think is Klaus in one of the camps."

Bryk scanned the remaining two pages of the report. "You've been busy. When did you want to leave?"

Eitan grinned. "I have a reservation on El Al for this evening."

Bryk smacked his lips skeptically as his eyes bored into Eitan's. "Keep in mind who you work for. Give up as little information as possible and get all you can." He signaled his approval with a nod and a wave.

Eitan rolled his eyes even as he shot Bryk a thumbs-up on the way out the door.

Burly called Atcho's office on a secure line from an FBI field office outside Washington, DC. "We might have a nibble in Buenos Aires."

"When do we leave?"

"You tell me. You could be gone a while. Do you have someone who can run the company in your absence?"

"He's already on the job. Let's leave tonight."

4

Iguazú Falls, Argentina
Four days later

Atcho gazed across the magnificent Iguazú Falls spanning the border between Argentina and Brazil. Tons of water rushing furiously over rugged cliffs on both sides of the river created clouds of spray as far as he could see, their pounding on the surface below filling his ears. The resulting droplets worked their way into his hood and down his back, soaking his shirt despite a heavy rain slicker. He shivered.

Only ten miles to the left of where he stood with Burly and Eitan was the border of Paraguay. "This is gorgeous," he yelled at Eitan over the roar of the falls, "but what are we doing here?"

"Enjoy," Eitan called back. "We're tourists, and we need to look like tourists. Smile, take pictures, look amazed. Point at things. We'll talk later."

Atcho's shoulders slumped. As he turned to view the falls again, he caught Burly's eye and telegraphed his skepticism.

The three men sat in a small hotel in Puerto Iguazú, Argentina, on a veranda away from prying ears. Two hours had passed since their trip to the falls.

"Why are we here?" Atcho asked politely, though his impatience showed. He refrained from glaring at Eitan, who appeared twenty years his junior.

Startled, Eitan shifted his eyes toward Burly. "I thought you wanted to track the man you showed me in the picture."

Burly leaned back and smiled. "Sorry. Atcho flew down from Texas, and I came in from DC. We flew separately from Buenos Aires to the Tri-Border Region. We haven't had a lot of time to talk."

Eitan looked back and forth between Atcho and Burly, his expression inscrutable. "I know some of your background," he said to Atcho. "Burly sent a summary and I went through what's in the public record. He told me some of your training and operational experience. I'm taking his word that you can handle yourself. I should tell you that we are already in the middle of intelligence gathering, and mistakes here could be fatal."

Atcho sat back, feeling chastised but not quite understanding why. "I'm sure you know what you're doing," he said with a tinge of sarcasm, "but we're after a man with powerful weapons intending to lay waste to both of our countries. He specifically threatened me and my family. I don't have time for sightseeing."

Eitan fought down exasperation, but his expression did not change. He turned to Burly. "Are you sure he's up to this?"

Burly froze, and so did Atcho. Burly alternated his view between his two companions. The air suddenly felt thick despite the seasonal chill of approaching winter and the high altitude. "This is my fault," he said. "Atcho is new to working with the Mossad. I should have taken time to explain."

"Then let me enlighten at the outset," Eitan cut in, his voice icy. "We wouldn't be having this conversation here, in this place, if members of the local team hadn't already cleared it. I don't know who they are, and we'll probably never meet, but if we do, we'll use aliases. They are out now, as we speak, gathering the intelligence we need, and they're doing it at personal risk. I'll get a report tomorrow via a dead drop.

"Meanwhile, our job is to get a ground sense of the area. We're tourists, and we'll drink and laugh and act silly, but not so much that we draw attention. While we do that, we'll take in every detail we can. Do you know anything about this place you're in?"

Dumbfounded, Atcho returned Eitan's steady gaze with an unfamiliar feeling of uncertainty. "I-I can't say that I do. I—"

With barely concealed disgust, Eitan cut him off. "Then let me educate you. It's important for you to know what you've wandered into."

Atcho leaned forward. "Go ahead," he said evenly.

Eitan glanced quickly at Burly before addressing Atcho. "This area is called the Tri-Border Region because—"

"That much I know," Atcho said. "It's bounded by Puerto Iguazú in Argentina, Foz do Iguaçu in Brazil, and Ciudad del Este in Paraguay."

"Exactly," Eitan said, his agitation ebbing a bit, "and if not for the borders, the three towns would almost form one good-sized city. This is an area where all three countries are sovereign, but no one rules. Laws are not enforced except as required to protect the tourist trade, and the bad guys will even help out on that when needed, like the mob did in the early days of Las Vegas. The intent is to keep tourists in the dark about nefarious activity.

"This is where Nazi war criminals escaped to after World War II to evade trial, so it has a history. The borders create opportunities and attract illicit activity. Hell, you can walk between the three countries here without carrying papers."

Eitan paused, gathering his thoughts. "Most people can't show you on a map where Paraguay is, but this Tri-Border Region is a big deal. The population is over half a million and growing at boomtown rates. It's a free-trade zone with established banks, but the area is largely lawless, a great environment for terrorist and criminal activity, and when their interests meet, well..." He shrugged. "The Brazilians and Argentines like it because it's a cheap place to buy electronics. The region is a melting pot of cultures, including Portuguese and Spanish, of course, but also Chinese and Korean.

"One of the largest Muslim populations in South America is here too; most are from Lebanon, but a lot are Palestinian. They have their own schools and clubs, and they live in gated communities, so penetrating them is difficult. We have specialists who take care of that. On the Brazilian side are Syrians, Egyptians, and some from other Arabic countries. They are prosperous and influential here.

"We're getting reports of duty-free transactions conducted by both Hezbollah and Hamas. They supply Colombian consumers with cheap products, and the profits fund their terror enterprises." He leaned back and wiped his eyes as if to shut out the scale of what he had described.

"Tourism is big," he continued, "especially with the Iguazú Falls only ten miles away, so the population is always transient. That's the legit side, and the authorities, such as they are, cooperate with the darker elements to ensure an atmosphere that won't turn tourists away.

"On the illegal side, drug smuggling, money laundering, gunrunning, prostitution, human trafficking, and document forgery are everywhere, but most of the money coming into the area is from Lebanese donations— Hezbollah. Paraguay has a weak, corrupt government, and all three countries have poor banking transparency laws. That makes this a perfect place for terrorist and organized crime financial networks to operate undetected, exchange tactical tradecraft, raise and launder money, and cover their trails, with huge sums sent out every day. In fact, we've identified local agents of Al-Qaeda, Hezbollah, Al-Jihad, and al-Muqawama. Iran's active here too."

"I get the picture," Atcho broke in. "What does that have to do with us?"

Eitan inhaled, curbing a retort. "We think this is where the planning and coordination for the attack in Buenos Aires took place. If Klaus had any involvement with it, he would have been inserted into the operation here." He stopped talking, eyeing Atcho in silence.

Atcho leaned back and stretched, looking out at the cold night sky. "I understand. Now, will you tell us what's going on while we're being tourists?"

Eitan smiled wanly. "Burly told me some of your story. I know you came from Cuba, and about your actions at the Bay of Pigs, your years in prison, and the assassination plot you aborted. I know what you did in Siberia, in Berlin when the Wall came down, and what took place in Kuwait."

"That's great. I know nothing about you."

"I'm not important. What is important is that you understand how Mossad works. We admire your confidence and successes, but if we were to describe them in a word, it would be 'cowboy.'"

Atcho chuckled. "A Cuban cowboy. You wouldn't be the first. My wife accuses me of rushing in where only fools go. In my defense, I didn't get involved with intelligence willingly, and I never sought out a mission. They always seem to find me." He tilted his head in contemplation. "Come to think of it, I did set out on this one deliberately. We have to find and stop Klaus. Get those bombs away from him."

"I'm going to brag on you a bit, Eitan," Burly interrupted. "I think Atcho would feel a lot better knowing your pedigree." He chuckled. "You *do* look a little wet behind the ears." Without waiting for a response, he turned to Atcho. "Are you familiar with the Kidon?"

Atcho shook his head.

"'Kidon' means 'the tip of the spear.' It's the name of the most secretive department of the Mossad. There's a lot of myth mixed in with some truth about foreign operations, assassinations, and the like, but when those activities are ascribed to Mossad, most people don't know that they mean Kidon. To apply for Kidon, a prospective recruit will have been active in the Israeli Defense Forces for many years, culminating in training and serving with the Israeli special forces. Out of the best of those, Kidon takes its few. Eitan is one of those."

Atcho turned to study Eitan while Burly continued.

"Once selected, the new Kidon recruit goes through two years of extensive training on surveillance, counter-surveillance, and hand-to-hand combat more intense than your basic commando. They learn and practice spy craft from every angle, and when finished, they're assigned to teams, mostly operating far from home, and usually for a three-year stretch.

"The Mossad believes that the people at the top must come from field operatives, because only then can they make smart decisions based on first-hand experiences. They know what their people in the field go through.

"Eitan has already done all that. He's assigned to headquarters because it's his turn. My point: he knows what he's doing."

For a few moments, the veranda was quiet. Atcho regarded Eitan with new respect.

"Wow," Eitan quipped, breaking the silence. "I'm impressed." He laughed. "Burly, how much do I owe you for that story? I don't know where you're getting your information and I won't confirm any of it." He turned back to Atcho. "Seriously, our service is charged with gathering intelligence and executing operations to keep our tiny country safe, and we're surrounded by people who openly swear to wipe us off the map. We can't take unnecessary chances. Sometimes, we seem slow and overcautious, but we get the job done, and usually, our people come home."

Atcho held his gaze. "Tip of the spear, huh?" he muttered, then broke into a wry grin. "So, now will you tell me why we're just twiddling our thumbs?"

Eitan laughed. "Fair enough. I'm a guest here during our Mossad team's intel gathering mission. The members know the streets, the personalities, and the locations. For me to insert myself would be the height of arrogance and could prove counterproductive, if not catastrophic, to our undercover guys. We provided them with all the information they needed to find out what we want to know. Tomorrow, they'll give back a data dump of everything they've learned. Specifically, they'll find out if Klaus was here, and why.

"Meanwhile, we acclimate. This region is unlike any other. Not everyone thrives here. More crime of every sort is probably committed here per square mile than any place in the world, including terrorist activity, but because of the tourist trade, the local powerbrokers keep a lid on it. It's a good place for introductions into the underworld."

The next evening, the trio met again on the same secluded veranda. "This is what we know, but it isn't much," Eitan said, opening the conversation. He pulled out a clear photo of Klaus. "He was here. That's been confirmed. He was seen by two of our operatives and a few of their informants. He was here only a day or two, but he sat in on a couple of the coordinating meetings before the Buenos Aires bombing."

"Do they know where he went from here?" Burly asked.

Eitan shook his head. "Obviously he went to watch the mission, and that's why he was here—strictly to observe. We don't know where he went after that. His presence is significant, though. It's the first known instance of Al-Qaeda and Hezbollah collaborating. And we suspect we know his current location." He put another photo on the table between them. "This was taken at one of the Al-Qaeda training camps in Sudan."

Burly peered at the photograph. It showed a close-up of hooded trainees, their arms stretched between the overhead bars of a combat obstacle course. At the base was a man's uncovered face, observing the trainees. Burly looked closer. "Makes sense," he muttered, "and that looks like him." He lowered the photo. "If Osama bin Laden is looking to Hezbollah for technical know-how, he'd want to approach someone who's already in his own camp. How recent is this photo?"

"Within the past few days. I sent out inquiries right after you contacted me."

Atcho examined the grainy photo. "You're sure it's him?"

"We'll do a final confirmation, but I'm quite certain."

"Get me that verification," Burly said. "With that, I can get a contract with the CIA and bring in more assets. It's been less than two years since I left the last contract, so renewing my clearance should not be an issue."

5

Lima, Peru
June 5, 1992

A light blue 1964 Chevrolet Impala navigated through the tight streets and heavy traffic. When it reached the three-lane, one-way Jirón Luis Sánchez Cerro in the Jesús María District, it turned right and headed toward the upscale thoroughfare, San Felipe Avenue.

The driver wiped sweat from his brow. It ran in rivulets, stinging his eyes, but not from summer heat—the windows were closed, and the air-conditioner blasted cold air in his face. His breathing came faster, even spasmodically, as the intersection came into view. He hoped no one noticed that the car hung low over its tires, weighted down as it was with one thousand pounds of dynamite.

He had scouted this area thoroughly but had been unable to find a suitable parking space near his target to accomplish the job, meaning he had to take extreme action. His heart pounded as he turned right onto the high-end thoroughfare. As soon as he rounded the corner, he saw the brand-new headquarters of Frecuencia 2.

The television broadcast company, founded in 1957, was one of the oldest in Lima and had gone through several changes in management, name, and program format. Most recently, it had moved from its original headquarters; and, most dangerously, it had begun transmitting a ninety-second news report that was repeated and updated throughout the day with a longer, more in-depth version in the evening.

Unfortunately, the ownership and management were independently minded people who called the news as they saw it and proffered opinions counter to the cause that the driver served. Further, they had ambitions of becoming the first station to broadcast all across Peru. With their philosophies and supporting actions, that could not be allowed to happen.

The Impala drew nearer to the station. To his right, the driver saw full-color images of the television personalities side-by-side on huge placards lining the front of the building for at least half a block. He passed the side cargo entrance, a place he had discarded as a detonation point because it was far from the organization's heartbeat.

He maneuvered into the right lane. A fountain on his left marked the T-intersection with Olavegoya Avenue. He continued on San Felipe, past the fountain, intersection, and the Frecuencia 2 stars' smiling faces.

When he reached the end of the placards, the curb gave way to a driveway leading into the headquarters' inner confines. This was as close as he would get to the offices where the station management mingled with its talent.

The driver pressed a button to turn on his hazard blinkers and pulled across the driveway. He exited the car, raised the hood, and pretended to make adjustments to wires and hoses on the engine. Moments later, he left the car, crossed San Felipe, backtracked toward the fountain at Olavegoya, turned right, and walked briskly along a row of multi-colored high-rise apartment buildings. Thirty seconds later, he ducked into one of them. Just before the door closed behind him, he reached into his jeans pocket and pushed the button on a small remote control.

The explosion tore off Frecuencia 2's face, shredding the placards, ripping into the depths of the edifice, and sending shockwaves and dust clouds along the streets, stripping leaves off the tall trees in the medians along the avenues. When the noise receded, the dust cleared, and people dared to emerge from their shelters, Frecuencia 2's new headquarters lay in ruin, its news editor and two security guards lying in bloody heaps.

6

Riyadh, Saudi Arabia
One week later

"What did you think about the operation?" Yousef scrutinized Klaus' face, observing a subdued expression of disgust. They were once more sipping tea on the couches in Yousef's courtyard.

"I don't understand why we're working with these people," Klaus retorted. "The *Senderos*." He snorted his disgust. "They are not dedicated. They're infidels. And they leave too much to chance. What was I supposed to learn there? Three people dead—that's all—and the station was back on the air within twelve hours."

Yousef smiled, amused. "My brother, you can be so impatient. I'm glad you had a safe trip back."

"Please, explain. Why are we working with them? They're communists. I escaped Soviet communism. They have no god. They are worse than most infidels."

Yousef chuckled. "We aren't working with them. We are learning from them. We share common enemies and the objective of bringing down the last remaining superpower. Pressures in Washington are growing. What did you learn?"

Klaus sighed. "As I said, the *Senderos* are not dedicated. I watched from the top of a building down the street. I saw the driver park the car across the driveway, open the hood, and fiddle with the engine. Anyone could see the car was weighted down beyond its capacity—it's a wonder the axles or the suspension system didn't break.

"He parked too far for maximum damage, and then he walked away. He's lucky a station guard didn't come out to see why he blocked their driveway. As it was, someone might have seen him and given investigators a description. Has he been caught?"

Yousef leaned back. "I don't know." He sipped his tea. "What would you have done differently?"

Klaus sat up, resting his elbows on his knees, his hands clasped loosely between them. He sighed. "I've thought a lot about that. It's important to control all aspects of the attack right up to the moment of execution. In this case, the driver should have detonated as soon as he parked across that driveway."

"A suicide bombing? You don't want to be a martyr. Why should he?"

"I'll gladly be a martyr for the right target," Klaus retorted. "With my weapons, I won't waste my life on a small-time hit—he only killed three people and didn't even put the station out of business." He shrugged. "There wasn't closed-in parking that could assure the driver's getaway without his being stopped or seen. And he should have used a truck, not a car. If he had broken down on the way to the target, he would have failed the mission."

"You failed. Three times."

Klaus grimaced. "You keep reminding me."

"What would you have done differently on your missions?"

Klaus took a deep breath. "Day and night, I think about that." He tilted his head to look at Yousef. "In Texas, I should have detonated as soon as I knew Sofia was in the house. If I had done that, Austin would be a wasteland, the entire Colorado River below Lake Austin would be contaminated, and Atcho would be a widower grieving not only his wife but also his unborn child. By waiting, I left him time to figure out what I was doing and take counter-action."

He looked down at his hands and shook his head. "In Kuwait, I should have sent in suicide bombers—I could have been one myself. I missed that opportunity." He looked up again and made eye contact. "I let my desire for revenge get the best of me."

Yousef pursed his lips and nodded somberly. "And in Berlin?"

Klaus smirked. "I was an underling then, but that's where I learned the lesson of staying in control. I set the bomb, but the Russian general held the remote two miles away. We should have detonated as soon as I was a safe distance from the blast area. If we had, the Wall would still be there, East Berlin would still rule East Germany—"

"And that Russian general might have made the Soviet Union stronger and able to survive," Yousef said. He gripped Klaus' shoulder. "Don't trouble yourself, *habibi*. Allah's will was done. You learned from those experiences—and more importantly, you brought us the bombs."

The phone rang in the basement lounge of Atcho and Sofia's house on the bluffs overlooking Lake Austin. Atcho looked up from playing on the floor with his ten-month-old son, Jameson, and his nearly four-year-old granddaughter, Kattrina.

Sofia, sitting on a sofa with Atcho's daughter, Isabel, answered. "It's Burly," she said after a moment, and handed him the receiver.

Atcho arched his brow. "What's up, Burly?"

"Can you get to a secure line? We had a sighting. We need a teleconference."

"Give me two hours. Can I bring Sofia along?"

"We'll need her insights."

Two hours later, Atcho and Sofia sat in a secure conference room inside the FBI's Austin field office. He called Burly on a speakerphone over a classified line to an office in the Old Executive Building within the White House compound.

"I've got Eitan on the line at Mossad headquarters," Burly said as soon as contact was made. "This is a difficult connection, so we'll skip niceties. Eitan, I have Atcho and Sofia on the speakerphone." He gave a quick summary of Sofia's background. "Based on what we learned on our trip to

Argentina, I've accessed CIA resources. I'm under contract again. Both Atcho and Sofia are cleared. Since we're chasing a nuclear threat, interest here goes all the way to the top. Tell us what you've got."

"Greetings from Israel," Eitan enthused. "And Sofia, congratulations on the baby. Atcho told me about him in Argentina." They heard rustling papers, and then Eitan continued in a serious tone. "I called about last week's bombing in Lima. The Shining Path terrorist group claimed responsibility. The Spanish term for the group is *Sendero Luminoso*. They call it *Senderos* for short.

"They hit a television station that was growing rapidly in influence, killing a news editor and two security guards. That's tragic, but beyond the deaths, their success was marginal. The station was back up within twelve hours."

"Excuse me," Sofia broke in. "The *Senderos* are a communist group. What do they have to do with Islamic terrorism?"

"We asked the same question," Eitan said. "It's an interesting turn of events. We saw evidence of Al-Qaeda cooperating with Hezbollah in Buenos Aires, and now with the *Senderos* in Peru? It's an open question, but when you see what I have to show you, you'll know it's a question we have to pursue. Did you look at the pictures I sent?"

"I saw them. They looked like they could be Klaus," Atcho said. "I'm not certain."

"No problem," Eitan said. "I only sent two for ease of transmission, but all of them were time- and date-stamped just before the bombing took place. Klaus took a walk south along the sidewalk in front of the television station. He crossed the street just past the driveway where the car had parked, then headed east on Olavegoya and entered the closest apartment building. It was out of the blast area. Fortunately, the station's surveillance cameras' storage devices survived, and we were able to extract these and others. Klaus seems not to be much aware of the electronic surveillance capability. One of the pics captured a long shot down Olavegoya and caught him on the roof. We had to magnify it considerably and it came out grainy, but it's him, and he's watching the TV station."

"Do you have any other confirmation?" Burly asked.

"From our undercover guys," Eitan replied. "Based on these photos, we had them pinning down whether he was in the area and why."

"What did you get?"

"Not much. He flew in, stayed a few days, and flew out shortly after the bombing. The Shining Path guys didn't like him much. They described him as aloof—like he thought he was better than them."

Eitan smirked. "That's the Muslim-among-infidels coming out in him. Where did he go?"

"We don't know. He didn't fly on a commercial carrier. At least not from Lima. He didn't arrive that way either. We're checking private flights, but so far nothing. Keep in mind that crossing borders in Latin America is easy. He could have driven anywhere and then taken a commercial or private flight."

"What's your take on his cooperation with Hezbollah and the *Senderos*?"

"If I may," Sofia cut in, "this is from a purely analytical point of view. We know he's a hero within Al-Qaeda, meaning he's firmly ensconced with them. He might like to be a lone wolf, but they provide financial and logistical support he can only dream of on his own. They're moving him around. That's why he enters and leaves countries at will.

"He's a fighter and wants to be in the thick of things. He wouldn't choose to be an observer of his own accord. That's against his instincts. Since that's what he did, Al-Qaeda must be handling him, and he's acquiescing. The question is: what are they up to? Is he the guy forging relations with these other entities? Is he advising these groups? Or, is he scouting out or learning techniques for a mission of his own, sponsored by Al-Qaeda in cooperation with another group? We need to figure that out."

"You zeroed in on those fast," Eitan said in an admiring tone. "Those are the same questions our analysts came up with."

Sofia shrugged off the compliment. "Any guesses about where he is or where he'll show up next?"

"I wish. The best we can say right now is that the plot thickens."

Atcho had sat listening quietly to the discussion. The conversation receded to silence, and after a beat, he broke it.

"Eitan, how much presence does your organization have in Lima?"

"Not much. I can't give you exact figures, but there's no organization in

Peru that threatens Israel, so we monitor through the embassy. We sent a couple of guys up from the Tri-Border Region to ferret out the confirmation on Klaus. They have dual capability to interact as Arabs or Latin Americans."

Atcho thought about that a moment. "So, you already have inroads to *Senderos* in Lima?"

From his right, Atcho felt Sofia fix her stare on him.

"We do," Eitan replied, "but I wouldn't call them extensive."

"What about CIA, Burly? What are its assets in Lima?"

"We've kept active surveillance on *Senderos'* activities. President Fujimori is fighting them hard. He suspended Peru's constitution and its congress last month—he's promised elections to restore constitutional government next year. Meanwhile, he's going after them in force, but they're fighting back."

"Do we have undercover assets there?" Atcho asked. He looked up and met Sofia's eyes; they flashed horror and anger.

"No!" she pronounced before Burly could answer. "You're not going down there. Get that out of your head."

"But—"

"I don't want to hear 'buts.' You have a baby son and a toddler granddaughter who need you, not to mention a wife and daughter who have already had you ripped out of their lives for too long. You can handle this from a distance."

"Honestly, Atcho, I don't know what we have in Lima," Burly interjected cautiously. "I'm sure we have sufficient people there to do anything we need done."

"You didn't have enough to stop the bombing the other day or the one in Buenos Aires," Atcho retorted. He held up a hand to stop Sofia from speaking. "Listen to me. We stopped Klaus three times because we know him—how he thinks, what he can do, and how he does it."

He stopped and returned Sofia's dismayed expression. "We're talking about a nuclear threat. Truck bombs are a poor man's air strike, and they're effective, but so far nothing compared to what they would be if they included a plutonium bomb. I promise that Klaus hasn't given up on hitting the US or getting revenge on me. He was in Lima for a reason, and we need someone on the ground to figure out what he's up to. Who else is better qualified than me?" He chuckled. "I even speak the language."

The conversation descended once again to silence. This time, Burly spoke first.

"Are you thinking of going undercover?"

"That's the plan."

"I'm not sure I can get support for that. You're a private citizen."

"CIA didn't mind using me for bait in Berlin," Atcho countered. "What about Mossad, Eitan?"

While he spoke, Sofia left her seat and circled behind him. She cradled his head with her arms and pressed against his back. "Please don't," she whispered.

Atcho reached up and squeezed her arm.

"We don't even know where Klaus is," Burly interjected.

"That's easy," Atcho replied testily. "He's either in Lima or back in Saudi Arabia, close to his bombs. I suggest you increase surveillance in Lima and get our own guys or Mossad's to act independently of the Saudi government to put eyes on that *hawaladar*, Yousef. We need to know what contact he's had with Klaus."

"Atcho, this is Eitan. I don't know if Mossad would support your mission. It's irregular, and we succeed by being deliberate, leaving nothing to chance. I'll run it up and see what happens."

"You do that. Tell your guys that my neck's in the noose, not theirs." Atcho stood and turned to embrace Sofia. She buried her face in his chest.

"Hear me well, CIA and Mossad," he said into the speaker. "My mind's made up. The only question is, will either of you support me—or not? I leave in two days. Get back to me with a cover story by then, or I'll figure I'm on my own." He reached for the phone and terminated the call.

"Eitan, are you still on the line?" Burly asked.

"I'm here. Atcho's a willful guy."

"He learned that from hiding his identity in Cuba's prisons for nearly two decades, and then being forced to be a sleeper agent in the US for the

Soviet KGB for seven years. He had no one to rely on but himself. He's been incredibly effective—"

"I know. I read the CIA dossier on him. Sad what happened to his family. Castro took everything from them. What are you going to do now?"

"I'll raise it upstairs and see what happens. Our president knows him and what he can do, so we have a good shot. What about you?"

"Operating Atcho's way is outside the Mossad's modus operandi, but we're better positioned to support him—our undercover guys are already placed in the Tri-Border Region. They could insert him, but if he trips up, they could be exposed. That could ruin years of asset development in that area. I'll push my boss, but I can't promise anything. Even if I could get it done, it could take a few days, and he leaves in two. We're on the other side of the world. That means he could go within thirty-six hours from now. That doesn't give us much leeway."

"Keep me posted. I'll do the same."

Atcho and Sofia rode home in silence. When they arrived, Isabel had already put the children to bed and sat alone in the ground-floor living room, watching TV. She sensed the tension when they entered.

"I have to speak with Sofia," Atcho told her brusquely. "We'll go downstairs."

In the lounge, Atcho crossed to the entertainment center at the far end of the room and felt along the wall behind it until he found a button. When he pushed it, the console swung away, revealing a room stocked with weapons, ammunition, water, food supplies, and other items required for an emergency.

They stepped in and closed the door, and Sofia whirled on him. "How could you do this again?" Her cheeks flushed with anger and her eyes flashed. "We're in no immediate danger."

"That we know of," Atcho responded, holding his own irritation in check. "We don't know Klaus' location or plans."

"Good point. So, what do we do if he comes here while you're gone?"

Startled, Atcho stared at her, then broke into an involuntary laugh.

"Who are you, and what did you do with Sofia?" He reached up and caressed her cheek. "I'd pity Klaus in hand-to-hand combat with you, but I'll read Ivan into the situation and get him to increase security around the house. I'll tell him to put a tail on you when you're out and about. When are Isabel and Kattrina going back home?"

Sofia's expression had morphed to sheepishness. "They leave in a few days. I'll hate to see them go." She reached up with both arms and hugged his neck. "I'll worry about you, and there's not much I can do to help you from here."

Atcho embraced her. "Are you kidding? You've got the biggest job of all —keeping those kids upstairs safe and making sure I have a home to come back to."

He brightened. "My gut tells me I'm yesterday's news to Klaus. He still wants revenge, but he wants his major strike against the US just as much. Otherwise, he wouldn't be tooling around in South America. He's not going to waste another bomb on me—he'll try to get me another way, another time."

7

Eitan hurried into Jaron Bryk's office. Mossad's head of operations looked up with feigned annoyance.

"Do you ever set an appointment, knock, or wait to see if I'm busy?"

"Sorry, sir," Eitan responded while striding across the room with an attitude that belied his apology. "We need fast action." He related his conversation with Burly, Atcho, and Sofia.

Bryk leaned back in his chair, hands clasped behind his head. "If we support Atcho, we could blow some assets. If we don't, this Klaus character could do incredible harm to us. Is there another way?"

Eitan sighed. "Probably, if we had time to ferret out all the risks and planning factors. We don't. Klaus could strike anywhere at any time. We have to find him and get those bombs away from him. Atcho knows his mind and is the best chance we have of getting him soon." He glanced out the window, continuing to think out loud. "The undercover assets in the Tri-Border Region must be protected. What do you propose?"

"That we detach two of our covert guys to insert Atcho. Spanish is his first language, and we can build a cover story that puts him working for Castro—the *Senderos* will like that. I'll go down to run the op…"

Bryk listened intently as Eitan explained his plan. When he had finished, Bryk contemplated a few moments before speaking.

"We'll need a longer-term plan in case Atcho fails. I'll handle that. Before exposing the undercover assets, I'll need minister-level approval and probably the prime minister's too. My boss will have to inform them anyway, since we're talking about a nuclear threat. I'm sure the PM will want to confer with the US, so I'll get a briefing prepared." He shook his head. "We're talking bureaucracy. This could take a few days."

"That might be all the time we have."

"I know." Bryk leaned over his desk, pressing his fingers into his forehead. "Let's do it this way." He lifted his eyes to meet Eitan's. "Fire off a warning order to the case officer in the Tri-Border Region and tell him to extend it to the undercover guys. You go down there ASAP, but don't do anything until you hear from me. I'll get our director to speak with the head of the CIA and tell him our plans and status. Let your counterpart at the CIA know, so he can prepare. What's his name?"

"We call him Burly. Can I pre-position our undercover guys in Lima?"

Bryk took a deep breath. "That's even more risky. They'll have to explain their absence from the Tri-Border Region and their presence in Lima. Can you live with just the warning order until we know when and how they'll link up with Atcho?"

Eitan nodded, his reluctance evident.

"Then go. I'll move things along here as fast as I can." He lifted the phone and punched a button. "Get me an appointment with the boss," he said, then turned back to Eitan. "I'm on it."

8

Two days later, Klaus and Yousef once again settled on the couches in the inner courtyard of Yousef's palatial mansion. A light breeze floated through the palm trees, and the fountains babbled. Yousef's servant hurried away for tea servings.

"We need you to return to Lima." Yousef's face tightened in anticipation of Klaus' reaction. "That's where the next strike will be. We want you to observe again."

Klaus took in the implications, expressionless. "Do you think I'm a trainee?" he said at last. "I know what I'm doing."

"No, no, no." Yousef extended a fleshy hand, palm out, to assuage Klaus' irritation. "You know that part of every successful operation is exploitation —extending the effect. The *Senderos* did that in Lima. They've been in running gun battles with the government all over the city since the attack on the television station. A major crisis is brewing there." He nudged Klaus. "The next attack will be huge. We want to see the effect first-hand." He smiled enigmatically. "Think of it as a rehearsal for a future strike."

Before Klaus could respond, Yousef reverted to a businesslike demeanor. "We have another reason for sending you."

The boy with the tea tray appeared, poured the hot liquid into little glasses, and handed them to Klaus and Yousef. The aroma of mint floated on the vapor.

"You know we've made inroads with Hezbollah in Argentina," Yousef resumed after the boy had retreated.

Klaus acknowledged his words with a nod.

"We want to establish a presence in Peru as well. Islam has been there since 1560, but the Catholic Church persecuted it almost out of existence. The faithful claimed to convert, but they secretly kept Islam alive. It resurrected in 1948 thanks to Palestinians and Lebanese fleeing the Arab-Israeli war. Both Sunni and Shia are there, and we think we can use *Senderos* to recruit Muslims into their cause, and then convert the effort to *jihad*. The organization's leaders have already met you. This will be a second contact. You can stick around awhile afterward."

Klaus, leaning back in his seat, now studied Yousef with steady eyes. "Do I have to stay there?"

"Go in early, watch the big event, and stay a few weeks afterward. Make contact in the Sunni community beforehand and meet with them after the explosion to show solidarity with *Senderos*. We will make good Muslims out of the communists after we kill the Great Satan. You are going to play a big part in that."

Klaus rested his chin on his chest and gazed at Yousef. "Do I have time for a stopover in Texas?"

Yousef frowned. "We would rather not risk the mission. As soon as you return, we will start preparation for your operation. Believe me, it will be worth the wait."

Klaus groused, "You can't tell me anything about it now?"

Yousef shook his head. "I don't know anything about it, but Osama bin Laden sent a personal message to beseech your patience."

Klaus folded his arms across his chest and scowled. "Give me something," he exclaimed. "I've been babysitting at the camps in Sudan for more than a year—most of those recruits are only good for cannon fodder. I didn't join the *jihad* to go on a world tour or watch others carry out operations." His eyes flashed. "You want me to wait until next year for my next mission? Allah give me patience." He looked up at the ceiling and then glared at Yousef. "I have a right to revenge. I'll leave Atcho alone for now, but I want to take care of him personally. Meanwhile, let me send someone to take out his wife and son."

Yousef peered at Klaus, then poured himself another glass of tea and stirred sugar into it. He shifted into a more comfortable position on the couch and fixed his eyes on Klaus again.

"We are not ready for highly visible killings in the US," he said. Then his face broke into a benevolent smile. "The operation has to be clean. No beheadings, no yelling 'Allahu Akbar,' or anything of the sort. If you can make it look like an accident untraceable to us, that would be perfect."

"There was a man in the camps. The Soviets had trained him to spy in Texas. Supposedly he looks, acts, and sounds like a Texan, and he won't hesitate to kill. I want him, and he'll need a team who can watch Sofia at her house."

"Consider it done."

"You'll handle it for me?"

Yousef met Klaus' anxious eyes with a look of benevolence. "If you can hold your impatience in check, that's the least we can do. I will coordinate through Kadir, our friend in Berlin. He is familiar with the parties in Austin and will know how to direct the team. That way we keep the plan as far away from here and Osama as possible."

Klaus stood and looked around the courtyard, taking in the palm fronds swaying in the breeze and listening to the fountains' musical notes. Then he turned back to Yousef. "When do I leave?"

9

Lima, Peru
Late June 1992

Atcho spun on the ball of his right foot in the waning light of dusk, then crouched low, extended his left leg, and swept the feet from under his first assailant. The other attacker grasped at the empty air formerly occupied by Atcho's upper body, lost balance, and fell into his partner. The first one pushed off, leaped to his feet, and stood back in a fighting stance while studying Atcho, who had backed off a safe distance to prepare for the next onslaught. The man remaining on the ground sprang up, and Atcho noted that both were agile and physically fit trained fighters. He looked for an escape route but, seeing none, waited to see which man threatened first.

The attack had occurred within minutes of leaving Jorge Chavez International Airport. Atcho had arrived dressed down and immediately altered his clothing to blend in with the general population. He had thought he had done well, but something must have stood out.

Intending to find a cheap room in a downscale place to stay, he had headed toward the town's poorer areas, but was attacked immediately upon entering the edge of a slum. The assailants had chosen a place where foot traffic was light, and their initial assault had driven him into a vacant building, dark and out of sight.

One of the men moved in. The other stood his ground but blocked the exit. Atcho prepared to fight.

As the first man edged in, Atcho half-crouched, ready to deliver a blow.

"Eitan sent us," the man hissed in Spanish. "We're here to help."

Startled, Atcho stared at him while holding his stance. "What?"

"Eitan and Burly sent us. Don't fight. Follow us."

The man straightened and stood watching Atcho. He was tall and lithe with deeply tanned skin, a narrow face, and dark eyes.

"You can call me Jaime," he said, then gestured toward his companion. "You can call him whatever you want to. I call him Danilo." He chuckled. "It means 'God is my judge,' and that keeps him in a sober mindset."

In the half-light, Atcho could see only that Danilo wore loose clothes over a medium build. He said nothing, keeping a wary eye on Atcho.

"We can't talk here," Jaime said. "We'll lead you to a safe house." He grinned. "Look hurt. Stagger a little. Keep a distance, but don't lose us."

Atcho remained silent, still crouched, ready to fight, and keeping a close eye on both men.

"I hear you prefer Glocks," Jaime said. "I'm going to reach to my belt, pull one out with two fingers, and hand it to you. It's fully loaded, and if we don't measure up, you're free to use it." He moved one hand to his side.

"Put it on the ground and back away," Atcho growled.

Jaime complied. Atcho picked up the pistol, checking the magazine and chamber before sliding it in his belt.

"Lead away."

Atcho sat on a wooden chair at an empty table with Jaime and Danilo in the kitchen of a sparsely furnished safe house. A lone clock ticked above a refrigerator humming in the corner. A lightbulb hanging from a bare wire provided the only light. "Why didn't you just come up and talk to me in the street?" Atcho asked. "I wouldn't have attacked."

"We couldn't know that," Jaime said. "You were in a strange city, alone, and as far as you knew, you were on an unsanctioned mission. You had to figure that someone might be watching you, and we had to see it that way too. Fortunately, you walked straight into a part of town where we could make it look like a mugging, and no one was going to interfere."

"From what I've seen of Lima so far, that's easier to do than walk into a safe area."

Jaime nodded. "Sad but true."

Atcho considered Jaime's words. "Are you telling me that I now have support? From whom?"

"Mossad at your service, for what it's worth." Jaime grinned, and Atcho noticed the wild look in his eye. "Out here in the field, we can be crazy. Especially him." He gestured at Danilo.

Atcho scrutinized Danilo. "Does he talk?"

Danilo scowled.

"Sometimes too much," Jaime said with a laugh.

He stood, moved behind Danilo, and clapped him on the shoulder. "You can come out now."

Danilo jumped up, whirled behind Jaime, threw a chokehold around his neck, and jerked his head down.

In a flash, Atcho sprang to his feet, pulled the Glock from his belt, drew back the slider with a metallic click, and trained it on the two men. They looked at him and burst into laughter. Danilo released Jaime's neck and the two shoved off from each other jovially.

For the first time, Danilo spoke. "You can fight *and* use a gun. That's good to know." He extended a hand to Atcho. "In our world, we like to know all we can about anyone we meet, especially if we're supposed to work with them."

Atcho accepted the handshake with uncertainty. "Should I be amused or angry?"

Danilo crossed to the refrigerator. "Sorry. We don't have a lot of time to size people up. You left the US without touching base with either Eitan or your guy Burly. You want a beer?"

Atcho nodded. "One of those two guys was supposed to get back to me with a cover story," he groused. "Neither of them did. I figured I was on my own." He sat back down at the table, and the other two men followed suit.

Danilo slid the cold beers across the table. "They both tried to reach you on your cell phone in Austin, but their calls went straight to voicemail."

"Damn cell phones," Atcho growled. "Austin is in hilly country and reception is spotty. I should have guessed."

"They spoke with your wife on your landline," Jaime cut in. "She couldn't reach you either."

"Regardless, we've never met Burly or Eitan, and don't want to," Danilo said. "I'm sure neither of them uses his real name. Our commo with them comes through our handler in the Tri-Border Region. My cover story is that I'm a *Senderos* fighter willing to cooperate with the Islamists to bring down Fujimori's government.

"Jaime's is that he's Lebanese and a member of Hezbollah. He's here to offer support to *Senderos* and help connect it to the Muslim community. For this mission, he speaks no Spanish and I speak no Arabic, so in public we'll communicate in broken English. By the way, we both speak Spanish and Arabic fluently, and either of us can pass for an Arab or a Spaniard. For this mission, I'm a Peruvian from the far north. We were here a few weeks ago in our aliases and made our way up the *Senderos* chain, so we can get back in without difficulty.

"Our story is that we were both in Cuba for training and brought you back with us. Your cover is that you're a mid-level instructor in guerrilla tactics for the Cuban Army. The tale goes that Castro had come to our site to observe training. He had been impressed with the June 5 bombing in Lima and the running gunfights since then. When Castro heard that I was from Peru and Jaime was from Hezbollah with an interest in Peru, he asked to meet us. You introduced us, and he immediately assigned you to come as his emissary to offer training and tactical assistance."

Atcho sucked in his breath. "That might work. Won't *Senderos* check?"

"Maybe," Jaime chimed in. "We'll use a slow-fast approach. Danilo and I will go in together for a couple of days to re-establish contact. We'll talk about our training in Cuba and meeting Castro and his interest. We'll say you're on your way and talk you up. By the time you arrive, they'll think they know you."

"Why aren't I on scene already? Won't they ask why I didn't come back with you?"

"You're a great son." Jaime chuckled. "You stopped in to see your ailing mother before you came down."

"Are we talking about *Senderos*? They're vicious. They boast about having no regard for human rights and killing anyone who opposes them. They push for social rights, which means Maoist theory. Remember Mao? He choked the Yalu River in China with tens of thousands of dead bodies."

His face grim, Jaime shrugged. "They'll hold you in high esteem because you come from Castro. Either they'll accept your story about caring for your mother, or they'll give up the technical expertise Castro offered by sending you. If they do the latter, they risk offending him. At least, that's what they'll think."

"I'm sure they'll check me out more thoroughly."

Danilo laughed. "They'll do their best, but their capabilities are limited. We'll run interference. On the other hand, if they find you out, the time until your extraction will be unpleasant."

Atcho crossed his arms, blowing air out of puffed-up cheeks while nodding. "Who extracts me?"

"The CIA. This is a cooperative mission. They don't have undercover officers here, but they do have an active presence that can mount a rescue. We don't. We'll walk you through the signaling methods and give you time to study the details of your cover story. That's why your mother's sick, God bless her."

"One thing I'm not clear on yet," Jaime interjected. "What exactly is your objective? Don't tell us anything more than what we need to meet our mission—the less we know, the less we can give up if we're compromised—but make sure you're thorough." He grinned. "And by the way, when you go back to the US, we will never have known or heard of you, and don't want to see you again until after we retire."

Atcho grimaced, then took a moment to consider how best to respond. "If you hear of a Chechen anywhere around *Senderos*, let me know ASAP. That's critical."

Danilo scraped his chair back, rose to his feet, and disappeared into an adjoining room. He reappeared moments later holding a photo and tossed it on the table in front of Atcho. "Is that him? We got this just before we came after you. We're supposed to be on the lookout for him."

Atcho stared down at Klaus' black-and-white face. "That's him. He's why I'm here. If you see him or find out what he's up to, get to me quick."

The other two men studied the photo. Only the tick-tock of the clock and the hum of the refrigerator broke the silence. Then Jaime slammed a hand down on the table. "Let's talk about how we do this."

10

Austin, Texas
Early July 1992

"Rawley" spoke in rapid Arabic to Kadir in Berlin. "I've contacted the surveillance team. They tell me that Miss Sofia has guests staying with her —another woman and a child."

"Do you know who they are?"

"We're working on it. I'm going over to observe for myself."

"Don't include them. Hitting Atcho's wife will be a sensational news story. We don't want it traced."

Rawley hung up and walked into the convenience store in a strip mall where he had made the phone call. He was a gangly blond with light blue eyes and wore enough Texan attire to look authentic without pressing the point—denims with work boots, an untucked Western shirt with sleeves rolled to the elbows, and a Houston Astros baseball cap.

"Where's the beer?" he called to the clerk in a flawless Texas accent. As he paid for a six-pack of Lone Star, he asked, "Can you give me directions to Mt. Bonnell Road? I need to make a delivery."

Rawley's journey through life to arrive at this point had been long and circuitous. He was born and raised in Afghanistan to a tribe with features that sprang from Alexander the Great's ancient foray there. The iconic general's soldiers had dallied with local women before being among the first great armies brought to heel in that barren land. They left behind a large progeny.

During the Soviet's ill-fated adventure there, Rawley had caught the attention of military intelligence officers, who took note of his looks and cleverness and recruited him as an interpreter. While he was still young and malleable, they sent him to Moscow to train for assignment in Texas. Upon completion, he infiltrated the menial labor ranks of contractors serving NASA's Johnson Space Center south of Houston.

Rawley also trained as an assassin and had been diverted for short-duration operations in other parts of the world. His skill of blending in with Texans and sending treasure troves of space-related secrets back to Moscow had earned him respect within Soviet clandestine services.

With the dissolution of the Soviet Union foreseen by its retreat from global engagement and its withdrawal from Afghanistan, Rawley sought other sponsors. Having strayed from Islam, he made overtures through several mosques in Houston to rejoin the faith and make inroads into Middle Eastern terror groups, pointing out his value as a field operator with a successful background in representing himself as a Texan.

Before long, he caught the attention of both Sunni and Shia organizations and found he could operate as a freelancer, doing jobs for the highest bidder. He did not care to aim his weapons at women and children, but after speaking with Klaus in the Sudan camps and learning of Atcho and Sofia's incursions against Muslims in Berlin and Kuwait, he was happy to oblige.

The convenience store clerk directed him to Mt. Bonnell Road, and Rawley made his way back to his delivery van. He drove to the address he had memorized, Atcho and Sofia's home overlooking Lake Austin. He drove past it, noting the horseshoe driveway lined with mature oaks, the shrubs in front of the house, and the wide expanse of lawn. *If I can find the right place, this should be an easy shot.*

He waited an hour, and then drove past again. This time, he observed two women arrive in a sedan. They parked the car under a *porte-cochère*, exited, and removed two children from the back of the vehicle—a toddler boy and a little girl a year or two older.

Rawley left the neighborhood again, deciding that he had taken enough risk of exposure for one day. Then he thought better of his decision. *I've got to hit the right woman. She's there now.*

He first went to check that his getaway car was undisturbed and had plenty of fuel. Then he drove nineteen miles to Lakeway Airpark. He walked out to the single-engine, red-trimmed Cessna Cardinal he had parked there, opened it, and ran through the pre-flight checklist—twice—to save time later. That done, he retraced his route.

Rawley had considered bringing in a team but decided against it. Doing so would take time. Not only would that increase the odds of discovery, but Kadir had also impressed on him that the hit was urgent. He knew of Sofia's background but felt that, with surprise on his side, he should be able to handle the job on his own.

The sun had begun its slide on the western horizon, meaning he would have to take off illegally from Lakeway—the runway shut down at sunset. But he did not expect to fly far on the first leg—just enough to be out of the immediate search area.

He drove back through the neighborhood, his heart beating faster, his hands sweating. Between houses, he saw the waters of Lake Austin, a widening of the Colorado River forced by a dam farther downstream. He approached the driveway and turned in.

A green-lettered sign on Rawley's van read, "Mt. Bonnell Flowers." He parked so that it was easily seen from the front door. Circling to the back of the van, he removed a bouquet and carried it to the house.

Rawley rang the doorbell and stood back, his hand checking the Beretta 70 in his belt at the small of his back. He heard a female voice call, "I'll get it," and then the door swung open.

As soon as Rawley's van left the neighborhood for the second time, Sofia's phone rang. "This is Ivan. We've seen some unusual activity in your neighborhood. Stay alert."

When Sofia hung up, Isabel asked, "Who was that?"

"Ivan. He's keeping watch while your father's gone."

"Anything to be concerned about?"

"Maybe. His security guys noticed a van that didn't belong circling the neighborhood."

Isabel's expression became fearful. "Is it that serious? The children."

"Exactly. Right now, it's only a heads-up, but there are people who would like to do your father in, and they're not fond of me either. We're taking no chances. Ivan will move his guys in closer, we'll turn on our outside surveillance, and you need to move into the safe room."

Isabel nodded, her eyes wide.

"Good. Get the kids and bring them down. I'll open the room and switch on the security cameras. If the doorbell rings, don't open it. I'll handle that. You make sure the kids are inside the safe room and then close it. Ivan will send someone to the hidden exit at the back corner to take you down the path to a boat on the lake. Got all that?"

When Isabel nodded again, Sofia saw that she was trembling. She cupped Isabel's face in both hands. "It'll be all right," she said, looking into her eyes. "It might be nothing, but if it's something, we have a great team to help us. Ivan is one of the best in security, and all the people who work for him are combat veterans. They love your father. I pity anyone who threatens his daughter, granddaughter, or son."

"What about you?"

Sofia chuckled. "Me too, but they know I can take care of myself. Now go."

Isabel hurried away, and Sofia went to the safe room. There, she turned on all the cameras, checked the monitors, and called Ivan.

"We're set. Have you checked the waterfront?"

"We have, and there's no sign on either side of the lake. Our guys are watching for other team members in the neighborhood, but so far there's nothing suspicious."

"Good. Get that boat over here. We have to get Isabel and the babies out."

"And you?"

"No one's going to push me out of my home. If this is a real threat, we're going to deal with this guy. Did you find out anything more about that van?"

"It has a sign on the side—Mt. Bonnell Flowers. Looks nice, except there is no such flower shop. I checked."

"Keep me posted. I've got to keep Isabel calm. She's not used to this."

"I'll have her taken to my house. Lara would love to see her and the kids."

"Sounds like a plan. If this flower guy comes here, let him get to the door. I'll have my weapon out and my headset on. You'll hear whatever is going on and be able to speak to me."

"That'll work. I'll reposition several men to within yards of your front door. The rest will be on the lookout for accomplices. Our guys will be invisible."

"I think we have all the angles covered. Now it's a waiting game."

As the sun sank in the western sky, Ivan called Sofia again. "We've spotted him. He's headed your way. My guys are in position. We'll notify authorities as soon as he makes his move. There's still no sign of others working with him."

"That's fine, but Ivan, don't mention this to people at the company or to Burly. Do you understand? I don't want Atcho hearing about this."

Ivan sucked in his breath. "You're putting me in an awkward position."

"Humor me. He doesn't need to worry about what's going on here. He's got his hands full, and we can handle this. Where's the boat?"

"It's almost there."

"Tell your man to cut the engines and come in silently. Does he have an electric motor?"

"He's using it now. Take a look at your driveway monitor. Your visitor just turned in."

"I see him." Sofia grabbed a Glock from the gunrack and headed out of the safe room. "Get in there and close it," she told Isabel. Together, they hurried the children into the room. Sofia watched to make sure the entertainment center swung back into place before heading upstairs.

"You're my eyes now," she said to Ivan through her headset.

"We've got him. He parked the van in front of your entrance."

Sofia reached the foyer and unlocked the door. "Tell me when he's on the other side."

"He's taking flowers out of the van now."

Sofia's heartbeat thundered in her ears.

"He's almost at your door. He's reaching for the doorbell."

Sofia took a deep breath and pressed herself against the wall beside the entrance. She jerked involuntarily when the doorbell rang.

"I'll get it," she called out.

"He's taken a step back," Ivan intoned in her ear. "His hand is going to his back. Gun!"

Sofia threw the door open and leveled her pistol in Rawley's face. Simultaneously, two men moved out of the shadows with guns aimed at his chest.

Astonished, Rawley froze, taking in the weapons, his pistol still gripped behind him. He dropped the bouquet and opened his other hand, moving his finger away from the trigger. Then, he lowered his weapon carefully to the ground.

Sofia glared at him, her cheeks crimson with rage. Without a word, she stepped forward and delivered a solid kick to Rawley's groin. He screamed in pain and reached for his crotch, but before he could drop to the ground, Sofia high-kicked and brought her foot crashing down on the side of his face. He dropped, barely conscious.

Sofia grabbed him by the hair and jerked his head up. "Do you know what happens to *jihadis* who die at the hands of a woman?" she hissed in his ear. "No Paradise." She shook his head. "If you come near me or my family again, you're going to find out what that means. Make sure your buddies know it." She thrust his head down onto the concrete and stood over him.

Ivan appeared, walking up the driveway. "The FBI is on the way to pick him up. They'll decide what to do with him."

"Tell them I'll be at the interrogation, and you can cancel the boat."

11

Isabel emerged from the safe room, her eyes wide with uncertainty. The two children clung to her legs.

On seeing his mother, Jameson rushed to her, arms extended upward, begging to be picked up. She scooped him up and buried her face in his neck.

"Is it over?" Isabel asked.

Sofia took a breath to regain her composure. "We got him," she said. "He won't bother us again. I'm sending you home, though. Someone else could show up, and you don't need to be around if that happens."

"Bob's not home yet," Isabel objected.

"Then go stay with a friend." Sofia faced Isabel, placing both hands on her shoulders and meeting her eyes. "You have a child to think about. This place just became dangerous. You need to leave."

"You have a little boy to worry about too," Isabel retorted. She reached up and caressed the toddler's back. "At least let him come with me."

A look of horror crossed Sofia's face at the thought of being separated from her baby. She started to object, but then the germ of an idea formed in her head.

"Let me think about it. Make your travel arrangements. I have to go to the FBI office."

Ivan was still briefing the FBI agents when Sofia arrived at the field office. Above them, a TV monitor showed Rawley sprawled in a chair in an interrogation room.

"He's still recovering from that pounding you gave him." Ivan grinned.

"What do we know about him?" Sofia asked. "Who is he?"

"A bit of a mystery," one of the agents replied. "We already know that he's worked on a maintenance contract at Johnson Space Center for a number of years. We have documentation of a minimal background check that had to be run for that job, but because he was not expected to be in contact with classified material, it was a cursory check looking for criminal activity. He came up clean. He has a record of other jobs before NASA, but when we dug in, we found closed companies, unavailable references... Based on Ivan's briefing of who his target was—you, with your background —we sent a team to his apartment in Houston. They should be there by now."

Sofia looked up at the screen again. Rawley had not moved.

"Let me question him," she said. "There's one piece of information I want."

Startled, the agent raised his palms in protest. "Ma'am, I can't—"

Sofia stepped toward him. "That man just threatened my family," she said tersely. "I want to know —"

Before she could finish her sentence, the phone rang. The agent answered, and when he hung up, he turned to Ivan and Sofia.

"That was the lead investigator in Houston." He gestured toward the monitor. "This guy's careless. As soon as they entered his apartment, they spotted stolen and forged IDs giving access to classified areas of the space center."

Without another word, Sofia strode to the interrogation room door and entered. Surprised, the agent watched her go but did not attempt to stop her.

On hearing the door close, Rawley looked up. Seeing Sofia, he leaned back and grinned. His hands were cuffed to the table in front of him.

"Wow, lady. You sure know how to greet a guy. All I was doing was delivering flowers." He lowered his jaw to his hands and rubbed the spot where Sofia's foot had struck him. "I'm going to love the lawsuit I'm bringing against you and..." He looked around. "Were those FBI guys who brought me in? Deep pockets. That's going to be a great lawsuit." He laughed.

Sofia walked over and yanked his head back. "You attacked my family. You're on video pulling a gun from your belt before I opened the door. Attempted murder. You're going away for a long time.

"Let's talk about your background. You came out of nowhere, got a job at Johnson Space Center, and somehow got all those IDs to access classified areas, then left them on the nightstand in your apartment.

"You're a foreign agent, bud. Your attack on me was a terrorist act." She extended her right hand, palm up, and shoved it near his face. "You just disappeared." She blew air over her hand and splayed her fingers wide. "Like a puff of wind."

Rawley scoffed. "I know my rights."

"I'm sure, but I just gave you your safest option. Another thing we could do is spread the word that you exposed a plot to assassinate me. Who knows what else you might have told us? We could drop you in Moscow, Iraq, or Saudi Arabia. How about Palestine? You don't exist in the United States, so who's going to miss you?"

As she spoke, Rawley visibly stiffened. His expression turned sullen, but he remained silent. Sofia headed toward the exit.

"The first option is only good until that door closes behind me. Then I'll get the word out and prepare your transportation. Do you have a preferred destination?"

She walked deliberately to the door and made a show of opening it.

"Wait." Rawley's voice sounded hollow, desperate. "I'm low on the totem pole. I don't know much."

Sofia stopped. "Don't waste my time. Give me a name."

Five minutes later, Sofia told Rawley, "You're about to be dead to your Islamic masters. Unless you want to be dead for real, I would never let them know you're alive. You're not the type for the martyr thing."

She left the interrogation room and found Ivan. "Kadir sent him— Klaus' *hawaladar* in Berlin." Then she turned to the FBI special agent. "He's all yours."

"I don't understand why you don't just stay with us," Isabel protested. "You're going to fly with us to New York, leave Jameson, and go home?"

"This isn't easy." Sofia sighed. She picked up Jameson and held him close. "I want more than anything to stay home and be a mother. But I want him in a safe place, and you don't need to be handling two small children in airplanes and airports by yourself. But I need to be home. The bad guys could come again."

"Exactly," Isabel retorted, her eyes flashing in exasperation. "You should stay with us, where it's safe."

"No place is safe while Klaus is out there," Sofia replied distantly. "I'm trained for this, and I can't stand by and wait for the threat to reach our doorstep again." She finished packing the car for the trip to the airport.

12

Berlin, Germany
Two days later

Sofia walked off an early morning Lufthansa at Berlin's Tegel "Otto Lilienthal" Airport in the capital of a reunited Germany. She'd last visited the formerly divided city a little over a year ago, shortly after reunification, and wondered now what changes she would see. Certainly, the sense of traveling freely into the former East Berlin would feel strange, and she guessed that international investment and West German largesse had already begun transforming those streets closest to the old Wall site.

Almost as soon as she stepped into the terminal, she saw a grinning Joe Horton, a US Army major and the man she had called to await her arrival. Dressed in his uniform, he commanded respect, and he nudged through the crowd to greet her.

"Little lady," he chortled, his Texas accent cutting through the air. "What brings you back to this side of the lake? Cain't be good, since you came without Atcho or the baby. If it was to see my smilin' face, you're gonna have to take that up with my better half."

Sofia could not help laughing. "Ah, Joe. I've missed you." She hugged him, leaning her face into his chest. "I *wish* I were here only to see your smiling face."

Horton stood back and held her at arm's length. "So, it ain't about a trip to Tahiti? I told Atcho last time we was together that I didn't want anything to do with either of you unless we was all going for rest and relaxation on Tahiti. My wife is lookin' forward to that." He studied Sofia's somber face. "Oh no. Are you here for another one of them clandestine things?" He glanced up at the ceiling in mock vexation. "Figures. I should've guessed when you wouldn't tell me anythin' on the phone. Let's go somewhere where we can talk."

Horton sped a Peugeot through Berlin's streets. "Sorry about this little clunker. Since you're not here on official business, I couldn't get an army sedan to pick you up." He pointed down the street. "You'll get a kick out of seein' somethin' I want to show you."

Ahead, the thoroughfare widened in front of the magnificent Brandenburg Gate. He pulled to the side of the street and parked.

"Ya see, little lady, it's gone. The Wall." He jabbed a finger at her and then himself. "We did it. You and me. We brought it down." He grinned and pointed toward the gate. "Right over there's where you had the temerity to make me an' Atcho wait while you greeted your long-lost family from East Berlin—and me bein' all shot up an' all." He laughed, and then the corners of his eyes creased as they tightened into mock seriousness. "Did you notice how I just threw in that big word, 'temerity?'"

Despite her somber mood, Sofia laughed. "No wonder Atcho loves you so much," she said. "You lift spirits at the worst times." Her eyes misted as her face tightened.

"Don't you start doin' that on me, ma'am," Horton said. "Let's get out and walk around and you can tell me what's eatin' you."

As they walked along the sidewalk toward the gate, Sofia told Horton about Atcho's intent to hunt down Klaus, the sightings in Buenos Aires and Lima, Atcho's trip to Lima, and the attack in Austin. "They sent an assassin to our house," she concluded, her fury palpable.

"Let me guess," Horton said. "Atcho doesn't know you're here, and neither does anyone else."

Sofia wiped her eyes and nodded.

Horton looked up at the gate's tall pillars towering over them and put his hands together as if in prayer. "Hell, little lady. Ain't you ever gonna learn that goin' off on your own ain't never a good idea? You get folks all worked up and worried."

"Don't go there, Joe," Sofia said evenly. "I've done it before, and things worked out." Her face broke into a smile. "Remember, you and I brought down that Wall because I went off on my own."

"Sorry to correct you, Miss Sofia, but that was one time you didn't go off on your own, and you got all shot up too."

"You're making my point."

Horton's eyes widened, and he nodded sharply. "Oh. You're right. Well, what have you got planned this time? I thought you was retired."

"I am, but I need to find that *hawaladar,* Kadir. He's the one who hired Rawley, the hitman who came to my house. As I recall, you and that German police detective, Berger, pressured him to tell you that Klaus had moved his money to Libya."

Horton looked dismayed. "That's true, we did. But you need to understand that things have changed in Berlin. I don't have the same authority. We're not even doing the Flag Tours anymore. There's no East German and West German governments. There's just Germany, and the federal government here is firmly in control." He cocked his head. "You know I'm retirin' in four months. I'm so short now I cain't barely see over the tops of my boots. Are you gonna go and mess that up for me?" He chuckled. "Not that it would matter, but Ziggy might object."

"Ziggy?"

"My wife."

"I never knew her name. Of course I'm not going to mess up your retirement. I'll tell you what I have in mind, and you tell me the boundaries."

"Hell, you already know the boundaries—whatever we can get away with." His face broke into his unique grin.

Sofia laughed. When she had finished describing her idea, Horton scratched the back of his head and scrunched his face.

"If I help you with this, Atcho will skin me alive."

"If you don't, he might do that anyway."

Horton bobbed his head with a blank expression. "That's reasonable. Just so ya know, I'll have to bring in Berger. If all's we need is muscle"—he flexed his right bicep and chuckled—"I can do that, but if we need legal clout, it's his show." His expression morphed into a pout. "I sure miss the old days when we ran this place." He shook his head in fake regret, and then his face brightened. "Berger might want to bring that German intel guy in too."

"Whatever it takes to get the job done. Will either of them object?"

"Doubtful. Remember"—his eyes crinkled in another grin—"you and me, we brung the Wall down. We're heroes. You turn that charm of yours on them, and they'll melt like soft butter on a hot griddle at high noon on a summer day in South Texas. I'll call and get 'em to meet us here."

While they waited below the Brandenburg Gate for Detective Berger and Gerhardt, the German intelligence officer, Sofia contemplated Horton. She was frequently surprised at yet another element of his past or a skill he possessed that neither she nor Atcho had known about. As he was somewhat old to be a major, she had correctly surmised that he had enlisted in the army and later earned a commission as an officer.

His promotion into the officer ranks, however, had come after a nearly full career as an enlisted man, where he'd risen rapidly to sergeant first class. While still a young enlisted soldier, he served several tours with Special Forces in Vietnam, was on loan to the CIA for covert missions, and trained the Montagnards in the Vietnamese highlands. In addition to Vietnam and Germany, he served in Saudi Arabia, Afghanistan, and who knew what other parts of the world. He spoke German and Arabic fluently, with a smattering of Pashto.

Most endearing to Sofia was that he had rescued Atcho out of East Berlin just weeks before the Wall fell. He had then been the team leader for the US Flag Tours, a special intelligence unit of the US Army housed in the former West Berlin. His job was running patrols inside East Berlin to maintain US rights to freedom of movement authorized under the Four-Power Treaty, which had governed Germany post-World War II until reunification a little over a year ago.

Horton then accompanied Atcho on a raid into the dreaded Stasi head-quarters on the night the Wall fell. The mission was dangerous and impossible, but they had succeeded and survived, although Horton took a bullet in his leg.

Subsequently, they had gone on a perilous mission to Kuwait. Once again, Horton carried a sense of humor that sometimes seemed ill-suited to the current situation. His humor was generally self-effacing, and he some-times befuddled his superiors with an air that was simultaneously irrev-erent and completely respectful. Regardless, they often described him as the man they would most want with them in a foxhole.

"That's his secret," Atcho had once told Sofia. "Horton lulls people into underestimating him, but he's always alert, aware, knows what to do—and is deadly effective. He pulls it off because he's got a big heart, but he spares nothing in meeting his mission. He's a legend within army ranks on both scores."

Sofia noticed that Horton's humor had rubbed off on Atcho, and for that she loved him. Atcho's years in Cuban prisons and living in shadows as a Soviet sleeper agent had left him impenetrably serious, self-reliant, and almost humorless.

Under her nurturing, Atcho's personality had softened, but not his physical capability or skill. Around Horton, he had learned to poke fun and receive it, to joke, and to converse just for the sake of conversation.

She had loved Atcho from their first meeting for his nobility despite the incredible pain he had endured. But pulling him out of his shell so that he could enjoy life had been beyond her. Horton had accomplished that, and she could never thank him enough.

"What are you thinking so hard about?" Horton asked, interrupting her thoughts.

Sofia smiled. "That I'm glad to see you and that you're still here in Berlin."

Horton glared at her. "Don't you go gettin' mushy on me." He grabbed his chest. "My heart cain't take it. Besides, those guys just arrived."

The two men who approached both spoke flawless English with the peculiar German accent that was almost British. Sofia had noticed on a prior mission with Gerhardt that he invariably preferred to use proper grammar, almost never condescending to contractions or colloquialisms. Berger shared no such qualms.

They exchanged pleasantries before Sofia launched into her explanation of the current situation. They expressed concern for Atcho and the family.

"Thanks. We don't know Klaus' plans, but we do know what he's capable of. And he still has those nukes—we think three of them."

"What do you want from us?" Berger asked.

As Sofia told them, the two men exchanged looks of Germanic solemnity. When she had finished, neither spoke for a few moments. Then Gerhardt broke the silence.

"You have no official position here, is that correct?" he asked Sofia.

She nodded. "That's true, but I think we can construe one, and do it in such a way that Major Horton can participate in his official capacity."

Horton's head swung around to her in surprise.

Berger asked, "What do you have in mind?"

"The way I see it, this man Kadir ordered a contract on me from here in Berlin. That makes it a criminal matter in which the Berlin police should have an interest. I was the intended victim, so of course Detective Berger will want to interview me and learn all he can. We know from last year's operation that Kadir is somehow tied in with terrorist groups in the Middle East, but we don't yet know the ins and outs.

"Same with Rawley. He does a good Texas act, but he was born in Afghanistan, has Soviet and Middle Eastern backgrounds, and was contacted for the job by Kadir. That should bring in German intel, and since Rawley is stateside, that brings in US intelligence and Horton. He knows the situation and the players."

The three men listened intently. No one stirred when she finished, each thinking through her analysis.

"Remind me never to be on the opposite side of a situation with her in it," Horton said at last. "On second thought, no need." He tapped his head and smirked. "I'll remember." He glanced back at Sofia. "I'm in. I'll square it with my boss."

"The BND will cooperate," Gerhardt said. "Of that I can assure you."

"We've kept a close eye on Kadir for over a year," Berger said. "We haven't seen him do anything criminal. This might be what we need to reel him in."

"This might be an opportunity to turn him," Sofia added.

Horton regarded her with a smirk. "Like I said, I never want to be on the side opposing you—for any reason."

"I'll set things in motion," Berger said.

13

Same day

While Sofia discussed plans with Horton, Berger, and Gerhardt in Berlin, Atcho drummed his fingers on the kitchen table at the safe house in Lima. Danilo eyed him from across the room while Jaime rummaged in the refrigerator.

"Was that run-through good enough?" Atcho asked with a slight edge to his voice. "I didn't come here to sit around for days."

"Don't let impatience get in the way of success," Danilo said.

Atcho held back a retort. "I've been in secret operations in Cuba, Berlin, Siberia, and even Washington, DC. None failed, and none had time for preparations like you're imposing."

"Imposing?" Jaime slammed the refrigerator door and ambled to the table. "I hope we're not imposing." He sat down and scooched his chair forward. "We're trying to keep all of us alive in a sensitive operation. Tell me if I'm wrong: this guy Klaus knows you. He would recognize you and maybe your voice."

Chagrined, Atcho nodded. "Any sign of him?"

Danilo shook his head. "No, but we can't inquire about him. We're not supposed to know he exists." He locked eyes with Atcho. "Let me ask you a question. Did you ever operate undercover in any of these other operations? Were you ever among enemies, passing yourself off as one of them?"

Atcho lowered his eyes to his outstretched feet and shook his head.

"These are not nice people," Danilo said. "They'll cut your heart out and feed it to you in a second. If you hesitate about a single detail of your backup story, or if you say something in a language you're not supposed to know, that could be enough for someone to cut you down. This group is not well-disciplined. The leaders might take a second longer to allow for human frailty, but some of their hot-headed followers will look for any excuse to blow you away—and they would rather apologize for a mistake than ask permission."

"We trained for our roles for two years, and we've been in them for three," Jaime interjected. "If you're found out, we're exposed. That would be bad for Israel. We won't let that happen." He reached across and grasped Atcho's hand. "Listen to me carefully. If we think you're about to do something stupid that will reveal our cover, we'll take you out ourselves."

Atcho looked into two sets of unblinking eyes, then leaned his elbows on the tabletop and rubbed his eyes.

"I hear you loud and clear."

"Good." Jaime grasped Atcho by the shoulder and shook him. "Nothing personal. We like you, but mission comes first."

"I wouldn't have it any other way."

Danilo locked eyes with Atcho. "You're as ready as you can be for a short-notice mission. We just gave you our 'go forward and do great things' graduation speech. We'll take you in tonight."

"Let's go over this one more time before we head in," Jaime said. "Who is Abimael Guzmán?"

"He's the founder and leader of the *Sendero Luminoso*. His fighters refer to him by his *nom de guerre*, *Presidente* Gonzalo. He was a college professor who split off from a sub-group of the Peruvian Communist Party. Lots of young Peruvians joined his classes, drawn by his radical Maoist views. In

1980, he formed the Revolutionary Directorate with both political and military objectives. He sent guerillas into strategic areas of Peru with orders to start an armed conflict, and he set up a military school to teach strategy, tactics, and weaponry."

Atcho continued to recite the history of Gonzalo and the Shining Path, finally ending with, "He's a ruthless man running an equally cruel organization whose followers will kill anyone without blinking."

"In your undercover role, he's a hero you admire," Danilo cut in. "Got that straight?"

Atcho nodded unhappily.

"You could meet Gonzalo tonight," Jaime said. "He asked for an introduction. Be ready. Why are you here?"

"Fidel Castro sent me to offer technical assistance as an expression of solidarity with *Senderos*."

"Have you ever met Castro?"

"Twice. Once in Havana when I helped capture and kill a traitor of the revolution, and once at the training facility where my two companions, Jaime and Danilo, trained. He observed my class and asked to meet them. When I introduced them—"

"What is Jaime's Islamic name?"

"Abdul Kareem, but he prefers to use 'Jaime' in Latin American operations in order not to draw unwanted attention to himself."

"What name do you answer to?"

"Domingo Suarez."

"Who is Atcho?"

"I've never heard of him."

Danilo questioned him on Domingo's place and date of birth, parents' names, number of siblings...

"Why is Jaime here?" Danilo asked. "He's Hezbollah, not a communist."

"But Hezbollah wants to bring down the US. Besides, in economic philosophy, Islamic tribal practices are not far removed from communism, and we share similar strategies and tactics."

"That's good," Jaime broke in. "You said 'we.' That means you've internalized your role. Be sure to lean into your Cuban accent. It adds authenticity." He stood back and looked Atcho over. "Your hair and beard grew out.

You look like a Cuban revolutionary." He handed Atcho a well-worn Cuban Army cap and a pair of shaded wire-rimmed glasses. "Wear these. Keep the glasses on. They hide your eyes. If you run into Klaus, they could be the difference between life and death."

———————

At dusk, Danilo parked a battered Volkswagen along a street on Lima's eastern edge, then the three men walked two blocks to a house. Atcho noted dark places along the way where gunmen could hide.

Danilo knocked on the door. They heard movement inside, and then someone uncovered a peephole and peered through.

"Get your weapon out and be ready to hand it over when we go in," Danilo instructed. "Better you give it to them than they find it."

Atcho complied. The door opened, and the three men entered. Inside, three armed guards stood, feet spread apart, rifles held loosely pointed at them, fingers on the triggers.

Atcho watched Jaime and Danilo surrender their weapons to one of the guards, and he followed suit.

Wordlessly, the guard turned, indicated for them to follow, and led them down a dark hall. The remaining two guards trailed them. The lead man opened a door into a medium-sized, poorly lit room and gestured them inside. Furnishings were sparse, but a few chairs were set around the periphery.

"Wait here," he told them in Spanish, then left, closing the door behind him.

Atcho, Jaime, and Danilo sat down. No one spoke. Five minutes passed, and then ten.

Winter air had permeated the room and now seeped through Atcho's clothing. He shivered. The room reminded him of the dank prison cell he had occupied in El Moro in Havana.

The door opened, and three men entered—two of the guards and a third man who bore an air of authority. He stopped inside the entrance to study Atcho, the guards flanking him on either side.

"*Capitan* Domingo?"

When Atcho nodded, the man approached, hand extended.

"I am Carlos Marka, chief of operations for *Senderos. Presidente* Gonzalo sends his regrets that he could not stop in tonight. He's busy with the gunfights in the city."

Atcho grasped Marka's hand and shook it. "I'm not here to get in the way."

Marka grunted and glanced at Jaime and Danilo without comment. "We have a technical issue we hope you can help us with. We have an operation coming up, but we have not run one like this before. Are you an explosives expert?"

Atcho steeled himself against a reaction. "I've worked with them, but that's not my area of expertise. I train soldiers in hand-to-hand combat and small arms targeting. Fidel thought that might be most helpful with your city-fighting."

"We're trying to build bigger bombs," Marka growled. "Transporting them safely on these rough roads and ensuring they detonate at the target is a challenge. Would you take a look? I'll have these guards take you to the building site."

"I'll do what I can."

Marka turned to Jaime. "One of your fellow Muslims is on his way to observe the operation. He's overdue, but should arrive within the next few days. If *Capitan* Domingo can't resolve the issue, maybe he can. You might know him. His name is Sahab Kadyrov. He was here to watch the bomb attack last month. He says American Intelligence calls him 'Klaus.'"

"Your progress seems slow," Yousef told Klaus over the phone.

"You picked this route and mode of travel," Klaus groused. "I had a weather delay in Algiers, I'm sitting on a long layover in Caracas, and I still have to go through the Tri-Border Region and then overland to Lima. That could take days."

"I know. I apologize. We would have sent you on a private jet, but that is expensive for an observation assignment. The issue we have now is that our friends in Lima have a problem with their latest project. The objective is much larger than the last, and they are hoping you might have expertise to finish it out."

Klaus grimaced, hoping he had correctly deciphered Yousef's words. They conversed with caution in case intelligence monitors were listening to telephone conversations. "I might be able to help, if you can get me there sooner."

"We have a large community in Caracas. Let me see what I can put together. Maybe you can go straight into Lima and avoid the Tri-Border segment. Have you heard from Kadir?"

Klaus' ears perked up. "What's up?"

"Call him, but whatever he says, keep the communication directly between you two and don't mention me. I can't say more."

Annoyed, Klaus hung up and called Kadir. He related Yousef's comments. "Tell me what's going on."

Kadir breathed heavily into the phone. "Our man in Austin disappeared."

"What do you mean he disappeared? How could he disappear?"

"He had the highest recommendation, as you know. On the day he went to complete the job, he called to inform that he was on the way. That is the last we heard from him."

"Did he do what he was supposed to do?"

"We don't know. We sent a local contractor to observe the place. No one was home. It has been empty for days. If he completed his task, he was in and out and did not report back."

Klaus, burning with anger, called Yousef again. "When this project is over," he snapped, "I'll take care of that matter personally."

"I understand," Yousef said in a soothing voice. "You are owed that. Do us a favor, though, and come back here before you take action. We're prepared to brief you on the next project, and it might give you a different perspective—one you'll like."

"Fine," Klaus snapped. "Get me to Lima, and get word to that chief of operations, Carlos Marka, about when I'm supposed to arrive."

14

Berlin, Germany
One day later

Kadir controlled his annoyance as he sat alone in an interrogation room at BND headquarters. He was a large man, swarthy, with fleshy facial features and big hands, and he was dressed in a crumpled business suit without a tie. He wiped a hand over his thinning curly dark hair.

Sofia watched him over the closed-circuit television monitor, one arm across her waist, her opposite hand at her mouth. She turned to Horton, standing next to her. "He's upset."

"Let him stay that way a while longer," Gerhardt interjected. "He has no idea why we brought him in. His business associates will wonder where he is. That will be a good thing."

An hour later, Detective Berger arrived. Together with Sofia and Horton, he watched the monitor as Gerhardt entered the room carrying a Styrofoam cup.

"I thought you might like some tea," Gerhardt said.

Kadir scoffed but took the drink and sipped it. "It's barely warm," he said in disgust, setting it back down. "Why am I here?" They both spoke in German.

Gerhardt smiled. "You were a big help last year in tracking down Sahab Kadyrov, otherwise known as Klaus. We want your help again."

Kadir half rose from his seat, obviously angry but also nervous. He glanced around. "You threatened my business," he snapped. "I only told you about a pilot who had recently flown to Greece. You did the rest. I'm done."

"Shut up and sit down," Gerhardt growled. He walked around the table and shoved Kadir into his seat. "You participated in a terrorist act. Don't tell me what you will or won't do."

Watching from the next room, Sofia raised an eyebrow in surprise. Gerhardt always spoke so politely and properly. She had not considered his ability to get rough with detainees. Berger entered the interrogation room and stood over Kadir.

"What is this?" Kadir demanded, his eyes baleful. "I'm a businessman. I don't have time for terrorism." He smirked. "But I wish I did."

"You solicited murder," Berger said.

Kadir's head jerked up. "Are you crazy? My business runs on trust. I can't afford to kill people." He smirked again. "Lucky for you."

Berger leaned down and put his face close to Kadir's. "You're going to help us," he said, "and you'll do it happily. That's my prediction." He straightened up and looked at his watch. "It's lunchtime," he said to Gerhard. "Let's go. I'm hungry."

Anger rising, Kadir stood up. "I'm a German citizen," he stormed. "Charge me or let me go."

Gerhardt pushed him back into his seat. "I'll tell you when you can get up."

"Spend the time thinking about your recent activities," Berger added. "The criminal case will come later. Right now, the BND is concerned with an intelligence matter. Sit there and enjoy your tea. We'll get back to you."

Four hours later, Sofia, Berger, and Gerhardt watched Kadir on the monitor once again. He paced back and forth, periodically glancing at his watch.

Gerhardt re-entered the interrogation room while the others observed.

"You're costing me money," Kadir bellowed. "My customers will wonder where I am and why I'm not responding to them. Tell me what you want."

Bemused, Gerhardt gazed at him. "That's simple. We want you to work for us."

Kadir stared at him. Then his face broke into a grin, and he guffawed. "You want me to spy? Should I get a business card marked 007?" His expression turned sullen. "Let me out of here, now, or the lawsuit against the German government will be epic."

Gerhardt shook his head, exhaled, and gestured toward the overhead surveillance camera. "I think you'll change your mind."

The door opened, and Berger walked in with a set of handcuffs. "Kadir Dogan, you are under arrest for soliciting the murder of Sofia Stahl-Xiquez." He circled around and grabbed Kadir's wrist from behind.

"Forget that," Kadir said, jerking his hand away.

"If you want to add resisting arrest to the charges," Berger said, "go ahead. You might want to consider more carefully, though." He waved at the camera. Moments later, Sofia entered. Astonished, Kadir stared at her.

She stood across the table from him, arms crossed. "We've never met," she said in fluent German, "but I know a lot about you. Rawley gave you up."

The blood drained from Kadir's face. He leaned over the table, eyes fixed on Sofia's face, and offered no further resistance when Berger pulled his wrists behind him and cuffed him. Then he slid into his seat.

"We know you arranged the hit on me," Sofia said. "We know about your connection to Yousef in Saudi Arabia, and his links to Osama bin Laden." Her stern voice gained ferocity. She moved around the table and brought her face close to Kadir's. "Rawley came to kill me at my house. My baby was there." Her eyes burned with rage. "Was Rawley going to kill him too?" She grabbed Kadir's lapels and jerked him forward. "Did you order my baby to be murdered?"

Gerhardt moved behind Sofia and held her by the shoulders. "We have it now," he said gently in English. "Let us do our jobs."

Sofia shoved Kadir away. Berger sat down opposite him.

"If we take you to trial," Berger told Kadir, "we'll win, and you'll be in prison for years. Even if we lose, your associates will wonder how we learned about Rawley and where you've been all day today. Either way, your business is finished, and you could die a slow, painful death.

"Have you ever seen a pig gutted? They start just under the sternum, stick a knife in and pull it down through the stomach. All that stuff comes rolling out, making a squishy mess—and it's worse when you're alive. All the blood." He paused for effect. "Then again, your friends could just slit your throat or behead you."

He watched as sweat beaded across Kadir's brow and ran freely down his face. The man's eyes looked dull, almost trancelike.

Gerhardt sat on the table and grasped Kadir's shoulder. "We're here to help," he said softly. "We don't want to destroy your life or disrupt your business."

Kadir raised his eyes, despair mingling with hope. "What do you want me to do?" he croaked.

"We've arranged for you to be released from the emergency room close to your house. You were brought there after collapsing on the street this morning. You fainted from dehydration after an attack of acute gastroenteritis. You'll go home or to your office and carry on normally. You will willingly inform us of anything and everything that involves terrorist activity that comes your way—and we have a lot of catching up to do on what you already know. You'll volunteer for bugs on your phone, in your house, in your car, and you'll wear a wire whenever we tell you to. You will also wear a tracking device, so we know where you are. If you disappear, we will find you and start the criminal case. Is all of that understood?"

Kadir nodded. "What happened to Rawley?"

"We got him," a new voice responded.

Kadir's head jerked up. He had not noticed the bull of a man enter the room.

"I'm just another intelligence guy at your service," Horton said in fluent Arabic, smiling, "and we own Rawley, just like my German friends own you. He's in a safe place, but the official record will show that he was hit broadside by a drunk driver and didn't survive the accident. It was in all the newspapers. You didn't hear about it?"

"He folded fast," Sofia said.

"He's soft," Horton replied. "He's peripheral to terrorist activity, valuable for moving money and services but not ever getting his hands dirty. He never thought Rawley would get caught and point at him."

He nudged Sofia's shoulder. "What now, little lady? We got this situation tucked in. If Kadir sends someone after you again, we'll sock the guy away somewheres." He squinted, and then laughed. "This could be good for business. If Kadir kept sendin' bad guys, we'd keep catchin' them and puttin' them away."

Sofia smiled through her fatigue. "I haven't thought far enough ahead about what to do next. My main concern was turning this guy into an early warning system. Now we need to get the information that Rawley had about the camps in Sudan. He trained with Klaus in one of them."

Horton's eyes widened and he whistled. "Well ain't you full of surprises. Why didn't you tell Burly?"

"I didn't want him to know what I was up to over here. He'd try to stop me. Maybe you can get the information to him."

"I can do that—and also into the intelligence channels far and wide." Horton turned with a genuinely serious expression. "My advice to you is to go home. Your baby needs you."

Sofia nodded but said nothing.

Horton studied her face. "You listen to me and you listen good. It's like my mama used to say." He chuckled. "Hell, I don't remember anything my mama used to say, but it was good advice, and you should take it."

Sofia laughed in spite of herself. "You used that joke on me a year ago."

"Huh? Oh well, it was still good advice." Horton chuckled again, then grew serious. "Listen to me. Go home. We got things in hand in Berlin, and Atcho knows what he's doing."

He watched her face, which remained expressionless. "I don't know what you got cookin' in that noggin'," he said, 'but whatever it is, let it go." He leaned back, hands on hips, as another thought struck. He peered at her more closely. "Don't you even think about doin' nothin' without me. Tell me what you got goin' on."

Sofia stared into his eyes. "Remember last year when the reporter, Tony Collins, was murdered in Saudi Arabia?"

Horton nodded. "Yep. I was in Collins' room when Atcho found the note leading to the identity of Klaus' contact in Riyadh, Yousef the *hawaladar*."

"We *think* Yousef is Klaus' main contact," Sofia corrected him.

"So now you're gonna get all snippety and accurate with me." Horton grinned. "You win. We haven't proved a connection between Yousef and Klaus." He widened his eyes. "But it's damn close."

"I know. I think it's him too." Sofia took a moment to compose her thoughts. "What I'm seeing is that Klaus is connected to Al-Qaeda through Yousef. Kadir is just a messenger. He moves things under orders or as part of his regular business, but he's not connected as an active participant of Al-Qaeda.

"The reporter saw Klaus and Yousef together in the hotel. That's probably why Klaus killed him. After Klaus met up with Yousef, his 'career' accelerated. He suddenly had Al-Qaeda backing his moves. But I don't think he's been around long enough to be fully trusted at the highest levels. He's still a maverick."

"I'm intrigued." Horton grinned. "Did ya see how I used that word—'intrigued?' So, where are you headed with this?"

"If we're going to stop Klaus for good—get his bombs and stop him from coming after Atcho and my family—we've got to isolate him. Cut him off from his support. We need to find out where he's keeping his personal money and close down his access to it, and we have to separate him from Al-Qaeda."

Horton pulled back and whistled, looking at the sky in disbelief. "Lady, you sure don't dream small. Just how are you fixin' to pull all that off?"

"I'll need your help and Burly's, and we have to go to Saudi Arabia."

"Ain't you forgettin' one thing?"

"No," Sofia replied. "We still have to recover three nuclear bombs."

15

Lima, Peru
One day later: July 16, 1992

"Were you able to help those guys with the explosives?" Danilo asked.

"No. I had to maneuver fast to keep my credibility," Atcho replied. "I taught them some street tactics. Nothing fancy, just things they weren't doing, like using rendezvous points and maneuvering at night without losing anyone." He shook his head. "I worry about the good guys who will die because of what I showed the bad guys."

"You can't think about that. Did you get a good look at the bomb?"

"Two. Big trucks. Big bombs."

"We'll get word back through our contact in the Tri-Border Region," Jaime interjected. "Did you get an idea when or where they'll detonate?"

Atcho shook his head. "They've got the technical issue with the bombs and they're waiting for Klaus to get here, hoping he'll resolve it. Meanwhile, they're happy to keep up the gunfights in the streets. I tried to get close enough to do some damage, but once I convinced them of my limited knowledge on explosives, they wouldn't let me near them again."

"And they don't know when Klaus will arrive?"

Atcho shook his head. "He was held up by weather and missed his flight connections."

"So, we don't know when to watch out for him."

"We do," Atcho countered. "All the time."

Jaime raised an eyebrow and pursed his lips, then nodded. "We're going to have to destroy those bombs."

"I'll go in again this afternoon," Atcho said. "I promised to teach some techniques in hand-to-hand combat."

"We'll come along for the camaraderie." Jaime laughed at the irony. "Maybe we can damage it." They put their heads together over the kitchen table to brainstorm.

Two hours later, the three returned to the house at the edge of Lima. On entering, they noticed an air of expectancy, an energy not previously present. The guards exuded enthusiasm.

"Why the excitement?" Danilo asked one of them.

"The Al-Qaeda man," he replied. "He arrived last night and fixed the bombs."

Instinctively, Atcho reached up, touched his darkened wire-rimmed glasses, and pulled his service cap as low as possible on his forehead. His hair had grown below his ears and his beard hid most of his face. He slumped and walked with a lumbering gait.

"Marka wants to watch your hand-to-hand combat class," the guard said, leading the way. "He said he might stop in to observe. Right now, he's working with the bombs."

When Atcho started the class, Jaime and Danilo hung around until the guards returned to the front and then ducked out. They moved quickly through the house and grounds, not concerned about being seen—they had been around enough to be recognized as friends of the *Senderos'* cause.

They noticed that the headquarters, usually teeming with people, was almost empty.

Atcho had given them directions to the garage where he had seen trucks loaded with bombs, but when they entered, it was empty. They quickly retraced their steps and headed off in a different direction.

The house, though narrow, was three stories high. *Senderos* had taken over several adjacent buildings, including the garages. Jaime and Danilo proceed through the buildings, searching unobtrusively, but found nothing. The backyards were tiny but opened into a wide field that stretched far into the distance and was used for training. It too was empty.

After an hour of searching, as Danilo and Jaime returned to the training room, they saw Marka walking with another man. Before he noticed them, they turned into an adjoining hall and pressed into the shadows. After Marka and his companion had passed, they entered the training room.

"Come at me," Atcho urged a volunteer from among the *Senderos* fighters. "What's your name?"

"Basilio."

"Use your knife and come at me, Basilio. Don't pretend. Attack to kill me."

Basilio looked dumbfounded, but then he grinned and turned for his comrades' approval.

"I never liked Cubans," he said. "They think they know everything." He turned back to face Atcho, knife in hand, eyes gleaming, and half-crouched, ready to pounce. Slowly, he circled, maintaining eye contact with Atcho, watching for an opening.

He lunged.

Atcho blocked with crossed wrists against Basilio's forearm. He slid one palm behind the knife-wielding hand and pressed a nerve. Basilio yelped and opened his fingers. Atcho seized the knife handle while simultaneously jamming a foot behind Basilio's ankle and throwing his shoulder into the man's chest.

Basilio fell to the floor on his back. Atcho straddled his chest, pinning his arms, and held the knife at Basilio's throat.

The other fighters were silent in astonishment, and then roared their approval. Atcho patted the downed man on the shoulder, released him, and stood up.

Basilio took his defeat good-humoredly and climbed to his feet, grinning. "Next time," he said.

Atcho turned to address the group. Just then, Marka appeared in the door with a companion whose muscles bulged under loose clothing.

Atcho sucked in his breath. *Klaus.*

Atcho cleared his throat and proceeded to fake a coughing fit. He stooped slightly, dropped his hands onto his knees, lowered his head, and continued to cough. Then, raising his head, he called in a hoarse voice, "Dust in the throat. Pair off while I drink some water."

He walked into the shadows on the opposite side of the room, lifted a clay jug over his head, and poured water into his mouth.

"I liked your demonstration," a voice behind him called. "I saw the end of it."

Atcho turned to find Marka and Klaus facing him. He fought down his shock, silently thanked Jaime for the dark glasses, and acknowledged the comment with a nod. "Please excuse the dust in my throat," he replied, keeping his voice hoarse.

"Teach my soldiers well," Marka said with only a touch of irony, "and you'll be forgiven. I want you to meet Sahab Kadyrov. He's here to observe our next bombing operation. He fixed our technical problem. His English is as bad as yours, but at least you two can say hello."

Marka turned to Klaus and made introductions in broken English. "This is *Capitan* Domingo Suarez. Fidel Castro sent him to train our fighters."

Klaus shook Atcho's hand perfunctorily. "Castro is a good man."

Atcho hoped the rapid beat of his heart did not show through his shirt and that his forced breathing was not too apparent. He thanked Klaus, generated another coughing fit, and drank again from the water jug.

Marka and Klaus moved away. Atcho watched them until they disappeared through the door, noting an urgency about them. Then he reassembled the class. A few minutes later, Jaime and Danilo appeared. They made eye contact with Atcho and shook their heads.

The three men discussed what they had seen and heard as Jaime maneuvered the little Volkswagen through Lima's crowded streets to the safe house. The sun slid to the western horizon.

"They moved the trucks carrying the bombs," Danilo said. "We looked all over for them. Nothing."

"Marka said that Klaus had fixed the problem with the bombs," Atcho said. "They're probably staging the trucks now."

A strange expression crossed Jaime's face. "Atcho, what were they trying to fix?"

Atcho reflected momentarily. "I know the fundamentals of demolitions, but not much beyond that. In addition to their concern about its stability—getting it from here to there without blowing it in the wrong place—they were concerned about shaping it." He suddenly looked stricken. "Oh my God, that's it. I should have seen it before."

His strident tone caused Jaime and Danilo to turn toward him abruptly. "What?" Jaime asked tersely while keeping his eye on the road.

Atcho spoke slowly, pulling his thoughts forward. "If the two trucks contain an equal distribution of explosives and all they've done is load them into the vehicles with no other preparation, the detonation will be immense, but the shock wave will spread evenly in all directions. The damage will be massive, but they must have been looking to cause even greater damage."

He put his hand to his chin while he reflected. "They want damping on the same side of both trucks, and they want the main shock of the explosion to hit high, well above the trucks' height. The force has to hit along a vertical band."

"A skyscraper," Jaime muttered. He jammed the little car into a lower gear and shoved the gas pedal to the floor. "That's what they're going for. With so much destructive power shaped that way, they could bring down almost any of Lima's tall buildings." He glanced at Atcho. "The US and

Israel are organizing a joint op with Fujimori's troops to raid *Senderos* and seize the trucks. They'll get here too late."

"Did you notice that hardly anyone was at the headquarters?" Danilo cut in, his voice anxious. "We didn't expect to be confronted, but there was no one to challenge us."

"Even the group I had to work with was small," Atcho observed.

On arrival at the safe house, Jaime hurried into the operations room to radio his contact in the Tri-Border Region.

"Those are garbage-size trucks," Atcho called after him. "We're talking two tons of explosives. President Fujimori needs to mobilize everything he's got to stop them."

Danilo turned on a television in the living room and stood watching news reports. The screen repeatedly flicked from scene to scene of running gunfights all over the city.

"You need to see this," he called. The warning tone in his voice brought Atcho and Jaime to his side. "They've had constant shootouts since the June 5 bombing," he said. "But this is different. Today they executed nonstop simultaneous attacks all over Lima. The police are spread out, trying to keep up."

"They're keeping the police busy," Danilo said. "The cops can't respond effectively to any specific attack."

Atcho took a deep breath. "*Senderos* is going to blow those bombs tonight."

16

Esteban, the driver of the lead truck, looked about nervously. Traffic was relatively light at this time of night, but still moved slowly. He looked in his side mirror for the umpteenth time. The second truck was following a few cars back.

Esteban had already made his final turn onto Avenida Larco in Lima's Miraflores district. His target was a few blocks ahead. He reflected on the fact that he was not far from the location of the June 5 bombing and grinned. *No one's seen anything like this.*

He honked at a car blocking his path and cursed at the driver. While he waited for traffic to clear, he listened absently to radio news reports of the gun battles that had plagued the city all day, but he was not worried. He knew no shootings would take place within many blocks of him.

The driver of the car in front of him gestured obscenely and drove away. Esteban took his foot off the brake and pressed the accelerator. As the truck struggled forward under its heavy load, he checked his mirror again for the second truck. Satisfied that it was still following, he proceeded along Avenida Larco.

Three blocks later, Esteban pulled to a stop next to the Central Bank of Peru at the intersection with Calle Schell. He punched on his emergency blinkers and climbed down from the cab.

Behind him, cars honked and drivers yelled. Esteban stood in traffic to hold open the next lane until the second truck lumbered in behind his.

A security guard hurried out from the bank. "You can't park here," he yelled, face red with aggravation.

"It's only for a few minutes," Esteban called back. "We have to make a delivery."

"Deliveries are on the other side of the building," the guard insisted. "Calle Schell is a one-way street, so you can't turn there. You'll have to cross over, turn right at the next intersection, and take another right on Calle Alcanfores, which will bring you to Calle Tarata. You can park there."

Esteban sighed. "Come on," he implored. "That's a lot of maneuvering for trucks this big, and it's a small delivery. This will take only a minute."

Although he could still hear horns and shouts behind him, Esteban ignored them.

"I can't let you park here," the guard said. "Look, a policeman is coming this way. He'll tell you the same thing."

Esteban looked up sharply and spotted a nearby police car flashing its lights. Esteban signaled to the other driver to follow, then hurried back to the cab. He looked at his watch. Five minutes after nine o'clock.

Ten minutes later, both trucks lumbered onto Tarata. Esteban and the other driver left their trucks in gear, allowing them to drift into the intersection with Avenida Larco. Then they jumped from their cabs and fled.

Three hundred meters down the avenue, a young couple was kissing goodnight when the blast shockwave hit them, hurling them against an apartment building. They slid to the pavement, arms interlocked in an eternal embrace, never hearing the thunderous explosion that rocked the city. The concussion tossed cars into the air, ripped the faces off nearby high-rises, and sliced a vertical gash many stories high in the Central Bank before its entire glass front crashed to the ground, sending dagger-like shards flying in all directions. The floors at its base lay demolished, reduced to heaps of dust and rubble.

Miles away at the safe house, Atcho, Jaime, and Danilo heard the explosion.

"We got here too late," Jaime murmured.

"We should have known," Danilo whispered. "When they told us that Klaus was on his way, we should have known that the bombing was imminent."

Atcho sat on a kitchen chair and buried his face in his hands. "I could have stopped it. Klaus was right there in front of me. I shook his hand."

"Don't do that," Jaime warned. "We were there too. We saw them both in the hall. Think about the timing. The trucks weren't there. They must have been on the way."

"Besides," Danilo said, "stopping that bomb wasn't our mission. We were here to locate Klaus and learn what we could about cooperation between Al-Qaeda, Hezbollah, *Senderos*, and the local Muslim community."

"And get Klaus' nukes and track him back to wherever he hangs out these days," Atcho interjected. "Got it—but understanding that doesn't make me feel better. We should have been able to stop it."

Danilo regarded him thoughtfully. "Time to move on. Let's walk back through each step we've taken. If we find something we could have done differently, we'll learn from it and then let it go. If we find we would have done things just the same, then we'll have to accept that nothing else could have changed what happened. Does that make sense?"

Atcho looked at him through haunted eyes and nodded.

"That includes not being heroic inside the *Senderos* HQ today," Jaime added. "With that many fighters, including Klaus, you'd have been overwhelmed. You'd be dead, the bombing would still have happened, and Klaus would still have his nukes."

Horrified, Sofia watched the news of the explosion with Horton in his Berlin office. "My God," she said, "a hundred and eighty-three homes demolished, sixty-three cars destroyed, four hundred businesses ruined, twenty-five people killed, and a hundred and fifty-five wounded." She stared at the screen. "It looks like Berlin at the end of World War II."

"Those guys are serious," Horton said without a hint of humor, "and they don't care who they hurt."

The phone on Horton's secure line rang. He answered it and then held the receiver out to Sofia. "It's Burly, returning your call."

Sofia grabbed the phone. "Have you heard from Atcho? Is he all right?"

"We heard from the case officer in Lima. Atcho is safe. He was miles from the explosion. The CIA was on alert to extract him. They weren't needed."

Sofia closed her eyes and breathed a sigh of relief. "What's his plan now?"

Burly hesitated. "Uncertain. He saw Klaus. He intends to go after him."

Sofia squeezed her eyes shut and shook her head. She felt her gut tighten and steeled herself to remain calm and clear-headed.

"Did you understand the proposal Horton relayed from me? I'm putting you on speakerphone so he can join the conversation." She flipped a switch on the base instrument.

"I heard it. I won't claim to understand it yet."

"I'm taking Horton with me to Saudi Arabia. His boss has already approved his travel. We turned Kadir, the *hawaladar* here in Berlin. He identified Klaus' contacts in Libya and Riyadh and confirmed that Yousef is Klaus' conduit to Osama bin Laden. I want heavy surveillance on Yousef without Saudi knowledge. If we're going to put Klaus out of business permanently, we have to isolate him from his own money and his Al-Qaeda support. We need something on Yousef to make him work for us."

Burly whistled. "You don't ask for much, do you? I'm still ticked off about your trip to Berlin without telling me."

"I got good intel for you," Sofia retorted. "Can we stick with the business at hand?"

"Fine," Burly replied angrily. "But you're suggesting that we spy on a private citizen of an ally. If we're caught—"

"We do it all the time," Sofia said. "If there's a threat, we need to know about it. The threat is confirmed." She felt anxiety rising and fought it off. "Listen to me, Burly. This is the third bombing in Latin America we know about where Klaus was present to observe. He has no interest in that part of the planet. He wants to strike Russia and/or the United States.

"I think he's been less aggressive coming after Atcho because Al-Qaeda has been holding him off. They're the ones who keep sending him on these observation missions. Why would they do that?"

Burly grunted. "I'm sure you're going to tell me."

Sofia ignored the jab. "Multiple reasons. Buenos Aires was a Hezbollah-backed attack, but they arranged for Klaus to observe. He's Al-Qaeda. The mission was arranged through the Tri-Border Region where Hezbollah and *Senderos* share relations. The first bombing in Lima last month was *Senderos*, and so was this one. Klaus' presence there had to be arranged through Hezbollah, meaning that it is cooperating more and more with Al-Qaeda. A logical conclusion is that both organizations seek areas of cooperation and want to extend relations into the Muslim communities in South America. Are you with me so far?"

"That's a little hard to follow, but it makes sense at this point," Burly said. "Go on."

Across the room, Horton sat down in a chair, leaned back, and extended his legs, then stared at the ceiling, expressionless.

"In Buenos Aires, the target was the Israeli Embassy," Sofia continued. "The cathedral and school were collateral damage. Last month, the target in Lima was a television station. This time it was the high-rise headquarters of the Peruvian Central Bank. They're learning to strike strategic commercial and communications assets — targets that do more than kill people in the immediate vicinity: they disrupt economies. The bombs are getting bigger, and so are the targets. This latest one was a quantum leap."

"Agreed," Burly interjected. "Where are they going with it?"

"Burly," Sofia said, her voice hollow, "Klaus was studying the effectiveness of delivery systems. The vehicular bombs keep getting bigger and bigger. Think of the devastation if one or more of Klaus' nukes had been in those trucks." She took a deep breath. "Al-Qaeda is planning something bigger than we've ever imagined. It intends to use Klaus' bombs, and I doubt the target is in South America."

Burly remained quiet a moment. "You know that getting into Riyadh isn't easy. You'll need visas and they don't take tourists. Maybe someday they will, but not now. Arranging your travel will take some time—we're talking days, possibly weeks."

"Work your magic," Sofia cooed. "This should be high priority. You got your contract with the CIA, right?"

"I did." Burly let out a resigned sigh. "I'll have to do some arm-twisting to arrange that travel."

"Then do it. Take it to the president. He already knows who Klaus is and what he can do. Remind him that sources inside the Saudi police have assisted in keeping Yousef beyond our reach already."

"Right. Out." Burly clicked off the line.

17

Horton looked grim when he swung by Sofia's hotel for the drive to the airport. They met in the lobby.

"You're in an unusual mood," she said. "What's up?"

"Our trip got nixed," he responded.

Sofia's eyes widened in anger, and her nostrils flared. "What happened?"

"You ain't gonna like this," Horton said, opening his palms in a defensive gesture. "Don't shoot the messenger. The CIA pulled its support. The Germans did too. My boss reversed his approval. I'm supposed to give you a message. This comes from whoever Burly worked with in DC. He said you won't be allowed into Saudi Arabia. If you go there, you'll be deported back to the US. Atcho is on his way back home. Burly said you should meet him there."

Sofia stared blankly at Horton, the flush of anger draining into dread as she struggled with the inevitable.

"We could get this guy," she rasped, her voice shaking. "I feel it. Yousef is the key. When we get the goods on him, he'll work for us, and he knows where Klaus is."

"I know, little lady," Horton said in mock solemnity, a twinkle returning to his eye. "I agree with you. I'm on your side." He rolled his eyes to one side and scrunched his lips together in an expression of jovial skepticism. "I have to say I thought the CIA lettin' you traipse into the Kingdom and spy on a Saudi citizen was a long shot, but I didn't want to say nothin'." He rubbed his balding head. "I value my scalp. My guess is the president didn't jump up and down with enthusiasm either."

Sofia stared at him, expressionless.

Horton held her stony gaze, his own face frozen in comical indignation.

The corners of Sofia's mouth crinkled slightly in a suppressed smile. Then she burst into quiet, involuntary laughter.

"Does anyone get to stay mad around you?" she said, then cuffed his shoulder. "I'm not ready to be pleasant."

"Well, ma'am, I got an idea." He looked around as if checking for anyone who might overhear them. "Let's you an' me go into one of them lounges across the lobby and down a bottle of Conee-yak. You know that's my favorite liquor. I'll call Ziggy and tell her to come pick us up off the floor when it gets late. Then she can truck you up to your room and drive me home. By tomorrow afternoon, after the hangover, we'll both feel better, and I'll drive you to the airport."

Sofia stared at him. "Major Horton, are you making a pass at me?"

Horton chuckled. "You ain't never met Ziggy, or you wouldn't ask. Besides, I know Atcho, and I'm partial to my hide. You could use a friend right now. I thought I was one. We won't talk high principles 'cuz I ain't got none."

Sofia grabbed Horton's shoulder and tugged him. "I could use a strong drink right now." She started across the hotel lobby. "Let's go. You're paying."

18

"That was more like it," Klaus told Yousef enthusiastically on greeting him at the front door of Yousef's house. He embraced his portly friend and kissed him on the cheeks. "We killed some infidels."

"And did damage to Peru's economy and weakened its president." Yousef smiled warmly and led him into the courtyard. "That was the main objective, and the *Senderos* were happy with the technical solution you provided." He signaled to his servants to bring tea.

"I didn't do much," Klaus replied, taking a seat on the couch. "They were competent with the explosives configuration. I showed them how to stabilize the platform better and how to shape the charge to accomplish their objective. They had most of it figured out and wanted confirmation."

"Well, they are lifelong friends now. We have a staunch ally in South America, thanks to you."

The tea arrived, and both men sat quietly while a young boy poured it. After the servant had retreated from the courtyard, Klaus leaned forward. His eyes burned with enmity.

"Now, tell me. What's the big target?"

Yousef smiled benevolently. "I said I would tell you on your return, and I will." He held up a hand, palm facing Klaus, face solemn. "First, you must promise not to breathe a word to anyone. I am allowed to tell you only for the purpose of managing your impatience, but then you will leave Saudi Arabia and not return until after the mission, and perhaps not until months or years after that."

Astonished and almost angry, Klaus leaned back. "You said the attack wouldn't take place until February. That's seven months away. Where will I go? What about my bombs?"

Yousef leaned forward in a placating gesture. "You have them in a safe place?"

Klaus nodded.

"Leave them where they are. You can make one trip back to Riyadh to retrieve them when the time is right. We'll make the security arrangements to get you to your destination."

"Meanwhile, what? The camps?"

Yousef assented. "Our recruits need to know what you can teach them."

Klaus sat quietly, his eyes flickering as he studied Yousef while controlling his own annoyance. "Let me hear what the target is."

Yousef shook his head. "You must agree first and swear an oath never to speak of it. You will be held to it." He gazed steadily into Klaus' eyes. "You know what that means."

Klaus leaned forward and dropped his arms between his knees. He held Yousef's gaze. "And if I don't agree?"

Yousef breathed heavily. "No one will blame you, my friend. You have done much for Islam. I will place your personal funds in a bank of your choice where you can access them. Your balance is over four-and-a-half million dollars now. And you are free to retrieve your bombs.

"However, *habibi*, think carefully before acting. If you choose that path, our association ends. We cannot provide you safe passage out of the Kingdom or into any country. Al-Qaeda will no longer support you, and I will not be allowed to be your *hawaladar*."

Klaus regarded Yousef with an expression indicating he had anticipated that response. "Those are tough conditions."

Yousef sighed. "You're an unusual fighter for Islam," he said. "Your training in the Soviet Spetsnaz makes you more of a lone actor than we usually see. That's not a criticism. It's a fact, and your talents are extremely valuable. But we're not looking for individual hits, despite how large they might be. We look at a longer strategy. Once your bombs are proven in action and we can reproduce them reliably, they will fit in."

Klaus looked around at the swaying palms and babbling fountains, the spray falling like diamonds in the sunlight. He exhaled.

"Can't I at least kill Atcho?"

Yousef frowned and shook his head. "Too much risk right now."

Klaus leaned back against the couch, his hands cupping the back of his neck and his legs splayed out in front of him. He stared up at the blue sky.

"All right," he said at last. "I swear on all that's sacred to Islam that I will never mention the target until you direct me otherwise. I will go to the camps in Sudan and train Al-Qaeda recruits until I am called for this great mission." He glanced at Yousef. "Does that satisfy?"

Yousef nodded.

19

Sofia watched through Atcho's conference room window as a metallic-green compact rental car stopped at the security gate below. A guard approached the window and spoke with the driver briefly, then checked a clipboard and waved the car through. It traveled a short distance to a parking lot and slid into a space. Then Burly's bulky, balding figure squeezed out of the small vehicle and headed toward the building carrying a valise.

Atcho stood next to Sofia, also watching Burly's arrival. "Are you still mad at him? It's been two months, and he's a good friend."

"I know," Sofia sniffed. "But I can't let him off the hook so easily. We could have had Yousef and maybe Klaus by now. What's he doing with that tiny car?"

Atcho chuckled. "He's on his own dime. And I don't agree that we would have caught those guys by now. With or without Burly, your mission in Saudi Arabia would have been scrubbed. The director was never going to sanction that, and if he had, the president would have had his neck. Anyway, Burly wouldn't tell me on the phone why he's here."

"Don't worry." Sofia kissed Atcho on the cheek. "I'll be good."

They watched Burly enter the building before turning from the window and taking seats at the conference table. Sofia poured coffee from a pitcher and added cream and sugar.

A few moments later, a secretary showed Burly into the room and closed the door, leaving him alone with Atcho and Sofia. They rose to receive him.

Burly greeted Atcho amiably, and then turned to Sofia. "You still mad?" He exaggerated a look of anxiety.

"Depends on what you have to tell us," she said with a pert smile. Then her expression warmed, and she extended the cup to him. "Your coffee, sir, just the way you like it."

Startled, Burly took the coffee and grinned. "A peace offering?"

"A truce, until I hear what you have to say."

Burly groaned. "Fair enough." He glanced around the room at the Western art on the walls and a bronze cowboy-on-a-bucking-bronco statuette on the table. "I'm always amazed at how a lifelong Cuban adapted so well to life in Texas," he told Atcho, then addressed Sofia. "We've located Klaus. Will that do?"

"What? Where?" Sofia replied, startled.

Atcho's eyes narrowed, but otherwise he showed no expression.

Burly moved toward the conference table. "I'll show you." He sat down and took a key from his pocket, then unlocked his satchel and pulled out another bag, which he proceeded to unlock as well. He looked up and caught Atcho's questioning glance. "The travails of carrying classified material," he muttered. Then he took a quick look around the room. "This is still a secure facility, right?"

Atcho nodded as he took a seat next to Burly. "We have our defense department contracts."

Sofia sat down on Burly's other side.

"We believe this is Klaus," Burly said, extracting a photo from the file folder. "This was taken a few days ago by Mossad at one of the camps in Sudan. It's a bit grainy, but the agent on the ground assured his headquarters that this is our guy."

He turned to Sofia. "That was good information you got from Rawley. I passed it on to the Israelis, and they located him." He paused. "I didn't shoot down your mission to Riyadh, but I didn't give it much probability of being cleared either. You must have anticipated that."

Sofia stared at him, then sighed and nodded in acquiescence. "Every time I try to do things by the book, I get shot down. That's why I go off on my own."

"Please don't do that this time," Burly replied. "Eitan Chasin's man in the field got this for us. He put his neck on the line—for real. Need I say more?"

Sofia shook her head. "Just so we get Klaus. What's the plan?"

Burly chuckled. "You'll be happy to know that I'm a bit off the reservation myself this time. I knew that the CIA higher-ups would nix your request for intel support in Saudi Arabia, but I keep my backchannels to members of the Mossad. They kept an eye on Yousef in Riyadh, watching him and monitoring his communications. One call came through that helped in finding Klaus. So, your conclusion that Yousef is Klaus' conduit to Al-Qaeda is confirmed, and now we know Klaus' location."

"Okay," Sofia cut in. "I'm properly chastened and you have my thanks. Again, what's the plan?"

"Israel's going to mount an operation to grab him. Obviously, since he has nukes, Israel feels threatened."

"The world is threatened," Atcho said. "Why doesn't the US go after him?"

Burly shrugged. "For the same reasons Sofia goes rogue. Bureaucracy. Al-Qaeda isn't perceived as much of a threat. Osama bin Laden is seen as a rich kid with a fortune to spend who likes toys that go boom."

"What makes anyone think Mossad can mount a mission before Klaus disappears again?"

"The Mossad is a bureaucracy too," Burly countered, "but because they're so much smaller, they have to conserve resources, including manpower. They have their own challenges with intransigence, inertia, and careerism, but not as severe as in the CIA. They eliminate as much risk as possible and have backup plans on top of backup plans to ensure success." He furrowed his brow and pursed his lips. "Frankly, they have an enviable record."

"I want to be there," Atcho said.

Sofia's eyes flashed.

Burly nodded. "And they want you there to confirm they've got the right guy."

"This is insane," Sofia said as she paced in their bedroom.

"No more insane than your intent to go to Saudi Arabia. My presence is sanctioned." As he spoke, Atcho stuffed articles of clothing into a light bag.

"By Mossad, not the US."

"By the people who are running the mission." Atcho's impatience flared. "They've done all the prep work, and my only task is to confront Klaus after they've nabbed him."

"You're going into Sudan," Sofia stormed. "That's a hotbed for terrorists. If you get caught, the things they'll do to you would be beyond imagination except they've already done them: beheadings, hangings, crucifixions..." Her voice trailed off.

Atcho tried awkwardly to comfort her. "I've seen as bad," he replied gruffly. A scene replayed in his mind of a fellow prisoner being bayonetted next to him and left to bleed out while Cuban guards stood around and watched. "I know what to expect from evil people."

Sofia's expression softened and then became stoic. She crossed the room, embraced Atcho from behind, and buried her head against the back of his neck.

"I know you do," she whispered. "I want you home, safe and sound."

Atcho turned to wrap her in his arms. "I'll be back. Make sure I have you and Jameson to come home to."

Sofia held him closely and then pulled away, the fire back in her eyes. "What do you even know about Sudan?"

"Not much," Atcho admitted, "but I'll be with people who know it intimately."

"It's a hell-hole." Sofia's voice rose. "It had a great civilization centuries ago. That's long gone. It's where Egyptian and Turkish traders snatched people to sell into slavery. The Brits took over Sudan more than a hundred years ago and set up a democracy, but they mucked it up with more lines on a map, like they did when they created Iraq out of whole cloth."

Atcho noted the anger in her voice, unsure if it was aimed at him or history. She continued unabated.

"The Brits criminalized migration from the south to the north and vice versa, and then opened the south for Christian missionaries. In no time, Christians and Muslims started fighting each other. The civil war killed people by the millions, and the last coup happened only three years ago. Omar al-Bashir is a dictator, and he just aligned with Osama bin Laden and let him set up terrorist training camps outside the capital. Do you even know what the capital city is?"

Atcho started to shake his head, but before he could say anything, Sofia put her head close to his, her eyes boring into his own, her inflection becoming more pronounced. "It's Khartoum. I was on the desk for that part of the world for several years. I studied Sudan. Khartoum makes the Tri-Border Region look as organized and civil as Switzerland. Sudan isn't Cuba, and it isn't Latin America. They kill people on the streets over any excuse. That's what you're wandering into."

Atcho held Sofia by her shoulders. "This isn't like you. Aren't you being a little extreme?" As he gazed at her, he saw that, under her ferocity, she was fighting back tears.

"Extreme?" Sofia jerked away. "I'll tell you what's extreme. It's the culture you're going into. They hate us because we're infidels. It's the culture that murdered my first husband." She whirled on him. "I won't lose another husband, and we have a baby son and a granddaughter to think of. I'm begging you. Don't go."

Atcho, feeling helpless, reached to comfort Sofia, but she tensed and stepped away.

"Why can't they bring Klaus here, or to Israel?" she blurted. "Somewhere safe."

"Burly explained that. They'll snatch him out of Sudan when they are sure they have the right person. If they have the wrong one, Klaus could get wind of it and disappear again, and they might expose informants and operators."

"You always have a reason why you have to be the one going in." Bitterness had crept into her voice. "Why can't you just stay home for a change and let someone else get their hands dirty? I'm starting to think you like the adventure."

Stunned, Atcho searched for words. "Adventure? Like it?" He held his creeping anger in check. "Have you forgotten that an assassin came to our front door? That the man we're going after has a sworn vendetta against me? He's aligned with Al-Qaeda, Hamas, and Hezbollah. They're hitting bigger and bigger targets, and he has a nuclear bomb. If I don't go after him, I'm consigning my family to death." He glanced at his watch. "I'll miss my flight. I have to go."

Sofia stood, unmoving.

Atcho kissed her on the cheek, then picked up his case and headed for the door, stopping at the threshold to face her. "Promise me you'll stay out of this." He paused, his face a mask of conflict. "Take Jameson and go stay with Isabel. She'd love to see you, and the two kids will have fun together. It'll be good for all of you."

Sofia walked over, embraced Atcho, and kissed him. "I love you," she said softly, and then turned away.

20

Tel Aviv, Israel
Two days later

"I trust your flight was pleasant? Burly, that tip you gave us about Klaus' whereabouts was terrific." Eitan turned to Atcho. "We'll take today to let you get over jet lag." He sat across from the two men in a bungalow along a broad stretch of beach by the Mediterranean. In the distance, skyscrapers reached into the heavens, and on the road between them, multiple-lane traffic bunched up as cars traversed both ways. Near the water's edge, vacationers soaked up the sun.

"Our men are rehearsing, and you"—Eitan indicated Atcho—"will need to be inserted into the team and brought up to speed quickly on your role during the operation. The next moonless night is in a week. That's when we go in."

Atcho stood, stretched his arms over his head, and stifled a yawn. "I'll be fine. Let's get on with it." He crossed the room, cup in hand, to refill it with coffee from a steaming pot on the kitchen island.

"We'll take it slow," Eitan responded, an edge to his voice. "We need you at your most alert. Things are rough in Khartoum, especially now. This is a difficult operation without much room for error. As we speak, a crew is preparing a dirt airstrip in the desert, capable of handling a large cargo jet. They have to work undetected—not an easy feat."

He turned to Burly. "We've set up an operations center on a nearby military base where we'll monitor preparations and the op as it progresses. Your living quarters are there. You won't have access to the rest of the base, and you'll have to enter and leave under escort. I hope that's acceptable."

Burly chuckled. "Nothing I didn't expect. Can you bring us up to speed on what's going on in Khartoum?"

"You'll get more in-depth briefings later. Atcho will rehearse how to interact with the team and members of the Sudanese public and security forces he might encounter, but I'll give you the quick and dirty now." He sipped his coffee. "Sudan has been in a deadly civil war for seven years, essentially between the Muslim north and the Christian south. When the Brits were here, they poured huge amounts of money into developing the north but very little into the south. That raised resentment on top of the religious divide.

"Since al Bashir's coup, he's been merciless, killing off rebels and political opponents, and he made the strategic mistake of supporting Saddam Hussein's invasion into Kuwait. That's left him very little foreign support. The US is furious with him. He had a huge military parade three months ago to celebrate independence from British rule, but about the only dignitary who came to celebrate was Yasser Arafat from the Palestine Liberation Organization.

"That said, oil was discovered a few years ago across the line that separates north from south. That should have benefited the south, but the pipelines are being built north through Khartoum. China is investing heavily there, and with projected oil revenues, al-Bashir expects plenty of money to finance his military operations."

Eitan sighed and crossed his arms. "So, al-Bashir's going nowhere soon, and in fact, he not only knows about the training camps outside Khartoum, he welcomed Osama bin Laden to set them up. They share similar views about infidels and establishing a caliphate."

"I heard," Atcho broke in. "My wife informed me."

Eitan nodded. "I recall that she's great at intelligence analysis." He shifted in his seat. "For your purposes, the result of that history is that

Sudanese society is in chaos, riots and killings occur regularly, and al-Bashir's henchmen are everywhere. To give you an idea of the danger, if Beirut is threatening to Westerners and Israelis, Khartoum is about ten times so. That's the environment our covert operators live in." Eitan fixed his eyes on Atcho. "That's the environment you're going into."

Atcho held Eitan's gaze. "Fine. I get that. But I'm curious: why Khartoum? I understand the interest in oil, but that's recent. I read up a little on the area during the flight over here. From what I can see, it's in the middle of the desert without much else going for it."

Eitan stretched and took another sip of coffee. "It's got the Nile going for it, and don't let the bleakness or current situation fool you. The history is ancient and rich. Egypt ruled here for centuries, and then Sudan ruled Egypt for a while. There's even a kings' graveyard here, with pyramids that no one ever hears about. Suffice it to say that before the Brits gave it up, Khartoum was the Paris of eastern Africa—before Sudan descended into chaos."

Atcho sighed. "A common theme the world over. So, let's get down to specifics. How are we going to pull off nabbing Klaus?"

Eitan smiled. "Two words. Think Entebbe."

"What's Entebbe?"

Startled, Eitan stared at Atcho. "You haven't heard of Entebbe?"

"He was in prison then," Burly cut in, "courtesy of Fidel Castro."

"Sorry, I forgot." Eitan looked sheepish, then studied Atcho. "Operation Thunderbolt was a rescue mission by the Israeli Defense Forces based on intelligence from Mossad. A group of terrorists had captured an airliner with 248 passengers, including 114 Israelis. The hijackers flew it to Entebbe in Uganda and threatened to kill every passenger if Israel did not release forty Palestinian prisoners. They wanted to free thirteen men in other countries too."

"The operation was sensational," Burly added. "The Israelis flew several C-130s at night, barely a hundred feet off the ground, for about 3,600 miles. They landed undetected but were eventually seen. To make a long story short, in a ninety-minute engagement, they freed most of the hostages with minimal casualties and brought them back to Israel. When you consider that they had to bring along armored personnel carriers and other heavy equipment and refuel along the way there and back, it was one hell of an operation."

Atcho listened, entranced. "And that's what we're going to do in Khartoum?"

"A variation," Eitan replied. "The planes will fly at night below radar. We have longer-range aircraft and less than half the distance to go than we did for Entebbe, but the aircraft is larger, and detection technology has advanced considerably. It's a high-risk mission."

He took another swallow of his coffee. "Most of our operators are already inside the country, and they've acquired vehicles for ground travel, but the operation is high cost. When it's over, we'll have blown the cover of several undercover agents and will have to take them home.

"We know where Klaus is. Two of our men are in the camp. You'll be inserted into Khartoum a day ahead of the mission and make your way there with an in-country operator. On the night of the mission, the assault element will take care of subduing Klaus and any resistance and get him to the full extraction team. You'll wait with the team leader. Whether or not Klaus leaves the country is on your say-so. If it's Klaus, the entire team will bring him back to Tel Aviv."

Atcho mulled over the plan. "What if it's not him?"

"You and the rest of the team will leave the way you came, and the aircraft will return with just the combat-support elements."

"What should I do between now and then?"

"Rehearse, rehearse, rehearse. Our guys will tutor you. Unless you can learn Sudanese Arabic in a few days, you've got to look and act like a Sudanese who is both illiterate and mute." He studied Atcho's jawline. "You'll need to grow some facial hair, get dirty, and start smelling like a street person. I suggest that if you take a shower tonight, it becomes your last one until mission complete."

Atcho shot him a wan glance. "Sofia would love that."

"One other thing," Eitan said. "Go on a starvation diet. You need to look hungry."

21

Sofia tossed in her bed at Isabel's house at West Point in upstate New York. She was worried about Atcho, but even more, she felt frustration at being unable to help him. A week had gone by since he had flown out to meet Burly and Eitan in Tel Aviv. He had called the night he arrived, and since then he had gone dark. She did not know where he was, where he was going, or any details of the operational plan. With Burly also gone, she had no way of gaining information and determining if there was a role she could play. She had exhausted her sources in the CIA and State Department, and she sensed that she was wearing out her welcome in both organizations.

She got out of bed and went to the kitchen to make coffee. There, she found Isabel sitting alone in the dark, already sipping a freshly brewed cup. The warm aroma took the edge off the tension. Sofia flipped on a soft light over the table.

She greeted Isabel with a hug. "You can't sleep either."

"No. Grab a mug and help yourself. There's plenty."

The two sat in silence for a time, each with her own thoughts. Then Sofia eyed Isabel with curiosity.

"Do you do this often? Get up to have coffee by yourself in the dark?"

Isabel gave her a distant smile. "More often than I'd like to think about."

She sighed. "Bob's teaching assignment at West Point was supposed to be a break for us, but he's constantly gone. All I know right now is that he's in South Korea doing some kind of special study he can't talk about. He'll be gone a few weeks." She laughed without mirth. "I'm surrounded by people who can't talk to me about what they do. You can't, Dad can't, Bob can't, his associates can't. And there's the not knowing what's going on with family members. Bob might be in danger. I don't know. Dad seems always in danger, I don't know where he is, and you're here because your home is threatened." She suddenly seemed on the verge of tears. "I admire you, Sofia, I really do, but I don't know how you do the things you do, and that's just the things I know about."

Sofia reached across the table and clasped Isabel's hand. "You have a daughter, our granddaughter—if I'm allowed to think of Kattrina as mine."

"Of course," Isabel murmured through teary eyes. "She loves you. I do too."

"Being a great mother is every bit as important as the things Atcho and I do. I'm falling down in that department. I know it." She sniffed as her eyes moistened. "If you weren't available to fill the breach, I'm not sure how I'd take care of Jameson in this situation." She squeezed Isabel's hand. "Never forget that our families are why we do the things we do."

"You're a wonderful mother," Isabel broke in.

Sofia sighed. "A lot of people think I'm a know-it-all bitch."

Isabel leaned forward and grasped her hand. "You're not. You're a very capable woman who loves her country and has put her life on the line over and over in its defense. And you're a wife and mother who will fight for your family with everything you've got. I wish I could be more like you."

Sofia wiped away a tear. "Being a mother is the best job I've ever had," she said, dropping her eyes, "but under these circumstances..." She brought her hand to her face and rubbed her forehead. "I took an early retirement package to be with Jameson, and I love taking care of him. But now this..." She sat quietly, her expression conflicted. "I'm a threat to him just by being around. I can't let that go on forever."

She sat quietly a moment. "I want to be a real mother to him," she continued, her voice catching. "I'm torn between staying put while Atcho and the others handle things..." Her voice trailed off as she struggled with her thoughts. "But I'm trained and good at what I did in my past life. I couldn't live with myself if something terrible happened because I didn't do everything I could."

The two women sipped their coffee in the quiet morning. Isabel broke the silence with a chuckle. "It's hard to think of Jameson as my half-brother —we're nearly thirty years apart. But you're so capable of defending him. If someone broke through my door—"

"You'd do whatever it took to protect your daughter. Do you have a gun?"

Isabel nodded.

"Do you know how to use it?"

"Yes."

"Keep it handy. My role, your father's role, and Bob's role is to widen the safety perimeter, to go after the bad guys before they get to your door. Between us and you are our military and police forces. Someone has to make sure the kids are warm and fed. And if the bad guy gets inside your door and we're not there, it's up to you. Otherwise, what we do is for nothing."

A look of horror crossed Isabel's face. "Sweet Jesus! You're scaring me." She crossed herself.

"I'm sorry. That's the reality of what we live in. It's better that you're prepared."

Isabel acquiesced with a nod, then looked thoughtful. "One thing I don't understand is why you go off on your own so much. I don't know a lot of details, but I overhear things sometimes, and you have a reputation for going rogue. You go off without telling the rest of your team."

Sofia laughed. "Guilty," she exclaimed. "I guess I've done that a few times."

"Why?"

Sofia was slow to respond. "It started when I met your father, although the instinct developed several years earlier." She paused, and the hurt in her eyes expressed her reluctance to continue.

"You don't have to say anything," Isabel said.

Sofia shook her head. "It's better that you know. I never want you or Kattrina or Jameson to think that I put anything above my family." She wiped tears from her eyes. "My first husband came home from a covert operation in a body bag. The funeral was closed casket because he was so mauled, but the CIA would never give me a straight story about what happened.

"When I started dating your father years later, I could tell something was wrong. He was so strong and noble, and people loved him, but he pushed everyone away, even me."

"I remember," Isabel interjected. "I thought he was crazy."

Sofia smiled. "My intel instincts kicked in. I went to Burly for help, and as things turned out, Atcho was being coerced to be a sleeper agent for the Russians, and he was resisting by doing the only thing he could—becoming a recluse."

"But he got out of that."

"True, but he almost got killed in the process, and a year later, the president wanted to send him into Siberia with no support. I was furious when I heard about it. We were engaged to be married, and I refused to accept that I might lose another man I loved to a spy mission. I was trained and capable and had some ideas about what to do. As things turned out, what I did helped.

"We had two more missions where I saw things that others didn't and felt like I had to act. Some people thought I was careless. I saw it as using the skills I had trained for and the experience I had gained to protect those I love most, your father and our family." She sniffed. "That might seem like an emotional approach, but" she shrugged and laughed "I'm a woman."

Isabel closed her eyes as if to shut out a fearsome world. "Are you going to stay with us this time?" she said, an edge to her voice. She opened her eyes and looked directly at Sofia. "Or do you plan on taking off again to places unknown? I know you didn't go home last time around. You went to Berlin."

As soon as she spoke, Isabel looked as though she wished she could take the words back. Sofia regarded her without expression.

"How do you know that?"

"I'd rather not say," Isabel replied, her tone slightly defiant. Then she softened. "I don't want to get anyone in trouble."

Sofia's mind furiously worked through a mental list of all her acquaintances who might have known about her trip to Berlin. She settled on one name.

"Ivan must have told you. There's no one else who could have."

"Don't be mad at him," Isabel cried. "I tried to reach you after you left here. Dad was wherever he was, and Bob was on travel. You were supposed to be at home, and when you weren't, I pushed Ivan to tell me where you were."

"It's all right." Sofia rose and moved to the other side of the table to reassure her, wrapping her arms around Isabel's shoulders. "Ivan is the one guy who can usually figure out where we are," she mused aloud. "How would he have found out?" She thought a moment. "He must have called Horton. He and Ivan worked with us on a mission in Berlin two years ago. They know each other and are close to Atcho and me."

"Who's Horton?"

"Never mind." Sofia's mind whirled as she considered who else might have information leading to Atcho's current location and activity. She released Isabel and downed her last bit of coffee. "I have to shower and get dressed. I'll be gone most of the morning."

Startled, Isabel called after her, "Ivan's not in trouble, is he?"

"No, but you gave me an idea."

By nine o'clock, Sofia was waiting outside the office of the West Point history department director. When she was finally shown in, she got straight to the point.

"Colonel Morgan, I believe my son-in-law, Bob Bernier, teaches in your department?"

The colonel nodded. "How may I help you?" He was an amiable man, tall with dark hair tinged gray, and he was in remarkable physical shape. Despite his warmth, he carried an air that brooked no nonsense.

"I need a secure line to call Berlin."

Morgan stared at her. "I'm sorry. I accepted this unscheduled meeting out of courtesy to Bob, but I—" His voice was firm, his speech refined.

"I'll tell you exactly why I need it," Sofia interrupted. "Does the name Atcho mean anything to you?"

Their conversation lasted fifteen minutes, after which Sofia sat alone in an office waiting for the secure phone to ring at the opposite end.

"Horton here."

The major's big, friendly voice brought welcome relief.

"Joe, it's Sofia. I'm glad you're still in Berlin. I know you're supposed to rotate out soon."

Horton grunted and Sofia smiled. She could almost see him leaning forward in his chair, his face mischievous as he calculated how best to respond.

"Yes, ma'am, I'm still here, holdin' the line against the Mongol hordes. Great to hear you." A moment passed. "You ain't never called me from stateside before — just to chat. This cain't be good. Are you aware that I'm gettin' ready to retire? You ain't gonna mess that up for me—"

"No." Sofia laughed. "I just need your help."

Horton huffed into the receiver. "Somethin' tells me that your no-account husband got hisself in trouble again. Cain't you put a leash on that guy?"

Sofia brought Horton up to date. "I just need you to get someone, anyone, to keep an eye on Yousef in Riyadh. Twist that *hawaladar* Kadir's arm there in Berlin. He can tell you how people come and go at Yousef's house. If this Mossad mission in Sudan gets close to Klaus and fails, he's going to be hopping mad, and he'll go to Yousef pushing for vengeance. Unfortunately, his revenge is aimed at our family."

"I see what you mean, little lady, but I wouldn't be bankin' on the Mossad failin'. They got a pretty good record."

"I'm not banking on it," Sofia said, stifling her impatience. "I'm playing 'what if?' If they do fail, they'll go home, make a report, and look for the next chance. But my family is likely to pay the consequences. I can't wait around to find out."

"All right, ma'am, I'll see what I can do." He sounded deliberately world-weary.

"Get the Germans to help," Sofia urged. "They're bound to have assets in Riyadh."

"I got it."

"Get them to interrogate Kadir again."

"I said I got this," Horton said brusquely. Then he laughed. "You know, if you mess up my retirement, there's gonna be hell to pay with Ziggy." He paused a moment. "Where are you?"

Sofia told him.

"Well, I suggest you stay right there and get to know your son a little bit. Your stepdaughter and her daughter too. Cain't hurt. And don't worry. I got your backside from here."

After hanging up, Horton stared at the phone. "What are you gettin' yourself into this time, Major?" he grumbled to himself. He rose, walked across his office to a cabinet, and extracted some blank forms. Returning to his desk, he grabbed a pen and filled them out.

Twenty minutes later, he was sitting in front of his boss, engaging in a heated exchange. Ten minutes after entering the office, Horton emerged with a satisfied grin, his request for a special intelligence mission to Riyadh approved.

"I'll push it upstairs," his boss said, "but it'll take a few days."

Horton's conversation with Ziggy that evening went as he expected. At first dismayed, then angry, then mollified as he cajoled her, she finally acquiesced with tears and hugs to an outcome she had known at the start was inevitable. Three days later, Horton boarded a plane for Riyadh.

Two hours after landing, he entered the headquarters of the General Intelligence Presidency just off Said As Salmi, a major Riyadh thorough-fare. He presented his US Army credentials and asked to see a particular officer. Then he sat and waited in a reception area.

An hour passed, then two. By that time, Horton had tired of studying the intricate design on the ceiling, discerning repeated patterns and counting their number while twiddling his thumbs. Another hour passed, and Horton took note of various people crossing the reception area and throwing glances his direction.

At last, he heard his name called in a heavy Arabic accent and looked up. A short, barrel-chested man walked toward him, hand extended. His smile wrapped from ear to ear over a jutting, clean-shaven jaw, and he had a straight nose with flaring nostrils and eyes a peculiar shade halfway between green and brown. His hair was cropped short.

"My brother," the man said, and laughed. "You should have told me you were coming. I would have told my wife to prepare a room for you at my house."

"Which wife, Iqbal?" Horton chuckled and shook Iqbal's hand. "The last time we met, you only had two."

Iqbal's face turned deadpan. "Yes, that's a serious issue, and now I have three." He looked skyward. "They all give me trouble. I should have stuck with just one—or maybe none." He broke into laughter again. "What are you doing here?"

"You already checked me out, so you know I'm here in official capacity."

"But you came straight to the Kingdom's intelligence headquarters without checking in at your own. How can I help my best brother?"

"Don't flatter me," Horton joshed. "You tell everyone they're your favorite brother. I'm tired. You could offer me some refreshment in a quiet place where we can relax."

Iqbal's eyes narrowed and he looked about. "Of course. You had a long flight. I'll take you to my favorite tea room."

They left the building and Iqbal drove Horton to a nearby plaza with a smattering of shops and eating establishments. Entering one, he greeted the owner like a long-lost relative and introduced Horton as his very best brother. Then he asked for a room where they could relax quietly without being bothered.

When they were seated in front of a pitcher of steaming tea on a low table, Iqbal glanced around the room. "These walls have no ears," he said. "My good friend, the owner, would not dare to compromise me." He fixed his gaze on Horton. "What brings my best cousin to Riyadh?"

"I thought I was your best brother." Horton grinned.

Iqbal poured the tea. "Brother, cousin, friend—it's all the same. I would give my right arm for you. I would take a bullet in the chest and—"

"Got it," Horton interrupted. "I've never had so much fun workin' with anyone than when I was assigned here—what was that, ten years ago?" He sipped his tea. "I need to call in a favor."

Iqbal's expression dropped. "You don't need to call in any favors," he said with an edge to his voice. "You are my brother, my friend. You have only to ask. If I can do it, consider it done."

Horton took a moment to order his thoughts. "There is a *hawaladar* here in Riyadh. His name is Yousef."

Iqbal nodded. "I know who he is. We track all the *hawalas* in Saudi Arabia. He is very well connected."

"Do you also know of a terrorist by the name of Sahab Kadyrov? Western intelligence calls him Klaus from a previous alias."

"We're cognizant of him. Tell me what you know."

Horton related his first awareness of Klaus as a Soviet Spetsnaz deserter and rogue operator in Berlin. He went on to describe Klaus' activities in Kuwait in the days after Saddam Hussein's invasion during the time when the wells burned, including his suspected murder of Tony Collins, an investigative reporter covering the war. He finished with details of how Klaus had attacked Atcho's home in Austin and later sent an assassin to kill his family.

Iqbal listened attentively. When Horton finished, he asked simply, "What do you need from me?"

"We believe the *hawaladar* Yousef is Klaus' conduit to Osama bin Laden."

"Saudi intelligence believes the same thing. Osama is a thorn in the royal family's side, but he has so far done nothing to cause us to take action against him."

"Do you know about his activities in South America?"

Iqbal shook his head. "Only peripherally. Maybe someone else in our agency knows more."

"He's been involved at a high level on each of three bombings." Horton related the details of the Israeli Embassy bombing in Buenos Aires, along with the television station and huge bomb in Lima. "That one killed over eighty people and took out a whole neighborhood and dozens of businesses. Klaus was present each time. We have positive identification."

Iqbal sat in silence for a while, then said, "What do you want from me?"

"Klaus is in Sudan now. We think he might have reason to come through here soon. If that happens, I need to know. He'll go straight to Yousef."

"Why hasn't US intelligence made a formal request for cooperation?"

"We tried that when the newspaper reporter was murdered, but your police force protects Yousef."

"Ah, yes," Iqbal agreed. "We do have that problem."

"I ain't askin' for nothin' fancy," Horton pressed. "I just want to know if Klaus comes through here in the next week or two. If that happens, I'll know why and where he's likely to go."

"And you won't tell me how you'll know his purpose?"

"Are you goin' to tell me everythin' you know?"

Iqbal chuckled. "That would take years. Why don't we just arrest him here?"

"If you can, please do. He's become wily, enterin' and leavin' countries at will, undetected. I'm expectin' that by the time you find out he's been here, he'll already be gone." *Besides, we're hopin' he leaves with the bombs. We don't want those fallin' into your hands.*

"All right. I will tell you only this: we have an informant in Yousef's house. We turned one of his house servants after a US intel request a few months ago."

Horton's eyes narrowed. *Thank you, Sofia.*

Iqbal continued. "I'll bring this matter under my personal attention. If we hear that Klaus has come to Riyadh, I'll call you. But"—he raised a finger "we will also attempt to arrest him."

"Fair enough." Horton grinned. "You must have been promoted a few times since I last saw you."

"Once or twice," Iqbal said noncommittally. "How's your family?"

22

Khartoum, Sudan

Atcho struggled to keep Jaime in sight, following from a distance as they wound through the crowded city streets. He had placed a small pebble in his shoe to induce a limp, and he wore a long, dirty, pastel robe—a *jalabiya*. Unkempt hair protruded from below his soiled turban. He stooped heavily over a worn walking stick, and he kept his head bobbing oddly to one side while his eyes burned with apparent madness. His week of fasting had left him looking gaunt—he did not have to pretend. That morning, he had eaten enough to take the edge off his hunger and keep himself mentally alert, but he still felt lightheaded.

As Atcho passed the teeming crowds, he noticed buildings that evoked the grandeur of a time long past, their walls cracking and crumbling and surrounded by lean-tos and shanties. Water pooled in low spots in the middle of the dusty streets, and the stench overcame that of his own unwashed body.

The condition of Khartoum reminded him of Havana the last time he had seen it, just after his release from prison: a formerly proud city, brought to ruin by Castro. Atcho wondered which part of Khartoum's history had brought it to this disorder.

Dismissing his thoughts, he looked ahead to keep Jaime in sight. So far, no one had approached Atcho, but he had practiced how to indicate that he could neither speak nor hear, emphasizing his feigned plight by throwing in a few unintelligible grunts.

A car had brought him to the edge of town at dawn. Atcho knew nothing of the driver, and they did not speak. He had already been in character, and on reaching their destination in an alley off of Omduram Souk, the largest marketplace in Khartoum, he had waited in the shadows for the car to disappear before emerging into the teeming masses poring over open displays of vegetables and other produce and haggling in a constant cacophony.

As he struggled through the throngs, he held his hand in front of him like a beggar and took up a position near a mosque on the edge of the *souk*. He stood there for nearly half an hour, begging, and a few kind souls had dropped coins into his hand.

At last, Jaime had come along. Atcho knew that his former teammate from Peru had been selected for the task because Atcho would recognize his face.

Jaime was dressed to pass as a Sudanese farmer. He had stopped in front of Atcho, muttered a recognition phrase, dropped a few coins in his hand, and moved off. Atcho followed.

As they trudged through the streets, Atcho relaxed into his role, recalling how he had similarly disguised himself to meet with a Soviet intelligence officer in Cuba a lifetime ago. *We're in a never-ending battle.*

He looked ahead. Jaime had just rounded a corner. Atcho hurried to catch up, reminding himself to do so in character.

He turned the corner. Jaime was nowhere in sight.

Atcho wheeled about slowly, searching. Then he heard a hiss.

Jaime's head protruded from a short stairway leading under a row of buildings. He made eye contact with Atcho and then disappeared down the stairs.

Atcho waited a short while and then followed. He entered a dark, dank, smelly passage that led into deeper darkness and made his way carefully, shedding his pretense of physical disability as he went. At the end, he found a door leading to another tunnel-like passageway that crossed at a right angle. He took the branch to the right as he had been instructed and followed it until it curved again to the right. Then he saw light ahead. Moments later, he stumbled into a wider space, where Jaime was waiting.

"Great to see you," Jaime exclaimed. "We're safe here. If anyone comes in, we'll get warning, but it's doubtful anyone will." He led Atcho through a door to the side. "These are access tunnels to the city's sewer system, but it's antiquated, so the tunnels are not used much. We've cleaned out a mainte-nance room for our use."

The chamber was sparse, nothing more than a table with light commu-nications equipment and a few cots set against the walls. "We'll rest here for the day and move to the staging site after dusk. You'll meet the rest of the team there and run through a few brief-back rehearsals. Do you have any questions?"

"I'm glad to see you. Is Danilo on this mission too?"

Jaime shook his head. "We both volunteered, but as you Americans say, I got the short straw." He grinned. "Besides, I do a better Sudanese than he does. Any other questions?"

Atcho shook his head tiredly. "I've been thoroughly rehearsed." He hesi-tated. "Well, just one question. What was the point of my disguise and walking all that way through the city?"

"Simple. If we get separated tonight, and you don't make it to the extrac-tion point, you've got to take care of yourself until we can get you out, and you don't speak the language. You needed to get the feel from the ground. Do you have that transmitter you were issued in Tel Aviv?"

Atcho nodded.

"Good. Tonight, we'll cross the Nile west of here and meet up with the assault team a few miles east of the camp. Anything else?"

Atcho shook his head.

"Good. Then get some rest. I'll wake you up when it's time to go."

23

A Training Camp Outside Khartoum, Sudan

Klaus raised his head and listened. Something in the pre-dawn hours had awakened him, but he could not discern what. His gut stirred. He sniffed the air, but nothing unusual drifted in the light breeze. Across the room, other men snored and puffed in their sleep, but no other sound caused alarm. From afar, he heard the call of a rooster, soon to be followed by the call to prayer.

Thinking of the latter, he rolled to his other side, annoyed. Although he considered himself devout, he sometimes admitted to himself that his religion's demands could be onerous. *Prayer five times a day!*

He dispelled the thought, but soon the sense of unease returned. *Am I becoming paranoid, or are my instincts warning me?* He reached under his pillow and grasped his pistol, then sat up and tried to look through the darkness. Only the sound of sleeping men accompanied their unwashed malodor.

Rising to his feet, Klaus thrust the gun into his belt and reached for his AK-47 leaning against the head of his bed. He headed for the door, opened it, and looked out. Behind him, two men rose from their cots and joined him.

Klaus looked across the compound. The sun, still below the horizon, cast its pre-dawn light against a sky just turning blue with wisps of elongated red clouds above the distant ground level. Seeing and hearing nothing amiss, Klaus was about to turn back when strong arms seized him from behind. One hand went immediately to his face and clamped a wet cloth with a sweet-smelling substance across his nose and mouth.

Klaus only had time to sense that his assailants were hardened, trained combatants before he slipped into unconsciousness. The two men behind him grabbed him under his shoulders and dragged him forward into the compound's open ground.

A small white pickup truck was parked beyond the door. The two Israelis pushed Klaus into the middle and took seats on either side of him. The man on the driver's side cranked the engine and drove at an unhurried pace toward the main entrance. Although vigilant, he was not worried about meeting resistance. Other members of the team had subdued security across the camp, including the main gate.

Once outside the compound, the driver mashed the accelerator and headed west into the desert at high speed, leaving a trail of dust billowing behind them. Aided by a flashlight and map, his partner navigated through the dunes and craggy, sparsely vegetated hills. After ten minutes of driving, they crested a ridge and descended into a long, flat piece of hard ground. At the near end, a Black Hawk helicopter idled, its blades whipping the air and throwing up dust around it.

The pickup came to a halt a safe distance from the aircraft. Behind it, other vehicles pulled in with the rest of the assault team and formed a perimeter around the small truck.

Klaus stirred. His eyes opened. He looked around, taking in the full scene, as comprehension dawned. He heard the steel-on-steel sound of weapons being armed. On either side of him, his captors held pistols to his head.

As full consciousness returned, he heard another sound, the low roar of an idling jet engine. Then he saw a C-17 cargo jet a short distance behind the helicopter, idling on a rough, makeshift runway. Its rear cargo hatch had been dropped to the ground, exposing a cavernous interior. Crewmen hurried about making preparations for taking on freight.

Meanwhile, a man emerged from the Black Hawk. He wore the tattered clothing of a Sudanese beggar, and although he looked gaunt, he walked with authority. He was joined by another man in Western garb.

The two men guarding Klaus exited the truck while keeping their weapons trained on him. He sat motionless, watching the Sudanese beggar and his companion approach. The two guards stood aside while the newcomers thrust their heads in to take a closer look.

"Is that him?" the team leader asked.

The sun had risen to the point that no additional light was necessary. The Sudanese beggar stepped closer and gazed into Klaus' eyes.

For seconds, Klaus and the beggar stared at each other. Startled recognition crossed Klaus' face, but his mind could not yet believe what he saw.

The beggar turned to his companion. "It's him," he said simply. "He goes with us."

On hearing the voice, Klaus reacted. "Atcho!" he screamed, and lunged, wrapping his hands around Atcho's throat.

On the other side of the truck, the driver leaned in swiftly. He crooked one arm around Klaus' neck, and his free hand brought the pistol to Klaus' head.

"Let go," he growled.

Meanwhile, Atcho landed a punch in the middle of Klaus' face that stunned him, causing him to release his hold. With the gun at his head and surrounded by overwhelming firepower, Klaus stared at Atcho, hatred glistening in his eyes. "I will kill you," he said. "You and your family."

Without expression, Atcho turned his back on Klaus and walked away. Next to him, Jaime thrust an arm into the air with a circular motion. Immediately, the vehicles ringed around the white pickup started moving toward the C-17. The Black Hawk's idling engine began winding down. Two crewmen prepared to fold its blades and winch it into the hold of the cargo plane.

The pickup driver grabbed Klaus by the shoulder and pulled him from the truck, while the guard on the passenger side rounded the truck and held his weapon steady, aimed at Klaus' chest. The driver pointed to the C-17 and shoved him toward it.

Suddenly, gunfire erupted from the left ridgeline above the aircraft. Klaus' two guards went down and did not move.

Next to Atcho, Jaime fell, a clean bullet hole through his chest. Atcho heard the spit of rounds whizzing past him, ran to a sand berm, and dove behind it.

The helicopter's engine spun up again, and armed men returned fire and ran from their vehicles to clamber aboard it. Others scurried to the back of the nearest C-17 and ran up the cargo hatch. Within seconds, the helicopter soared into the air, spun in the opposite direction, dipped its nose, and gained speed as it climbed into the sky and out of range of small-arms fire. Meanwhile, the large aircraft leaped into forward motion and began taxiing even while the cargo hatches were raised.

Klaus wasted no time. As soon as his two guards collapsed, he ducked, ran back to the pickup, and sped off. As Atcho watched from his hidden position, the little truck vanished in a cloud of sand.

Within minutes, the aircraft had disappeared. Except for the sound of wind springing up over the desert sand with the rising sun and morning heat, all was silent. Deathly silent. Atcho reached into a pocket and activated the tiny transmitter that would send out a location beacon.

24

Nessim had slept fitfully that night in the chamber next to the one Klaus occupied. His room was small, no more than a closet, and it doubled for his place of work during the day. His job was to keep records of each trainee's progress.

He longed to be a fighter as well, but his slight figure made that improbable. He was well regarded in the camp, even considered to possess superior intelligence, but no one thought of him as being effective on a battlefield. Perhaps he could be a martyr if the appropriate mission came along, but doing so did not require training in the other military skills, and he was not sure he wanted to take such extreme action before contributing to *jihad* in some other meaningful way.

Nessim's ambition had always been to be a *jihadist*, and he had arrived at the camp with that intention. However, he soon learned that the training cadre looked for trainees of at least average physical build, and his frame was slight. They humored him by allowing him to stay and take part in training if he did not get in the way, but they gave him noncombatant jobs that prevented him from being a full participant.

His favorite trainer was Sahab Kadyrov, the Chechen who had been a KGB officer trained by the Soviet Spetsnaz. Rumor circulated that he was wanted in the West, where he was known by an alias he no longer used, Klaus.

Sahab maintained a distance from trainees and other instructors, but Nessim found the man's breadth and depth of knowledge fascinating. Whether the subject was hand-to-hand combat, small-arms targeting, demolitions, land navigation, or any other of a myriad of subjects, the Chechen seemed to know all of it to a superior degree. Students also muttered that Sahab had a personal connection to Osama bin Laden, a distinction that gave him an almost mythical aura.

Nessim had contented himself with attending lectures whenever time allowed, and he took part in skills exercises every chance he could. His perspicacity had been recognized despite his size, so he maintained the respect of trainees and cadre.

He heard the rooster crow and anticipated the call to prayer that would follow. He sat up in bed, yawned, stretched, and got up to prepare for the day. He heard the door creak open in the next room and went to see who might be up. Entry to his room was on the opposite side of the building, but his window was angled such that he had a clear view of the door to Sahab's room. Nessim was pleased to see that Sahab was the first to rise and had stepped outside just beyond the door. *Not surprising.*

As he observed, two other men appeared behind Sahab. One Nessim recognized. He was a trainee who had been in camp for many months and did well at all his lessons. He was quiet and kept to himself for the most part, but he was friendly when addressed, and he helped other students who did not grasp training tasks as easily as he did.

The other man was one Nessim did not recognize. That surprised him because the man had not registered with him, yet he slept in quarters reserved for trainees and cadre. For a guest at the camp to stay in that room was unusual.

As Nessim watched, one of the men stepped closer and threw a hand over Sahab's face. The other immediately grabbed Sahab's arms and held them until they went limp. Then both men dragged Sahab to a white pickup truck.

Before the truck's engine had turned over, Nessim ran out his door, heading around the building. As he reached the front, the pickup drove off.

Nessim darted into the room where Sahab had slept. He tried to wake the other men there. They had been drugged.

He sprinted to the office near the front of the camp where someone was always on duty. He arrived there with heaving lungs in time to see the pickup clear the gate without being challenged.

Inside the small room that served as the duty office, a young man, really a boy, was slumped in his chair, also drugged. In desperation, Nessim ran to the headquarters building, yelling all the way. He pounded on the door until a tall bearded man opened it. From other buildings, men poured into the compound to see what had caused the commotion.

Speaking in precise terms despite being out of breath, Nessim told the camp commander what he had seen. With a wave of his hand, the commander ordered the camp to be rousted. Within five minutes, a quick reaction patrol of twenty trucks with heavily armed men rolled out of the gate in pursuit.

Nessim rode in the lead truck with the commander. The trail of dust lingering in the air made following the pickup easy. Looking ahead, they saw by the abrupt end of the dust cloud where the intruders had halted.

The commander ordered his patrol to the left of a ridge that would hide their actions. Then all the fighters dismounted and climbed up the hill, Nessim with them.

At the crest, they looked over. Several military vehicles had circled the white pickup. Two men, one in traditional Sudanese clothes, leaned into it, and two other armed men stood on either side of it. A Black Hawk helicopter idled below the ridge, its blades spinning. Beyond it, a huge cargo jet faced away from them, its cargo bays open.

Nessim pointed toward the white pickup and spoke into the commander's ear.

"Who is the Sudanese?" the commander asked.

"I don't know," Nessim responded. "He was not in the pickup when they took Sahab."

The commander designated targets to three snipers, set his other men in a line along the crest of the ridge, and gave the order to open fire.

25

When the mayhem had subsided, Atcho remained still for nearly ten minutes, listening. Then, from the far ridge, he heard voices. When he dared peek over the top of his meager cover, he saw armed men descending the steep, craggy slope on foot.

He eased back down, his mind racing. The only plan that came to mind was impersonating a deaf and mute Sudanese beggar again—he was already in costume and knew the part.

The weakness in his plan was that snipers had already seen him. That had been evident when they'd picked off Jaime and the two men in the pickup but had left Klaus and Atcho unscathed. *Did they shoot at me and miss, or did they assume I was a captive? Either way, they'll spot me. I can't beat them all, so I'd better join them until a better plan comes along.*

The ground behind him was flat, aside from a few low sandhills. He pushed himself backward on his stomach down a shallow sandy slope a few yards and stood up. Then, assuming the posture and gait he had used while traversing Khartoum on foot, he started up the bank toward the site of the firefight.

He first headed toward Jaime's limp body to check for breathing and to pretend to scavenge. On his way, he waved wildly at the men still struggling down the embankment. As he neared Jaime, he saw clearly that there was no life.

Casting aside remorse for the moment, he spotted Jaime's sidearm still in its holster. He reached for it, and then heard the rhythmic chopping of helicopter blades slicing the air, followed by long bursts of machinegun fire. From the back side of the ridge, the Black Hawk wheeled around and veered to the front, firing withering bursts that cut through the men, who now ran headlong down the slope seeking cover. Atcho estimated that they numbered between seventy and a hundred.

Its machineguns still doing their deadly work, the Black Hawk settled back to the ground. Immediately, armed men jumped out of each side. The ones nearest the enemy advanced toward them, sending a hail of bullets. The ones on the opposite side sprinted toward Atcho and the three dead Israelis.

Moments later, Atcho found himself running toward the helicopter among a group of rescuers who carried their dead between them. On reaching the aircraft, they clambered aboard, while the other element retreated to the opposite side and climbed on. All the while, the door gunner kept up his prodigious rain of steel.

The helicopter lifted into the air. Atcho took in the simultaneous roar of gunfire, thunder of engines, and odors of fuel, gun smoke, and bloody corpses. He glanced down at Jaime's still face, remembering their time together in Lima, in the rancid streets of Khartoum, and now on the bleak sands of the Sudanese desert. Against the chopper's throbbing vibration, he felt overwhelming sorrow.

He looked into the faces of the men who had mounted the original assault and risked their lives to rescue him and bring back their fallen comrades. Some watched the bodies. Others stared far away into the empty desert. All carried the same expression of unspeakable grief and failure buttressed by stoicism. No one spoke.

At the far end of the desert runway, the ground spilled into rough terrain, all but impassable for ground vehicles. Then it spread into flat, hardscrabble ground.

The helicopter flew on for a few minutes, then settled on the surface and cut its engines. Ahead of them, the C-17 waited with cargo hatch down.

Even as Atcho and the soldiers jumped from the Black Hawk and transferred to the larger plane, a crew ran to the helicopter to fold its rotor blades and winch it into the cargo hold.

Fifteen minutes later, the C-17 taxied over the rough desert floor and lumbered into the sky. Atcho settled in with the rest of the team for the long flight back to Tel Aviv, each man alone with haunting images.

26

A panel truck with three coffins awaited the C-17 when it taxied to a stop on a remote airstrip outside Tel Aviv. Atcho stood with the rest of the team to pay respect as the bodies were transferred. Burly, Eitan, and the head of Mossad operations, Jaron Bryk, joined them.

When the panel truck had departed, Burly and Eitan escorted Atcho to a waiting car while a bus drove the rest of the team away. Bryk and the mission leader walked separately to another waiting car, already in deep discussion.

Eitan shook his head sadly as he watched them. "Heads will roll over this cluster. What happened?"

Atcho described as best he could.

"What happened to the overwatch?" Eitan pressed. "And why was the Black Hawk on the ground? It was supposed to be providing air cover."

"I don't know what happened to the overwatch. I can say that the dust kicked up by the returning assault team hung in the air and created a smoke screen. A good guess is that the overwatch couldn't see the force in pursuit."

"Which the Black Hawk *should* have seen. So again, why was it on the ground?"

"It had a mechanical problem. The crew considered that it wasn't mission-threatening, but it took longer to fix than expected. It had something to do with locking the blades in place once they were unfolded. So, the assault got a late start. The leader decided to go for the capture rather than wait for air cover. Another few minutes and he would have had to scrub the mission because daylight was already dawning."

"He should have scrubbed it," Eitan observed. "We wouldn't have captured Klaus, but we could have had another chance. That's why the Mossad is deliberate." He closed his eyes momentarily and leaned his head back. "As it is, we lost three good operators, one on loan from Lima and two from Sudan. That's a huge intel hole in both countries, and we still don't have Klaus. Worse yet, he knows we're closing in on him."

He opened the car door. "There'll be an investigation. I'm sad to say that the mission leader is likely to see the end of his career. He'll live with this for the rest of his life." He sat in the driver's seat and started the engine.

"What now?" Atcho asked, settling into the back seat.

"Klaus has already scooted, I'm sure of that." Burly turned in the front passenger seat to look at him. "Who knows where?" He grimaced.

"He recognized me," Atcho said. "Now more than ever, he'll want revenge. He'll come after me and my family." He leaned forward and grasped Burly's arm. "Please get word to Sofia to stay put at West Point."

Burly nodded. "What are you going to do?"

"I don't know. I'll need time to think." He sat quietly a moment, and then leaned forward to speak to Eitan. "Out of curiosity, where did the Israeli Air Force get a C-17?"

"What C-17?" Eitan replied without turning his head.

27

Eitan pushed into Bryk's office uninvited and sat in a chair in front of his desk. Bryk barely acknowledged his presence, continuing to scribble notes on a pad. Eitan waited him out. At last Bryk looked up.

"Is there something I can do for you?"

"I've been debriefing our recovered undercover asset from the raid in Sudan. He's the guy who got our picture of Klaus in the camp."

"Any surprises?"

Eitan shook his head. "He said Klaus was a good instructor for technical competence, but he stayed aloof. Our guy tried to get close to him, but Klaus held him at a distance. It was as if Klaus was there against his will and biding his time."

"For what?"

"We don't know. Another bombing, maybe. But where?" Eitan shook his head again. "He's a bit of a legend inside the camp, with supposed contact with that new terrorist rich kid, Osama bin Laden, but so far we haven't been able to pin him against any known plans. Rumors there credit him with exploding a nuclear device in Afghanistan last year that caused those tremors we heard about, but that's not confirmed."

Bryk eyed Eitan irritably. "Then what are you doing in my office?"

"I'm trying to piece together Klaus' next move. Here's an interesting aspect. Before the raid, chatter was building with references to a Chechen, a bomb, New York, and the financial district. That all stopped after the raid."

"What do you mean 'that all stopped?'"

Eitan sat quietly a moment. "You know how it goes. The chatter is just that. Snippets of conversation along the lines of 'he saw,' 'she said,' 'I heard,' and the like. Quite a bit of it seemed to point to Klaus, and much of it was associated with New York and the financial district."

Bryk leaned back, his expression skeptical. "All the bad guys want to hit New York City, including King Kong and Godzilla. Do we have any confirmation or corroborating evidence of something imminent?"

"No, but there is a difference between what we have and chatter."

"And that would be...?"

"What our asset overhears inside the camp is a step up from chatter. He's hearing the same things, but not from anonymous sources on a phone line many miles away. He's hearing from flesh-and-blood people he trained with. And what he heard is that something big is going down in the New York City financial district."

"Then I ask again, what are you doing in my office?"

Eitan smirked. "Seeking the wisdom of greater experience?" He leaned forward. "Seriously, we haven't encountered a threat from terrorists as great as the one Klaus represents. Shouldn't we at least be making preparations?"

"That's been done. Anything else?"

"How about warning the US?"

"That's been done too. They've been tracking him as much as we have. How seriously they take the threat is on them."

Eitan nodded. "Do you mind if I back-channel Burly and Atcho? Klaus has a personal vendetta against Atcho. They're likely to pay more attention."

Bryk let out a long breath. "I don't see how that would harm anything. We're really just talking about your gut instinct, right?"

Eitan acceded, and Bryk went back to scribbling notes on his pad. He looked up a moment later. Eitan still sat in front of him.

"Is there something else?"

Eitan sighed. "Sir, what is going to happen to the mission leader on that raid?"

Bryk dropped his pen on the desk impatiently, though his eyes held compassion. "It's out of our hands." He picked up the pen and toyed with it a moment. "I hate losing good people, but he showed remarkably poor judgment against all his training. He can never be allowed to lead an operation again. Beyond that, I don't know." He glanced at Eitan's face. "Is he a friend?"

Eitan looked down in resignation. "No," he said slowly. "I just feel bad for him. He risked his life; he was the guy on the ground. I just wish we allowed for second chances."

Bryk rose from his seat, a gesture to end the discussion. "I understand, but when life and death are at stake, as they were on this mission—we lost three good men, and who's to say that if allowed another chance he wouldn't exercise similar judgment, or overcorrect by being too cautious? He's damaged, and we can't risk other lives for his sake."

Over eyes half-closed with regret, Eitan nodded and rose to his feet. "I suppose you're right. I also wish we could find a way to even the score with Klaus."

"Get that out of your head." Bryk spoke sternly. "We gather intelligence. We share it when and where appropriate. We mount operations. We even retaliate, but when we do, it's after careful thought about possible outcomes by taking or not taking action. And we never allow a desire for revenge to cloud our thinking. That's the way to ruin. Do you understand?"

Chagrinned, Eitan nodded. "Yes, sir."

Bryk gestured that he would walk Eitan to the door. "I've given you your leeway. If you want to see justice for the failed mission, put the information where it can best be used. That includes your gut instinct. And then back away."

Eitan thanked Bryk and returned to his office. There, he put in a call to Burly, but connected with an answering machine. He left a message.

28

Yousef awoke with a start. A light shined in his eyes, and he felt a hand clamped against his lips. Around him in his bedroom, all was dark.

"Shh, it's me, Sahab. Don't set off alarms." Klaus lifted his hand from Yousef's mouth.

Bewildered, Yousef looked about wildly. "Wh-who? H-how did you get in here?" He struggled to pull his wits together.

"Never mind that. I'm here. Or rather, I'm not here." Klaus snickered. "You taught me well how to move in and out of countries without being seen."

"What are you doing here?" Yousef hissed, suddenly angry. "You put us both in danger."

"Don't worry. I'll be gone before the authorities know I'm here. I've already transferred my money to my own control, and my bombs are safely outside the country."

Fully awake now, Yousef stared at him. "Why are you doing that? Did we do something to gain your mistrust?"

"Haven't you heard?" Klaus growled, matching Yousef's anger. "They came for me in Sudan, right in the training camp. They were taking me away on a jet. I came face to face with Atcho." His face contorted with rage. "If one smart trainee had not been alert, who knows where I would be right now." In vivid terms, he described the raid on the camp. "Our snipers killed three of them."

Yousef listened, almost disbelieving, except that Klaus' fury was genuine, and here he was, in the dead of night, having entered Saudi Arabia undetected on his own, not once but apparently twice—and he had taken possession of his money.

"I see why you're upset," he entreated when Klaus finished telling his story, "but don't blame us, and don't throw away our *jihad*."

"I'm throwing nothing away," Klaus stormed, "but someone is to blame. How did they know where to find me?"

Yousef thought for a few moments. "It had to be either the Americans or the Israelis. I think the Israelis. They have covert operators all through the Middle East and parts of Africa."

"But Atcho was with them."

"Maybe he was on loan."

"I'm going after him. I'm tired of his interference. He blew the operation for us in Berlin and then in Kuwait, he stopped me in Texas—and he killed my brother. He needs to go."

Yousef pulled his bulky frame out of bed, crossed the room to switch on a lamp, and then sat in an overstuffed chair. Klaus remained sitting on the edge of the bed.

"I understand your anger," Yousef said, "but why are you blaming us? Why did you pull your money and take your bombs away? We're on your side."

"I'm tired of waiting," Klaus snapped. "I spent months in the Sudan training camps. I made three trips to Latin America and then spent more months in Sudan. I want Atcho dead, and I want to blow a hole in America that will never be forgotten. I have the ability to do both, and I don't need Al-Qaeda's permission."

Yousef saw that Klaus would not be easily placated. "Then why did you return to see me? You have your money and your bombs. Why not just plant your bombs?"

Klaus took his time to respond, choosing his words carefully. "Because I have enough enemies. I don't need more." His tone seemed almost wistful. "When my brother was alive, we relied on each other. If I go alone now, I am truly alone. I don't wish to alienate you or Osama bin Laden. I just want my revenge and to hit my own targets, and I don't want to wait for anyone's permission. I think we can still cooperate."

Yousef studied Klaus from across the room. He observed a rare ferocity in him, but also a dampening of spirit, as if Klaus felt his isolation for the first time, or at least the depth of it. He climbed from his chair, walked over to Klaus, and leaned over, placing his hands on Klaus' shoulders.

"*Habibi,*" he said, "you are one of us. You have no need to ever be alone. We fight for the same things."

Klaus looked up at him defiantly. "You gave me ultimatums."

Surprised, Yousef pulled back. "I did," he said. "Maybe that was the wrong approach. You seemed about to take hurried action. We've succeeded by careful planning and execution.

"You know the operation we have coming up. We've prepared for years, but moving the pieces into place took a lot of time. It's almost ready. We didn't want you to do something impulsive to jeopardize it."

Klaus dropped his head into his hands. Yousef returned to his chair and sank into it. "So, what do we do?"

Klaus raised his head and regarded Yousef for a moment. "Just let me take care of Atcho. Now. More than two years have passed since he killed my brother, and he's taken a wife, and they've had a son. He's living life while my brother lies cold and desecrated by infidels in an unknown grave."

He cast a beseeching glance at Yousef. "I can make Atcho's death look like an accident. I'll even let his wife and son live, if you prefer. And whether I succeed or fail, I'll turn over my bombs to the people you already have in the US, and they can add them to the ones they're building. I'll show the leader how to detonate them. In return, I only ask for help locating Atcho. I doubt he went home to Texas. This way, I get my revenge, your plan goes forward, and we both get to strike a huge blow for Islam— the biggest ever."

Yousef's eyes widened in surprise. "You would do that?"

Klaus nodded. "You've already scouted the target. You know where to place the bombs for maximum destruction. I'll be happy to help."

Yousef sat in disbelief. "What happens afterward?"

Klaus shrugged. "I'll give you back my money to manage and go wherever Osama directs. I'll be his most loyal soldier. If the bombs work, I'll make as many as we can get plutonium for, and I won't ask for another thing." He stood and faced Yousef with fierce determination. "Atcho must die."

29

Sofia hurried into Isabel's house to answer the incessantly ringing phone while Isabel helped the children from the car.

"You were right, little lady. If I ever doubt you again, please remind me to check my sanity."

Sofia recognized Horton's voice and smiled despite the warning implied by his words. "What's going on?"

"Get to a secure line. I'll fill you in."

An hour later, Sofia sat in the same West Point office where she had previously called Horton. He picked up on the first ring.

"The mission failed," Horton said. "Klaus got away."

Sofia's heart dropped into the pit of her stomach. "Atcho—"

"He's fine. But the Israelis lost three men. Klaus went back to Riyadh."

"How do you know?"

"I have a friend in Saudi intelligence. Thanks to your shakin' the bushes when you came to Berlin, they recruited an informant inside Yousef's home in Riyadh. A man arrived there in the middle of the night, unannounced. He didn't use the doorbell. He broke in. It was Klaus. The informant eavesdropped." Horton chuckled. "Ya really shouldn't take the domestic help for granted."

He coughed and continued. "We have a second source. The *hawaladars* had a conversation. Yousef in Riyadh called Kadir in Berlin, who called us. You and the Germans turned him good. A guy by the name of Sahab wants help to locate Atcho."

"That's Klaus."

"Right. As I was piecin' this together waitin' on your call, I remembered that last year, here in Berlin, Kadir checked out you and Atcho for Klaus. He hired a detective agency in Austin and got pictures of you from an announcement in the Austin newspaper about your joinin' a garden club." He chuckled again. "Somehow, I have a hard time seein' you putterin' around in the roses and weeds with muddy gloves and rubber boots."

"Not now, Joe. What are you getting at?"

Horton's tone turned serious. "Klaus already has loads of information on you and Atcho. It's only a mental hop, skip, and jump for him to find out that Atcho has a daughter and granddaughter and where they live. He'll figure that Atcho will come to wherever his family is to protect them. It's good that you're at West Point. You should be safe there."

"I'm not so sure about that. Security is pretty loose here."

"Well, when you hear from Atcho, there are a couple of other things to talk about. There's some big operation planned inside the US. No mention was made of where, but it's been in plannin' for years, and they're goin' to execute soon." Horton sighed heavily into the phone. "I don't like tellin' you this, but you got to know."

"Just spit it out."

"Klaus offered to contribute his bombs to the operation in exchange for being cut loose to come after Atcho. At last count, he has three left. He'll deliver them to the stateside honcho for this operation, show him how to arm and detonate them, and then head Atcho's way. You nailed it, Sofia."

Sofia felt pressure against her temples and a roar in her ears as a sense of dread descended. Her hands became clammy. She took deep breaths to regain emotional control.

"Has our intelligence been advised?" she asked.

"The CIA, military intelligence, and even the FBI are hittin' their sources hard for whatever this operation is. So far, there's not much to go on, but they've heard chatter about it for months. I don't know where Atcho is now. Presumably, he's headed home. My guess is you'll hear from him today or tomorrow."

Silence ensued. "Ma'am, are you there?"

"I'm here. I was trying to think through all of this. Thanks for the help, Joe. You're a good friend to our whole family."

"That's mighty nice of you to say, little lady. Ziggy is just glad I get to stay home nights now, and soon we're headed into that promised land of retirement." He laughed. "Anythin' else I can do for you? Keep in mind that's just a nice way of endin' a phone conversation." He laughed again.

"Nothing for now, Joe. Thanks again."

"Seriously, if you need somethin', alls you got to do is ask. Us Texans got to stick together."

When Sofia arrived back at the house, Isabel looked anxious.

"Burly called," she told Sofia. "He wants you to phone him back first chance." She handed Sofia a piece of paper with numbers neatly written on it. "He wouldn't tell me anything."

"Don't worry. I'll fill you in." Sofia took the number and called Burly. "What's up?"

"Atcho's on his way home. We landed in the US a little while ago. He's fine. He asked me to get a message to you to stay where you are."

"I'm not so sure that's a good idea. I'm read into the situation. Security here is not great."

"Got it," Burly said, then chuckled. "There's no reining you in, is there? Just do me a favor and keep me in the loop."

"I will, Burly, but you've got to do me a favor. Call our friend Joe Horton and get him to brief you on what he told me. Then call Bob, Isabel's husband, on a secure line and fill him in. He needs to be home with Isabel while this is going on."

"Shouldn't that come from you, or Atcho, or Isabel?"

"Maybe, but you can locate him and get on a secure phone easier than I can, and we don't know how much time we've got."

"Roger. I'll shake some trees."

"Thanks." Sofia hung up and turned to face Isabel.

When Atcho arrived at Isabel's house that afternoon, he was surrounded by the overjoyed embrace of his wife, daughter, young granddaughter, and toddler son. He could not help thinking of the stark contrast in atmosphere and living conditions between being among loved ones at this stately home above the Hudson River and roaming the streets of Khartoum.

Isabel chided him. "Dad, those gray hairs on your head are multiplying. When are you going to stop this dangerous hobby of yours?"

Atcho did not reply. He caressed the side of Isabel's face and hugged her tightly. Then he stooped to pick up Kattrina and Jameson. With one under each arm, he bounded out onto the lawn, dropped to his knees in the grass, and rolled over onto his back amid the children's happy squeals.

Watching them, Sofia's chest swelled and her eyes moistened. She turned to Isabel. "Atcho has never had a malicious bone in his body. That's the life he yearns for and deserves."

Later, when they were alone, Atcho and Sofia exchanged details of their activities since Atcho's departure. Sofia related her conversation with Horton that morning.

"Your analysis was dead-on," Atcho told her. He took her in his arms. "No wonder they paid you the big bucks."

"Right," Sofia replied, snuggling against him, "and now we have to figure out what we're going to do. Klaus has something big planned inside the US, and he will never stop coming after us. We're going to have to end it."

30

Klaus called Yousef from Tripoli, Libya. "I'm in a safe place now."

They spoke in cryptic terms.

"Have you moved your cargo?" Yousef asked.

"It's on the way. I broke the individual objects into their component parts and sent them the way I did before. I'll find machine shops to do the parts of the frame I couldn't send."

"How will you travel?"

"I'll take exactly the same route." *Well, not exactly, but I won't tell you that.*

"When you get there, I'll put you in touch with our contact."

Klaus hung up and crossed to a window, deep in thought. He watched the blue waves of the Mediterranean crash against boulders far below. This was a moment of introspection, as if observing himself from outside his body.

Deciding not to reveal his real travel plans to Yousef had been an impulsive decision, based, he suddenly realized, on mistrust. Not that he believed Yousef would do anything to harm him or any other member of Al-Qaeda —the *hawaladar's* entire existence was based on trust. If he violated that, his fortune would collapse, and that would be the least of his problems. *But somehow, Atcho found me in Sudan.*

Klaus realized an emerging sense of independence greater than any he had known before. He had money, he had weapons, he knew tactics, and, just as importantly, he knew how to move around in the Western world unseen.

For a moment, his mind's eye glimpsed the man he had been, crawling through the smelly tunnels under Berlin a fearsome warrior, no doubt, but one taking direction from a higher authority and relying on brute force to take down enemies in his immediate vicinity. Now, he knew how to disappear into the fabric of societies as far-flung as Afghanistan, Peru, and even the United States, whether the occasion called for a *jalabiya*, tourist clothes, or a business suit. He smirked. *I've grown.*

Later that day, he met with Hassan, a local *hawaladar* who had introduced him to Yousef on Klaus' first trip to Saudi Arabia. So much had happened since then. Klaus had flown over the burning oil fields of Kuwait, he had smuggled himself with a lethal packet of plutonium into the United States, and he had traveled into several countries in South America to watch three separate bombing attacks.

"I need to move money and have it ready in three cities," he told Hassan, getting down to business after courtesies. "Make it one hundred thousand dollars in Caracas, the same in Montreal, and half a million in New York City."

Hassan made a note. "Anything else?"

"Get me a Libyan passport, an Argentinian passport, and a US passport. I need highest quality, and they should be well used with proper stamps. The Libyan one needs a visa to enter Argentina, and that one needs to get me into Canada too. The American one needs to show that I've passed through a legal port of entry—I don't care where."

"These could take several days."

"That's fine. One other thing." Klaus pulled a sheaf of papers from his jacket. "This is information that Kadir pulled together for me when I was in Berlin. There's a photograph of a man known as Atcho. You'll see his real name in these documents. They include newspaper articles about him and his wife, Sofia. I want to know everything about him, what family he has, where they live—"

"Should I go through Kadir?"

Klaus shook his head. "You'll see the name of a detective agency in Austin that Kadir used. Get a different one. I'll make my own travel arrangements. No one can know my movements."

Still taking notes, Hassan nodded as if doing routine business. "Anything else?"

"Just one. I need a contact in Montreal with a mosque that is sympathetic to *jihad*. Is that something you can arrange?"

Hassan nodded without looking up.

Klaus headed for the door. As he opened it, he turned back to Hassan. "I'll pick them up in three days." He glanced at Hassan's notepad. "Burn those notes."

31

Klaus looked about the small coffee shop on the Jersey City waterfront. The early morning crowds were finishing their last mugs before heading off to work. The buzz of chatter quieted amid the aroma of fresh brews mixing with cinnamon and nutmeg. *This is not an unpleasant place.*

Klaus had never heard of the man Yousef had directed him to meet, nor would Yousef tell him anything about the contact except to say that Klaus would be approached at this time on this date in this place. Despite the coffee shop's pleasant atmosphere, Klaus felt persistent unease, surrounded as he was by tall skyscrapers and roaring traffic on a scale beyond his experience, even in Berlin. Nevertheless, he was impressed with the opportunity that presented itself: *My bomb in this place would kill huge numbers of infidels.*

He reveled in the thought, but his mind turned to Atcho. *How do I get Atcho into the area where I'll place the bomb?* He dismissed the notion with a shrug. He could take out Atcho at any time. The hit did not have to occur in conjunction with the bombing, and Atcho might suffer even more knowing who had planted it and that he had been powerless to stop it. Klaus smiled.

He felt someone nudging his shoulder. A stoop-shouldered man stood there, young despite his posture. He had reddish hair that curled around his ears and an unkempt beard.

"Excuse me, sir. Do you mind if I read your paper—the part you've finished?"

Klaus studied him. The man had just given the recognition signal, but he was nervous in a way that bothered Klaus, as if that was his habitual demeanor rather than one generated by this clandestine meeting taking place in public view.

"I'm finished with the sports page. Is that the part you wanted?" Klaus replied, completing the sequence.

The man nodded and looked around, again in a manner that was too furtive for Klaus' liking. *He'll attract attention just because of his silly manner. Who sent him?*

"I'm sitting with a friend over there. Would you like to join us?"

Klaus stared at the man angrily. "No, I would not," he retorted, registering the man's startled expression. "I have a meeting to go to."

He shoved the newspaper into the man's hands, stood, and made a quick exit. He made his way to his hotel a short distance away and called Yousef in Saudi Arabia. It would be mid-afternoon there.

"They sent me a fool," he blurted when Yousef came on the line. "If I'm going to work with these people, I need to see someone with competence. Anyone would have noticed and remembered that idiot. If that's who's carrying out your mission over here, it's already a failure."

"I'll take care of it," was all Yousef said. He entreated Klaus to return to the same coffee shop at the same time the next day.

Klaus spent the rest of the morning walking the city streets. Around noon, he crossed to the other side of the Hudson River through the Holland Tunnel in a taxi. There, he asked the driver to point him to the ferry that would take him out to the Statue of Liberty.

He meandered along the waterfront opposite the coffee shop, taking in the sights and sounds of the bustling city. As he skirted by the World Trade Center, he stared up at the towers, taking in their full height and might. Then he scoffed. *Your days are numbered.*

His reaction was similar as the ferry broke the wavelets while approaching Liberty Island with its grand statue, the most famous in the world. Without emotion, he watched the people gazing up in awe at the crown, torch, and visage. He viewed them in the same light as a homeowner observing an anthill spoiling a back yard—a nuisance to be removed. *And I have the pesticide.*

The next morning, Klaus returned to the coffee shop. He arrived a little earlier this time so that he might have a better chance of getting a seat in a corner with his back to the wall, where he could better observe the morning crowd. Several minutes later, he noticed a man enter alone.

The newcomer was nondescript, wore tinted glasses, and dressed neatly in clothes typical of the area. He moved easily among the other customers, excusing himself politely when bumping into someone or having to reach across for items like sugar or cream. He did not look around, yet he seemed aware of where everything was in the room, circling tables, chairs, and other people with unobtrusive ease.

When he had paid for his coffee and a pastry, he made his way to a table not far from Klaus and sat with his back toward him. He lingered there as the crowd grew, satisfied its morning caffeine craving, and then thinned out—the rhythm of the city.

After a while, the man stood and walked into the restroom. When he came out, he stopped by Klaus' table.

"Excuse me, sir, if you are finished with parts of your newspaper, would you mind if I read them?"

Klaus looked up into a set of calm eyes. The man had removed his glasses, and he smiled mildly. "I don't mean to bother you," he continued. "I'll return them if you like."

Klaus studied him quickly. "Please sit. You can read them here."

"Thank you. My name is Ramzi Yousef."

The two men stayed in the coffee shop only long enough to ensure they had not been observed. Then they departed and walked along the street edging the waterfront, speaking in Arabic.

"I apologize for Salameh yesterday. He's my useful idiot."

"He needs a leash. He has no subtlety and he's all emotion. People will notice him, his strange behavior, and the people with him. I could not stay."

Ramzi nodded. "You are right. He's exploded things in my workshop and he even put me in the hospital."

"He what?"

"It's true. He drives like a maniac. One night a couple of weeks ago, he drove through an intersection on a yellow light. He was going too fast and was rammed by another vehicle. I was a passenger and had to be taken away in an ambulance." He grasped Klaus' arms. "These Americans are so stupid. I had all the bomb-making materials in the trunk of the car. Would you believe it? The police never checked. A few days later, two of our men went to the impound lot and told the attendant they needed to get some personal items from the car. The guard let them. They got everything out. No problem.

"I was in the hospital for a few days, but I had a telephone right by my bed and just kept working. I ordered some powdered metals I need to make the bomb more powerful. They will multiply the explosive effect by many magnitudes."

Klaus stopped Ramzi with a hand on his shoulder. "You're the bomb-maker?"

"I thought you knew that."

Klaus shook his head. "They wouldn't tell me much. Only how to make contact and that I would be briefed when I arrived."

They walked to the water's edge. "And there," Ramzi said, "is the target."

Across the river, the twin towers of the World Trade Center rose into the sky, gleaming in the sunlight.

"Can you believe it?" Klaus exulted. "Allah be praised."

"That's it," Ramzi affirmed. "In a little more than a week, we'll topple both of them."

"How?" Klaus asked, barely able to contain his excitement.

"Simple. We'll park the van next to one of the outer walls on an upper floor in the parking garage. We've already scouted and have the location selected. When the bomb blows, it will be of such power that it will damage the foundational structure of the first tower, causing it to fall into the second tower." He rubbed his hands together in exultation. "We'll get them both."

Klaus' eyes glowed with excitement. He leaned back so he could see the full height of the towers and imagined them collapsing into the Hudson River.

"Do you know why I'm here?" he asked.

Ramzi pursed his lips. "Not really. I was told only to expect you, how to find you, and that you should be treated as a peer. You come with the blessing of Osama bin Laden."

Klaus nodded. "True." As he explained his purpose, Ramzi's eyes grew wide with amazement. Klaus explained to him about his bombs, how he had come into possession of them, and how he had transported one into the US on a previous occasion. "I'm building a new one here," he said. "I'll have some parts machined in local shops; the other parts were delivered to an address here in New York. I think that address is yours."

Ramzi's cheeks contorted as he held back a smile. "I didn't know what they were for." He stood back and took a new measure of Klaus, then pointed across the river at the towers. "That," he exclaimed, "is the financial heart of the US economy. When we bring those buildings down, this abominable country might never recover. And with your weapon added to mine, thousands of infidels will die, perhaps millions. The black hole a mile wide in New York City will be a warning to all mankind of the power of Islam." He closed his eyes and breathed out slowly. "Surely, Allah brought you and me together for his *jihad*."

Then a questioning look crossed his face. "What about the nuclear fuel? Do you have it already?"

Klaus chortled. "Are you ready for some irony? I have it, and I stored it in a bank safety deposit box in that tower." He pointed at the one with the television antenna protruding from its top. "I think they call that the North Tower."

Neither man spoke for a few minutes, both taking in the sight of the soaring edifices across the river. Then they turned and retraced their steps past the coffee shop toward Ramzi's workplace.

"How did you enter the country?" Ramzi asked.

Klaus smirked. "It was so easy. I flew into Montreal on an Argentinean passport and took a boat from Kingston across Lake Ontario. I have a US passport that shows I traveled outside the country a while ago and re-entered a few weeks back." He laughed. "I'm legal. What about you?"

"I've been here since September. I came in on a fake Iraqi passport and was arrested coming through immigration at the airport. I claimed that my life was in danger in Iraq and requested political asylum." He shrugged and laughed. "I went in front of some minor official who scheduled a court date for me and let me go on my own recognizance." He guffawed. "I think I missed my court date."

They reached a long alley and turned to walk through its shadows. "You know what's even funnier?" Ramzi continued. "I came here with one of our men. He's more like Salameh, not the most intelligent person. The passport he presented at immigration had his own picture pasted over someone else's, and he had three other passports. He was arrested and sentenced to six months in jail and fined fifty dollars."

"Fifty dollars? That's all? In Saudi Arabia, they would have tortured him."

"Here's the funniest part," Ramzi continued. "He was carrying bomb-making manuals with him, complete with his own drawings. At his trial, he claimed that he had them because he was researching how to spot them among terrorists. The judge not only ordered that the manuals be returned to him, but also that if any of them were damaged or missing, the arresting officer would have to pay to replace them."

He shook his head. "Only in America. Anything goes here. He has a week or two remaining on his sentence, but we can't wait for him. If he's not out in time, we'll blow the buildings anyway. I don't worry about him, though. He's comfortable. He says the inmates just sit around watching TV or porno videos." He chuckled. "He claims to turn his head so he doesn't see and be corrupted, but I don't believe him."

They continued on through the alley. Then Klaus stopped. "I need help with another project."

Ramzi gave him his full attention.

"This project is sanctioned by Osama on condition that I don't let it interfere with our joint mission here." He recounted his running battle with

Atcho, the death of his brother, and Atcho's interference in his other attempts at raining death on infidels.

"Yes," Ramzi agreed when Klaus had finished. "This Atcho must die, and all those close to him. What do you want to do?"

"If I can't get him into the bomb blast area, I'll deal with him afterwards. Meanwhile, I want him to feel my reach, to fear the power of what I can do, to tremble at the knowledge that I am coming for him."

"How can I help?"

"I want to send him a message. He's at West Point. Have you heard of the place?"

Ramzi nodded. "Of course. It's about fifty miles upstream from the Twin Towers."

Klaus' eyes burned with malevolence. "That close? I hadn't realized that."

"What do you want to do?"

Klaus hesitated only a moment while he gathered his thoughts. "Let me have your best man. Atcho has a son and a daughter. They are at West Point now. I want them kidnapped and brought to me."

Ramzi shrugged. "We can do that, but do you think it's wise so close to executing our mission?"

"It will be a distraction for Atcho. He expects me to come, but he won't expect that. He'll be so busy trying to find them that he won't have time to get in our way."

"How old are the children?"

"His daughter is fully grown, and she has a daughter as well. Your man can bring her too, if he can manage all three."

"What about the son? Will he be a problem?"

"Only if you run out of diapers. He's a toddler."

"What will you do with them?"

"Sell them into the sex trade," Klaus said without hesitation, "or you can take Atcho's daughter back to Pakistan with you, if you like. Consider her a bonus. The son we can sell to a trader in Afghanistan. He can be a dancing boy there."

32

Atcho cleared security without difficulty at FBI headquarters in the Jacob Javits Federal Building on Lafayette Street in Manhattan. The largest federal building in the US, it was an imposing edifice with many small windows that made it look like an enormous, vacated beehive.

Burly met Atcho in the lobby and escorted him to an upper floor. "We're not getting a lot of takers on our story," he said as they rode the elevator. "Most people in the intelligence community or the FBI have never heard of Al-Qaeda or Osama bin Laden, and the notion of Hamas and Hezbollah cooperating with each other seems outlandish to them. That goes back to the Shia–Sunni chasm. If they killed every last infidel on the planet, that still wouldn't stop their *jihad* because they'd kill each other until one or the other of their belief systems reigns supreme."

"So, what are we doing here today?"

"Klaus threatened you and your family. We have to make sure we get all the federal protection we can. The special agent in charge at the FBI office in Chicago, Tom O'Brian, is an evangelist for counterterror and spends a lot of time researching it. I spoke with him by phone when we got back from Israel. He's proposing to his superiors to form a counterterror task force. He's a bit of a dandy and he rubs his bosses the wrong way. Rumor has it that he was granted the Chicago assignment to sideline him—get him out of his boss' hair."

Atcho's agitation sparked. "I'm not understanding. Don't they know that a ring of terror is closing around us, and if we don't stop it, we're going to be hit here at home, big time?" He took a deep breath and swung around to face Burly. "Three explosions. Three of them in the last year when Klaus was there, near the site, and they keep getting bigger. That doesn't even count the failed attempt by my house last year. The terrorists are testing methods and probing weaknesses, and they're getting better by the day. Do these smart intel guys think we're invulnerable?"

The elevator reached its destination, the doors slid open, and they stepped into a corridor. Burly led the way into a conference room. The view beyond the glass was dramatic, showing the vast cityscape that was New York City with its crown jewels, the twin towers of the World Trade Center, gleaming in the sunlight against a deep blue sky.

"The man we're meeting with is skeptical about the size of the threat," Burly said, ignoring the vista. "He'll be here in a few minutes to put us on speakerphone with O'Brian in Chicago."

"It's not just Klaus," Atcho said in exasperation, continuing their prior conversation. He glanced around the conference room and took note of the magnificent view, but he stayed on point. "Klaus is the tip of the spear, and an incredibly lethal one. Bad people are coming our way, and they intend to convert or kill us. In their view, we're all combatants: women, children, mothers, fathers—it doesn't matter. If we're infidels, we should die. That's the way these *jihadists* see things."

Burly gave him a sideways glance. "Do you think you might be getting a little paranoid?"

"Paranoid?" Atcho whirled on him. "You were the case officer when that suitcase nuke got loose in Siberia. You were in Berlin when the guy we're chasing right now, Klaus, escaped with one just like it. You came back out of retirement last year when he had ideas about using it in the Kuwaiti oilfields, and he had learned to make copies. And in each of my last three missions, including the attempt to capture Klaus in Sudan, *you* came to *me*."

Burly listened to him patiently. "Correct on all counts." He sighed. "I'm your friend, Atcho. We're on the same side. We have to stay objective, though."

"Meaning what?" Atcho fought to control his anger. Images crossed his mind of a dank cell in Siberia where he had been held captive in the dead of winter, of being aboard the near-crash of a huge cargo jet in Moscow, of crawling through dark tunnels under Berlin, and of flying through the black smoke clouds in a Black Hawk helicopter amid the flames of burning oil wells in Kuwait.

He squinted. "I've put my life on the line at your request several times, and you call me paranoid. Even if I were, that doesn't mean the danger isn't real."

Chastened, Burly backtracked. "Poor choice of words," he said. "But take another look. Siberia and Moscow were purely East-versus-West situations. Berlin was too, and only involved *jihad* because Klaus was part of that conspiracy.

"We're after one man with a bomb, not a whole movement. I'm not saying that there isn't a group of bad people wanting to do bad things to us, but their resources are limited. They can't pose a major threat to us."

Atcho's eyes bulged. He slid both hands over his ears to massage the back of his head. "I can't believe I'm hearing this. You thought the threat credible enough when Klaus put that suitcase nuke by my house last year—and activated the countdown."

Burly blew out a breath, his own patience waning. "Yes, I did, and the threat was real—from one man, with a weapon that still has never been proven."

Atcho contained his exasperation. "Are you serious? Do you recall that I nearly burned my hand off taking care of that bomb?"

"Agreed," Burly said, restraining himself, "and the device had plutonium, but we can't say definitively that it or any of Klaus' bombs were viable. They were never tested."

"What about the tremor in Afghanistan at Tora Bora? I recall you thought that might have been caused by a 'poor man's underground test.' I think that's what you called it."

Burly nodded. "We still think that might be the case, but we don't have proof. Some radiation leaked into the atmosphere, but that could have been naturally generated, and our teams couldn't go deep enough to find trace materials that would tell us the origin of any nuclear device, *if* that's what caused the tremor in the first place."

Atcho shook his head, defiant. "Then what am I doing here?"

"Klaus poses a real threat, particularly to your family. His device might actually work, in which case the danger extends far beyond you. As you said, you came to warn the authorities. I'm here for the same reason."

Burly paused. "There's one other thing I wanted to tell you when we got into a secure facility, like this one." He looked around the room as if double-checking. "Eitan called last night. He passed along that their asset inside the camp overheard that Klaus plans to hit the New York financial district. Mind you, that information is not confirmed and it's just above the level of chatter in terms of reliability."

Before Atcho could respond, the door opened, and a well-groomed man in a dark business suit walked in. "Gentlemen," he greeted them. "Sorry to run late. We're going to have to get right to the call. My name is Jim Dude." He extended his hand.

Atcho and Burly stared at him.

Dude returned their gazes with a shrug. "I get that a lot. That's my real last name. Will you please take your seats? My secretary has already placed the call and will put it through." A green light on a speakerphone in the middle of the table blinked. "That should be our man." He reached over and flipped a switch.

"O'Brian here," a disembodied voice intoned.

Dude introduced Atcho and Burly.

"It's an honor to meet you, Atcho," O'Brian said. "I watched the night President Reagan introduced you at the State of the Union Address."

"Thank you, but that was long ago. Can we get to business?" Atcho felt the heat of his anger still simmering and forced himself to be civil. "A few weeks ago, I was in Israel, where I participated with the Mossad in a mission to snatch a Chechen terrorist from Sudan. The man has a suitcase nuclear bomb, maybe as many as five, and his stated aim is to harm the US and, more specifically, me and my family. And I just learned he's planning an attack right here in New York City."

As Atcho spoke with passion, even fury, Burly leaned back in his chair and arched his eyebrows. Dude leaned forward in his seat, thunderstruck.

"If he succeeds in harming my family," Atcho went on, "he will simultaneously kill many other Americans. Depending on where that happens, we could be talking millions of casualties. Sorry to be so blunt, but I learned on the way here that the FBI doubts the severity of the threat."

A stifling cloud seemed to have descended over the room.

Dude cleared his throat. "Mr. Atcho," he began, his reluctance to speak evident. "This mission you say you went on with Mossad"—he glanced at Burly—"are we supposed to know about that?"

Burly shook his head slightly, looking dismayed. "Not necessarily," he said, just loudly enough for O'Brian to hear over the speakerphone. "I filed a full report with the CIA. If it's relevant to your efforts, you'll get the details through channels."

Startled, Atcho looked back and forth between Dude and Burly. "I don't understand. What do you mean you're not 'necessarily' supposed to know? How are you supposed to protect—"

"This is exactly what I've been talking about," O'Brian cut in over the phone. "That silly practice of not sharing information between the CIA and the FBI is going to get people killed. Lots of *American* people."

Atcho rose to his feet and leaned on his fists over the table. "Will someone please explain to me what the hell we're talking about?" He glared at Dude. "I came in to tell you about a man who has a nuclear device he intends to use inside the United States. The threat is taken seriously by the Mossad, and you talk to me about practices and whether you're supposed to know about something that could be critical to protecting our people? What kind of crap is that?"

"It's complicated," Dude responded in a low voice.

"Try me," Atcho snapped. "I'm just a dumb yokel from the general public, but I've been known to understand a thing or two."

"I'll handle this," O'Brian called, "and Atcho, I'm on your side. That's why I'm consigned to the hinterland in Chicago instead of meeting with you in person there in New York."

"Now, Tom—"

"I said I'd handle his question." O'Brian's voice assumed an icy quality. "I still outrank you, Jim, and I'm a participant in this meeting."

Dude started to protest.

"I want to hear him," Atcho said. He straightened to full height, crossed his arms, and cast a challenging glare at Dude. Burly said not a word.

"You know the CIA and the FBI have different missions," O'Brian said.

"Yes."

"The CIA is restricted to intelligence gathering outside the US, and the FBI is responsible for investigating crimes inside our borders."

"Got it. Tell me something I don't know."

"Because of the rise in terror worldwide," O'Brian went on, "I started this counterterror unit, but it doesn't have wide acceptance within the bureau."

"Now, Tom—" Dude interrupted.

"I'm just giving him the lay of the land," O'Brian said tersely. "I won't air our dirty laundry.

"Atcho, the hickey comes in when defining the dividing line between what is a threat to the US outside our borders and when it becomes a domestic concern. Your guy Klaus illustrates the problem clearly. He's on foreign soil, but he threatens us here, and more specifically you and your family. As you pointed out, if he succeeds, many people will die. I understand he attacked your house with a device a few months ago—"

"There's no physical evidence that was Klaus," Dude protested.

Atcho's head swung around, his anger palpable. "I fought with him. He killed one of your agents and beat a cop nearly to death."

"You say so," Dude retorted, "but where's the proof that Klaus did those things? You fought him at night, and no one else saw him." He looked at Burly. "So far there is no physical evidence confirming that Klaus was involved at all. Is that correct?"

Looking sheepish, Burly nodded and turned his attention to Atcho. "We found your fingerprints on the bomb last year. That was expected, because you fought with the assailant—"

"The assailant," Atcho glowered. "That's all he is? You and I joined in a full manhunt for him in Germany and Kuwait."

"That was overseas," Dude cut in. "Different ballpark, different game.

Here, inside the country, we need evidence of a crime to investigate. As I understand, the assailant"—he emphasized the term—"got away, and there's no physical evidence to say who the man was." He turned to Burly. "There was no match for the other fingerprints on that case. Is that right?"

Burly nodded. "Besides Atcho's, there was only one other set of prints. They were smudged, and there was no match in the database for the partials that were lifted."

Atcho stared in disbelief. "Burly, you were there. You know it was Klaus. You just got a call from the Mossad about an intent to attack here in the city."

Burly caught Dude's glance. "The call I got was unofficial," he said, his reluctance clear. "I was there when Atcho fought whoever it was, and I think it was Klaus, but I didn't see him, and we can't prove it."

Atcho had never seen Burly look so uncomfortable, even awkward.

"We think he's overseas now," Burly continued, "and involved with a terrorist organization that we know very little about. That makes it an intelligence matter, which is CIA."

Atcho's exasperation was unbridled. "So, the FBI is going to sit on its hands and do nothing in the face of a known threat? The same set of people blew up the Israeli Embassy in Buenos Aires. They did the same thing to a TV station and then a major bank in Lima. Their bombs are getting bigger, and they're hitting targets that are higher and have greater economic impact. To think they won't come here is silly."

"That's the battle I'm fighting," O'Brian growled.

Dude rolled his eyes. "It's not that we'll do nothing," he said. "We're a country of laws and we have a protocol. To protect our own people's rights, the CIA is not allowed to operate inside the US—we don't want the agency spying on citizens." He warmed to his argument. "When they've developed intelligence of a threat they judge to be credible, severe, and imminent, they'll let us know through proper channels."

"With all due respect," Atcho replied in a tone that indicated his respect had dissipated to a breaking point, "terrorists are not operating on your timeline or observing your protocol. They train, they rehearse, they improve every day, and they are gaining funds, technology, and advanced methods. You'd better stop regarding them as third-world wannabes and start seeing them for what they are: an increasingly sophisticated fighting force that wants to kill us. And you'd better find a way to get information back and forth between you and the CIA or..." He paused as though considering the gravity of what he was about to say. Then he straightened, looked directly into Dude's eyes, and pointed a finger at him. "Or you'll have lots of American blood on your hands."

He turned to Burly. "I'm done here. If I want to waste my time, I can find better ways to do it." He faced the speakerphone. "Mr. O'Brian, I wish you luck."

He looked Dude rapidly up and down. "Don't worry about protecting me or my family. I can do a better job without you."

With that, Atcho walked out.

33

Burly barely made it to the elevator before the doors closed. Atcho was already inside, staring straight ahead. They rode in silence down to the first floor. There, Atcho exited without a word and strode toward the street. On clearing the door, he kept going without slowing down.

Burly struggled to keep up. "Atcho, would you please stop? Let's talk," he called.

"I've heard enough talk for one day," Atcho retorted. "I have things to do. A thug is coming after me and my family, or hadn't you heard?"

"Atcho, don't do this." Burly stepped up his pace and turned in front of Atcho, stopping him. He lowered his head so his eyes were level with Atcho's and placed a hand on Atcho's shoulder, his lungs heaving. "I'm your friend," he panted. "After all that we've been through together, I shouldn't have to prove that."

Atcho looked away, his irritation still keen. "What do you want? I really have to go move my family. That's not idle talk."

"I know." Burly leaned back. "Let me catch my breath." Pedestrians moved around them on the sidewalk while morning traffic whooshed by only feet away, filling the air with the heavy smell of exhaust.

"I'm sorry about what happened up there," he said when he had regained his composure. "I saw it coming. It was worse than I thought."

"You mean the pigheadedness? What's wrong with those people? If they think that war we fought in Kuwait makes the world safe for democracy, they are incredibly naïve. Klaus and whoever sponsors him are breeding and training more goons like him every day."

Burly nodded. "Not exactly like him. There aren't any more we know of with their own money, expertise, and fighting experience."

"Maybe. Burly, I watched the training in Lima. Hell, I gave classes in close-in combat, and the guys who attacked us in Sudan were good. Not as good as the Israelis, but they'll get better. Their snipers took out three men with three shots. You can't ask for better than that. I didn't see inside the camp in Sudan, but they put together a quick reaction force in a matter of minutes." He shook his head and looked around at the tall skyscrapers looming overhead before returning his gaze to Burly. "If we don't recognize and identify the threat, we're in trouble. And if we won't share information with everyone who needs it, we're lost."

They headed up the street toward the parking garage.

"You surprised me up there," Atcho said. "I hadn't expected pushback from you."

"I didn't say I agreed with the practices," Burly replied. "I was trying to alert you to the facts of the world we live in."

"You called me paranoid."

Burly chuckled. "Lord help me for choosing the wrong words. I already apologized for that. Do you still want your pound of flesh?"

Atcho relaxed a bit. "No, but that policy had better change, or it's going to create the world we all die in together."

"What are you going to do now?"

"Get my family to a safe place, and then figure out how to get Klaus. We poked a sleeping tiger in Sudan, and he's mad as hell. He's coming. I can feel it."

"You don't think West Point is safe enough? By now, the superintendent has been alerted and will augment security. With the general terror threat elevated, that would happen anyway. There's a quiet alert going out. I'll speak with Dude and O'Brian again, and I'm sure they'll line up behind providing greater security for you."

Atcho scoffed. "For how long and to what degree? I'm not leaving my family's fate in their hands. My son-in-law will arrive home the day after tomorrow. We'll figure out what to do with Sofia, Isabel, and the kids. I'll get Rafael to put protection around the extended family, and Ivan can increase security around the home and our manufacturing plant. In Texas, we can still protect our property with guns, and those will be combat veterans pulling watch. If the country makes it through, so will we.

"Tell Dude not to get in my way. I won't do anything illegal unless I have to, but I'll do whatever it takes to protect my family, and I won't apologize for it. The government might not do its job, but I'll do mine."

They reached the parking garage and the point where they would part ways. Atcho paused. "I appreciate you, Burly, I really do. You've always been there for Sofia and me. Sorry I got hot under the collar."

Burly grabbed Atcho in a bear hug. "No need to apologize. We've been through lots of crap together. We'll get to the end of this. Anything I can do?"

Atcho thought for a moment. "Put me in touch with O'Brian. I want to know what he knows. Tell him I'll fly to Chicago if that's what it takes."

"I can do that. Mind if I tag along?"

Atcho smiled. "If you can get us there tomorrow, I'll buy the ticket."

34

Chicago
January 25, 1993
The next day

"I'm happy to meet you in person, Atcho," Tom O'Brian said, and then turned to the other man standing before him. "Should I call you Burly?"

"Might as well." Burly chuckled. "That's the name Atcho hung on me in the swamps of Cuba."

"I want to hear the story," O'Brian said. He was a tall man with a dark complexion, heavy facial features, and a receding hairline. His manner contrasted with his clothes: he was brusque, albeit courteous, though dressed immaculately in an expensive Italian suit with a pocket kerchief and matching tie, and perfectly coordinated soft leather shoes. "Come in. Sit down."

They were at the door of the special agent's office at the FBI Chicago field headquarters on Roosevelt Road. They crossed to a seating area with a couch and two leather chairs and sat down.

"Dude filled me in on the details of your personal situation," O'Brian told Atcho. His brow furrowed. "You rode him hard yesterday." He chuckled. "Not that he didn't deserve it. Now, what can I do for you?"

"I want to know what you know," Atcho replied. "Why are you met with such stiff opposition inside the FBI?"

O'Brian bobbed his head while considering how best to answer. "My bosses don't want to hear from me on the subject of terrorism mainly because our hands are already full, there's a wide ocean between us and where most of the bad guys hang out, and the CIA and department of defense are responsible for what's beyond our shores and borders. Our job is solving crimes already committed inside our borders. Once the terrorists act within our country, it becomes a crime and we investigate.

"I've been making the case that terrorists aren't just spies. They're fight-ers: they infiltrate, they don't wear uniforms, and they don't discriminate between civilians and military or police forces. To them, every man, woman, and child is a combatant." Passion rose in his voice as he spoke.

"I've been agitating to get ready for terrorism in the US because I think it's coming," he said. "The powers that be put me in Chicago to shut me up. They'd probably get rid of me if they could, but I'm the guy who broke that Tylenol case—you know, the one where this jerk wanted to off his wife, so he put Tylenol laced with cyanide in bottles and planted them on phar-macy shelves. He killed several people just so his wife would be among the dead, and since the victims got the pills from a pharmacy, he figured the investigators wouldn't trace the case back to him. Well, we did, and forever after, people are stuck wrestling with almost impenetrable plastic wrappers to get at their pills."

He smirked. "That's heinous. Anyway, that case protects me. Can you imagine the headlines if I'm fired?" He drew an imaginary banner in the air. "'FBI Sacks Agent Who Cracked Tylenol Case.' I'd get more attention and then maybe my ideas on terrorism would get out. That might be great in the short run. More people would hear about them, but the FBI would be embarrassed, and then I'd fade, and no one would listen to me." He furrowed his brow, winked, and wagged a finger in the air. "But mark my words, the terrorists are coming. They'll make an entrance in a big way, and I can do more good by staying in the FBI than I can if I leave it." He heaved a sigh. "Besides, I like my job too much."

He sat back in his chair. "Does that answer your question?"

Atcho leaned forward. "Something got you started thinking that terrorists are coming this way. What was it? I need to know everything you know on the subject."

O'Brian laughed. "That's precious little. I didn't say I knew a lot. I said I've been stewing that we don't know enough, and we'd better get up to speed before the threat becomes a tragedy.

"Look, those guys in the Middle East hate us. They hate us because we support Israel and because we don't embrace Islam. We're infidels—nonbelievers. To them, that's a sin punishable by death. This guy Klaus hates you because you killed his brother, but he'd hate you anyway."

He looked at Burly. "Is the New York office helping out with security?"

Burly nodded. "They've assigned a special agent to coordinate with local law enforcement and the MPs up at West Point."

O'Brian nodded. "And law enforcement is on a raised alert nationwide," he said. "So, it's not like nothing is being done." He regarded Atcho with an appraising look. "I think I've been a disappointment."

Atcho shook his head. "I hoped that you knew something that could lead to Klaus and what he's up to." He looked around the office, formulating his thoughts. "What made you think that terrorists are coming to the US—to the extent that you've alienated your bosses?"

O'Brian laughed. "Hey, I'm a charming guy," he quipped. "People like me if I'm not working for them." His smile disappeared, and he became serious. "It doesn't take a rocket scientist."

He extended his arm and pointed in the air. "Over there, they've been chanting 'Death to America' for years. They call us the 'Great Satan.' They hit US facilities in other places because they can get to them. But their targeting and delivery systems are becoming more sophisticated, and their bombs are getting bigger and more destructive." He jabbed a finger in the air to make his point. "Those two oceans won't protect us much longer. Our borders are wide open, and the bad guys are getting better educated and more technologically savvy." He shook his head. "It's only a matter of time, as your personal experience demonstrates."

He gave Atcho a curious look. "Do you really believe that was a nuclear bomb Klaus planted at your house last year?"

"No doubt about it," Atcho stated flatly.

Burly nodded in agreement. "We have the designer under protection," he said. "Atcho saw Klaus escape with one of the bombs, he was confirmed to have shown one to a credible source in Berlin, and the one he brought to Atcho's house was the same design. We took the plutonium out of that one and two others we captured."

He inhaled and exhaled audibly. "Klaus knows how to replicate them. His only limiting factor is getting the plutonium. The price has gone sky-high, but he's backed by huge petrodollars. As long as there's a source, he can get the money."

"What I don't understand," Atcho broke in, "is why the FBI isn't taking more concerted action. The president knew what was going on in Berlin and Afghanistan. His national security adviser coordinated support for the missions to stop Klaus in both places. Why doesn't he cut through the red tape and order closer cooperation?"

"It's comp—" O'Brian began.

"Don't tell me it's complicated," Atcho cut in. "We're talking about the safety and security of our country, and more specifically about my family."

O'Brian relaxed and chuckled. "You're right. The national security adviser is a friend. He's one of the few allies I have in the government, but he's overridden by the director of the CIA and the secretary of defense. Neither believes a threat to be imminent."

"So, we leave ourselves open to attack until one happens," Atcho said disgustedly. "Would someone please remind them of their oaths and their jobs?"

The room fell silent.

A knock on the door interrupted the brooding atmosphere. A secretary entered, brought a note to O'Brian, and left without saying a word.

O'Brian blanched. He stood and went to his desk, then picked up a remote and aimed it at a television on the opposite wall.

"More bad news," he muttered, "and it might be pertinent."

The television screen lit up to a scene of a multi-story building with large windows. Burly sucked in his breath. Scrolling text at the bottom of the screen read, "Shooting at the front gate to the CIA's Langley headquarters leaves two dead and three wounded. No suspects."

A young woman spoke into the camera. "We are told that a man steered his car into one of the two left lanes off the main highway that leads into the headquarters complex. Witnesses say he exited his car with an automatic weapon and walked down a line of cars, shooting into them. He shot only men, and when he was finished, he returned to his car. On the way back, he executed a man who was already wounded. Investigators currently have no suspects."

"It's begun," Atcho murmured.

"We can't say that for sure," Burly cautioned.

"Figure it out," Atcho said. "That was no spontaneous act. The man knew where he was and what he intended to do. Mark my words. The perpetrator will turn out to be an Islamic fundamentalist, and our august defenders will be afraid to call him that."

"I'm with you," O'Brian said, "but we do operate within constraints. Jumping to conclusions helps no one." He studied Atcho's face. "This attack might have nothing to do with your situation, but if they *are* related, we'll want to know about it. Meanwhile, you have a direct threat to deal with."

He stood next to his desk, hands in his pockets. All three men continued watching the television report.

"I'll tell you what," O'Brian said after a few moments. "A young special agent named Sam is assigned there in New York. I mentored him while I was there, and he stays in touch. He's kinda my back channel to know what's going on there, and he believes in my instincts. He's been chasing down the facts around the guy who shot and killed a Jewish rabbi a couple of years ago, keeping tabs on the shooter's acquaintances. I'll put Sam in touch. You might be able to help each other."

He turned to Burly. "What do you think? Does that make sense?"

"Can't hurt."

They continued to stare at the carnage at the entrance to the most vaunted intelligence agency in the world.

35

When Atcho returned to Isabel's house at West Point the next morning, his son-in-law, Bob Bernier, had arrived home from Korea and greeted him with open arms. Bob was tall and blond with blue eyes. He wore a perpetually friendly but skeptical grin, and his manner projected a warm heart constantly attuned to danger. Atcho knew him to always be ready to defend his family and his country: he had once broken the jaw of a man he had thought posed a threat to Isabel.

"Great to see you, Atcho," he boomed. "Sofia's been filling me in. That was some bad stuff that went down at the CIA headquarters yesterday. Do you think that's tied in with Klaus?"

Atcho shrugged ruefully. "I don't know. It could be a lone wolf acting spontaneously. Let me say hi to Sofia and Isabel. Then we can take a walk and I'll brief you on the details."

A few minutes later, they stood on the front porch of the stately house on a hillock near Michie Stadium, home of the West Point football team. From their vantage, they saw the rays of the waning sun glance off the waters of Lusk Reservoir, and far below, the wide expanse of the Hudson River carried its burden of broken ice chunks toward New York City.

Bracing against the cold, they started off at a good pace, walking through a thin layer of snow, past the reservoir and stately cadet chapel, and then descending a steep set of concrete stairs built into the side of the bluff overlooking the cadet garrison. Below them on a road skirting the rear of the barracks, young men and women in athletic gear ran together in small groups.

Atcho stopped and watched them with a melancholy expression. "It seems so long ago that I jogged that same road to the gym." His face brightened. "Would you believe I used to run these stairs to condition my legs for soccer?"

He turned and looked back up at the magnificent Gothic revival stone chapel, now outlined by the sky. His face receded to somberness. "The last time I climbed them was with my father on graduation day. We attended the wedding of a classmate." He sighed. "So much has happened since then."

"You were a better cadet than I was," Bob said. "I never attempted to run these stairs." He clapped an affectionate hand on Atcho's shoulder. "Let's keep going. I want to hear about this conundrum you've gotten us into."

They reached the bottom of the stairs and turned right toward Thayer Road. Now on flat ground, they could talk more easily, and Atcho recounted the entire series of events that had led to his visit to the New York City FBI building.

Sofia and Isabel watched as Bob and Atcho headed off together.

"They get along so well," Sofia said. "We're lucky for that."

"They admire each other," Isabel replied. "When Bob was still a cadet, he studied Atcho's actions in Cuba. That was before we knew each other."

"He mentioned that years ago. Time passes so fast." Sofia started toward the back door. "I need to run some errands. If you don't mind, I'll go while they're out."

Isabel shot her a skeptical glance.

"No, really," Sofia said, and laughed. "I need to get some things at the store. I won't be long."

Isabel consented with a smile, and then stood at the window watching as Sofia pulled the car out of the driveway. Below, the two children played on the front lawn. Isabel watched them for a few moments after Sofia had disappeared, and then took in the view of the sun filtering through the trees on its descent, reflecting off the surface of Lusk Reservoir.

She was about to turn away from the window when motion at the edge of the trees across the road caught her attention. Thinking she might see a deer or some other wild animal, she focused her attention in that direction and then froze.

A man emerged from the woods. He wore a deliveryman uniform, but Isabel could not make out the company, and no vehicle was parked nearby. As she watched, the man looked up and down the street, but his actions were furtive, as though he was checking to see if he had been seen rather than deliberately seeking an address.

A pit formed in Isabel's stomach. The man stared at her house and began walking toward it.

Spurred into action, Isabel rushed outside and called to Kattrina and Jameson. Her tone startled them. She ran to them, grabbed their hands, and hurried them back to the house. As they climbed the steps, she glanced over her shoulder.

The man was walking rapidly now. "Mrs. Bernier," he called. His accent was thick but indeterminate.

"Mrs. Bernier," the man called again. "I must speak with you."

Isabel pushed the children in front of her, then slammed the door and turned the deadbolt.

"Go to my bedroom," she ordered. Sensing her urgency, the children ran.

Isabel crossed the room to the mantel over the fireplace. Reaching behind a plate on a display stand, she pulled out a pistol and chambered a round. Then she hurried to the kitchen to lock the back entrance. Even before she returned to the living room, the man knocked on one of the front door window panes.

"Mrs. Bernier," he called, "I have a letter for you. I need your signature."

Isabel ducked behind the couch, grabbed the phone, and dialed.

"Go away," she yelled. "I'm calling the police."

She heard the door knob rattle as the operator answered her call.

"There's a man at my door trying to break in," she screamed into the phone. "I have children here and I'm armed. I'm Major Bernier's wife and we're in the residential area by Lusk Reservoir."

She heard glass shattering. A man's hand protruded through the broken window and reached for the deadbolt.

Isabel aimed the pistol and pulled the trigger. Her ears rang from the explosion. "He's coming in," she yelled to the operator. "He broke the window and he's trying to unlock the door."

"Help is on the way," the operator yelled back. "Can you get to a safe room?"

Meanwhile, Isabel dropped the receiver and stood up from behind the couch. She took aim with both hands, then steadied her stance and fired off three more shots at the man's hand. Then she raised the barrel and fired several more times through the door. She heard a groan—and a click as her pistol's magazine ran out of bullets.

Through a shower of glass, the man burst through the door, his left hand dripping blood and his eyes burning with fury. He strode across the room, grabbed Isabel by the neck, and shoved her toward the door. Her pistol clattered to the floor.

Isabel screamed, and then she heard Kattrina and Jameson whimper in terror from the other room.

"Shut up," the man snarled in Isabel's ear. He grabbed her hair and jerked it around, forcing her to look at him. "Or the children will die." Then he pushed her outside and down the steps to the woods.

By the time Atcho had finished relating the details of the threat Klaus posed, he and Bob had walked a full mile along Thayer Road overlooking the river, almost to Thayer Hotel. They turned right on Mills Road to head uphill and back to Lusk Reservoir from the opposite end.

"I think I've got a handle on the whole shebang," Bob said. "I'm not sure I agree that we need to leave West Point. What about Sofia? What's her role in all of this?"

Atcho grimaced, hesitating before speaking. "I need your help on that. I need you to keep her out of it. She has to stay with Jameson."

Bob pivoted in mid-stride and held his hands up by his shoulders, palms open, facing Atcho. "Whoa, buddy. I'll do almost anything you ask, but I'm not tangling with that lady. You want me to handcuff her to a radiator in our living room? Hog-tie and hand-feed her?" He belted out a laugh. "If she thinks you or Jameson is in danger, she'll be a hellcat, and short of putting my own life at risk, you tell me how I'm supposed to keep her out of anything."

Atcho heaved a sigh and smirked. "You're right," he said, a note of pride deepening his tone. "She's a handful and she's absolutely the reason our past missions succeeded. But..." Atcho's voice became serious, almost pleading. "If something happens to me, Jameson can't lose us both. She has to be here for him."

Bob placed both hands on Atcho's shoulders and lowered his head so that he looked directly into Atcho's eyes. "Count on me for this," he said. "I'll protect Jameson along with Isabel and Kattrina. Leave that to me and don't worry about it anymore. Your mind needs to be free so you can concentrate on Klaus. If anything happens to either you or Sofia, Isabel and I will take care of Jameson. He'll always have a home, and we'll treat him like our own child.

"I'll give Sofia my best advice, and I'll pass on to her what I just told you about Jameson, but if she's determined to do her thing, I won't stand in her way." He chuckled. "Not that I could anyway."

"Fair enough," Atcho said, his reluctance obvious. They resumed walking up Mills Road. "I talked with Rafael after I left Burly. He'll get security out to your extended family—"

"Your old Brigade 2506 buddies?"

Atcho smiled. "We're getting a little long in the tooth, but our guys can still fight. I wouldn't want to be on the opposite side of them."

Rafael Arteaga was one of Atcho's oldest friends. They had met more than thirty years ago in a firefight at the disastrous Bay of Pigs invasion in Cuba, when the US had deserted Brigade 2506. The unit had been a fighting force of more than one thousand men the CIA had trained to re-take the island country from its dictator, Fidel Castro.

Years later, after they had both been released from captivity in Castro's dungeons, Atcho and Rafael had reacquainted and worked together in several black operations. In the first, Rafael had organized and provided security to Atcho's extended family when they were threatened by a rogue Russian spy seeking to coerce Atcho's cooperation. He had recruited from among the veterans of Brigade 2506.

"I sure wouldn't object to any of them being in a foxhole next to me," Bob agreed.

"Ivan will secure our home and the manufacturing plant in Austin," Atcho went on.

"It sounds like you've got your bases covered."

"Not quite," Atcho responded. "I still think you should leave West Point."

Bob shook his head. "The superintendent knows the situation. He's beefed up security on the post, and he's specifically increased patrols around our house. If Klaus shows up here, we'll get him."

Atcho whirled around. "Listen to me, Bob. When there was still a wall in Berlin, Klaus found a way under it to go back and forth at will; he kidnapped me out of a hotel with US State Department security at my door; he moved around the battlefield in Kuwait freely; he smuggled a nuclear device into the US; and he escaped the country despite a nation-wide manhunt. He's gained knowledge and experience, and since I killed his brother, he has a vendetta against me. He'll kill everyone close to me if he gets a chance, and that includes you, Isabel, Kattrina, and especially Sofia and Jameson." Atcho's voice became urgent. "If we screw up, those we love will die."

Bob studied Atcho in the gathering dusk.

"Criminy, Bob," Atcho rolled on, "he tested a nuclear device in Afghanistan. It lowered the top of a mountain by thirty meters." He caught himself. "That's classified, and neither the FBI nor the CIA will confirm that's what happened, or that Klaus was behind it, but they know it and we know it."

They were about halfway up the hill, still on Mills Road, at a point where it curved left and continued uphill. Suddenly, they heard a single popping sound, followed by several more in quick succession. They could not be certain of its direction, but they both knew the sound from close-up experience: gunshots.

They glanced at each other, eyes wide, then turned and raced up the hill. Before they reached the crest, a military police sedan sped by, its blue strobe lights blinking. Moments later, another swept past them, its siren blaring.

Their lungs heaving, Atcho and Bob pushed uphill until they reached flat ground. Then they raced across a footbridge over the reservoir and loped the remaining distance. Four MP cars were already ringed in front of the house, their roof lights flashing.

As they sprinted toward the house, two MPs stepped in front of them. Bob pulled his ID from his pocket and thrust it at them. "I'm Major Bernier. I live here. This is my father-in-law."

Satisfied, the officers let them through. As they mounted the stairs, an MP captain walked out the front door.

"Major Bernier?" he said to Bob and introduced himself. "There are two children inside, very scared. You should talk to them. They're afraid of us."

"Where's my wife?" Bob demanded, still breathing hard.

The captain shook his head. "There were no adults in the house, and there's blood on the door." He spoke in rapid, clipped tones. "Shots were fired. The blood trail leads into the woods." He glanced at Atcho. "Who are you?"

Atcho jutted his jaw toward Bob. "His father-in-law. The little boy is my son."

Just then another car screeched to a halt down the street. Sofia jumped out and ran toward the house. An MP stepped in front of her.

"That's my wife," Atcho said. "Tell them to let her through."

Another MP emerged from the house. "I got the little girl to talk some," she said. "She says a mean man came to the door and took her mother away."

Sofia ran up the stairs in time to hear the MP, then rushed inside without stopping.

Bob and Atcho followed her. Inside, Sofia stooped to comfort the children while Bob strode into his bedroom. When he emerged, he was carrying a holstered Smith & Wesson Model 3 Schofield top-break revolver. He slapped the belt around his hips and, without breaking stride, headed for the door.

"This is the best I can do on short notice," he muttered, "but this just got personal for me too. I've got plenty of bullets."

Meanwhile, Atcho picked up Sofia's pistol from the floor. "Where's the ammo for this?"

Bob showed him. "Let's go."

The MP captain blocked their way at the door. "My people are on this. The post is already on lockdown. No one moves from wherever they are right now except for my MPs. We'll get this guy."

"That's my wife," Bob growled, shouldering past him. "Try to stop me."

"That's my daughter," Atcho echoed, and followed.

Isabel's heart beat wildly as she crashed through the underbrush down the steep slope of the bluff below her house. Her breaths came in short gasps and her feet stumbled over loose rocks and downed branches.

Her captor followed closely, prodding her in the back and cheek with a pistol he carried in his good hand. A good distance below was another row of houses, but rugged terrain and thick vegetation impeded their way. Whenever Isabel would pause to catch her breath or see where to take her next step in the waning light, he shoved her, causing her to stumble to the ground. Then he jerked her upright and pushed her forward again, down the mountain.

Above them the wail of sirens had risen to a crescendo and then ceased. Others sounded from every direction. Below them, the rush of the river mixed with leaves beating against each other in a swift wind, and the smell of half-decayed winter vegetation assaulted the nostrils.

Isabel barely noticed, her mind focused on a single thought—survival. Then, after several minutes that felt like hours, she heard the crashing of bushes and rolling of rocks above them. Her rescuers were on the way.

Another thought struck. *Will he shoot me before they can get to me?*

Her senses now fully engaged, Isabel pictured the ground ahead— steep, overgrown, rocky—and then a sheer drop-off behind the row of houses below, if she could steer their flight to the left of their current direction.

In the twilight, judging direction was difficult, but Isabel recognized the main area of the cadet barracks glowing to the left. She deliberately stumbled again, and when the man jerked her up, she turned slightly so they would veer closer to them. Two more similar falls and recoveries allowed her to move in her intended direction, and her captor seemed not to have noticed—his panic now evident as he reacted to the sounds of a narrowing pursuit from behind.

Two voices called, "Isabel!" She recognized them both. Atcho and Bob.

The man shoved his gun against her jaw, driving it into her teeth, and pushed his face close to hers while bringing one bloodied hand to his mouth as a sign to remain silent. They crouched and waited. The sounds of stumbling and the voices receded to the right and continued below them.

The man pulled Isabel up and pushed her to the left, away from the pursuers.

The pause on the slope had given Isabel a brief chance to study him. In the dim light, she couldn't make out any of his features but saw that he was not much bigger than her. The pain in his hand must have been growing— he had shifted his face to lean over and nurse it.

They continued downhill at a more deliberate pace, and Isabel noticed that his panic had waned, and he was now paying more attention to their direction of travel. She only hoped she had managed to steer them far enough to the left to provide her the advantage she sought.

Down, down they went, and she no longer stumbled or fell. Doing so could spell the end. She tolerated the jabs in her back as she stepped downhill, placing her feet carefully until she saw a break in the vegetation outlined by the glow from the distant barracks—and the edge of a sheer, high drop-off.

She deliberately stumbled again, and when the man reached for her, she rolled away, sprang up, and rushed him, her head low, aiming for his wounded hand.

She careened against him, jamming his injured palm against his leg. As he cried out in pain, she dug her heels into the rocky ground and shoved harder, driving him to the edge of the bluff.

Too late, the man realized her intention and teetered on the edge. He swung his arms wildly, then brought his pistol around to train on Isabel and pulled the trigger.

As his gun swung toward her, Isabel threw her arm up, deflecting his. The shot went wild, the sound muffled in the stiff breeze.

Isabel dropped to the ground, threw her arms around the man's ankles, and pulled with all her strength. Her breath came in gut-wrenching gasps.

With a scream, the man fell over the edge. Scarcely a moment later, Isabel heard a thud, and then all was quiet aside from the sounds of the wind, the leaves, and her own labored breath.

Isabel stayed in her prone position, breathing hard, until the icy fingers of winter began to wrap around her body. Then images of the children entered her mind and carefully, gingerly, she rose to her feet and began the climb back up to her home.

The entire family left that evening, including Atcho and Sofia, flying by military helicopter to nearby Stewart Air National Guard Base. They spent the night in guest quarters secured by Marines.

Many hours later, unable to sleep and still seething with anger, Atcho asked Sofia, "How do you think Isabel is handling this emotionally?"

"She's shaken up," Sofia replied. "She's never killed a man before."

Atcho nodded. "And when she climbed back up the hill, she didn't know he'd broken his neck. As far as she knew, he could still be after her. She's traumatized."

Sofia caressed his cheek, hiding her own rage. *Klaus attacked my family where we live—twice.* "She's strong. After all, she's your daughter. She'll be okay. Her confidence should take a jump. She knows she can protect her child. She's done it, and she kept her wits and saved her own life."

Atcho nodded. "Klaus won't stop."

Sofia shot him a glance. "We have to get him."

Atcho pulled back and studied her face. Her tone had carried uncharacteristic menace.

"What are you going to do?" she asked.

"I'm going back to the New York FBI office in the morning. We've got to figure out a way to draw Klaus into the open."

"You mean to make him come after you," Sofia said flatly, then sighed. "I suppose I can't stop you."

Atcho locked eyes with her. "I have to do this. He's not after just us. He wants to deliver a crippling blow to the US, and he can do it. If he needs to, he'll put me on a back burner, but he's still going to come after us personally. If I don't finish this fight, we'll always be checking our back-trail—after he's massacred millions. The more important question right now is what are *you* going to do? Isabel and Bob will have the same worries about Kattrina."

Sofia pulled back and gave him a preoccupied look. "Don't worry. Our kids come first. I'll help Bob stave off any onslaughts. Where he's taking us, Klaus won't know how to follow. Our family is off the table as a pressure point for Klaus to threaten you."

Atcho nodded. "That ranch of Ivan's up in Montana came in handy."

36

"I should have gone myself," Klaus groused. He had just listened to a news report about the death of a would-be kidnapper at West Point.

"You know that wouldn't have been a good thing to do," Ramzi replied. "If you had been captured or killed, your part of our plans would be dead."

"Why can't these infidel men teach their wives how to behave?" Klaus said in exasperation. "Their women dress to provoke when they go out in public; they go to jobs and drive to get there. And this daughter of Atcho's killed Aban. I should have known she could do that. Atcho's wife is a she-devil who beat up six men at once in Berlin last year."

"She did what?"

"Six men tried to detain her in Little Istanbul last year. She left all of them lying on the street."

"You're joking."

Klaus shook his head.

Ramzi grinned lasciviously. "Give her to me for an hour. I'll teach her proper respect. The daughter too."

Klaus heard him distantly. He pulled himself back to awareness and shook his head dismissively. "We'll never get close to Atcho's family now. He's warned and he'll move them. I'll deal with him later. For now, we'd better concentrate on the plan. We need to coordinate to make sure we get the most effect."

"And to make sure that if one bomb doesn't go off, the other does," Ramzi interjected.

Klaus looked at him sharply. "What do you mean?"

A cautious look spread over Ramzi's face. "No offense. I mean that if one system doesn't work, we've configured them so neither one interferes with the other."

Klaus' expression hardened. "Which system would you expect not to work?"

Ramzi's gaze turned stern. "We're brothers working for the same *jihad*," he said. "I meant no insult. I know what you did in Afghanistan, blowing up that mountain. If your bomb works like that one..." He shook his head. "You already have the respect of Al-Qaeda, Sheikh Omar, and Osama bin Laden, but the bomb is not proven operationally yet. We can't risk this mission. My bomb must have every opportunity to succeed, with or without yours."

Constrained anger clouded Klaus' expression.

"The same is also true about your bomb," Ramzi added. "Think, brother. We'll bring down those twin monsters across the river."

"You've been talking to Kadir," Klaus muttered.

"I don't know Kadir," Ramzi replied neutrally, "but I can tell you that while your weapon's potential is recognized in the Kingdom, it hasn't worked in a real situation yet, despite three attempts."

Klaus' eyes narrowed. "Because of Atcho," he hissed. "He's interfered every time."

"Which is why we can't let him get in the way this time."

The two men eyed each other for extended moments. Then Klaus nodded.

"What do you suggest?"

Ramzi exhaled. "The two bombs should be set to explode nearly simultaneously. Mine will go in the parking garage of the South Tower and detonate first. You should put yours a couple of floors above ground level. If it fails, mine will still topple one tower into the other one. If yours does succeed..." His eyes widened as a grin spread across his face. "It will have the effect of an airburst. Instantly, everything within a mile of the World Trade Center will be covered with radioactive fallout raining down on the city. Millions of infidels will be dead, and the US financial system will be crippled. Our bombs together will leave a black hole in the floor of Manhattan a mile wide, with nothing but rubble and dead infidels. That will be the beginning of the end for this wretched country."

Klaus listened, mesmerized. His eyes shone with the fervor of his mission.

"*Habibi*," he said, "it's so good to finally work with someone as dedicated to our *jihad* as I am. In Saudi Arabia, many men speak of *jihad* and they put their money in, but they leave the fighting to untrained fighters with no experience. You are here with me, and you have the wisdom, expertise, and experience to *do* something besides talk or throw money your family got out of the oil wells."

Ramzi smiled, a faraway look in his eyes. "Thank you, my brother. This is sacred work we do." He pulled himself from his thoughts. "How long until your bomb is ready?"

"About two weeks. I've located the machine shops that can manufacture the structural parts, but the tolerance levels are tiny, so I don't want to rush them, and I want plenty of time to test the bomb. I'm waiting for some electronic parts too, but they should be here by then."

Ramzi nodded in contentment. "That's good. My shipment of powdered metals should arrive around the same time, and then my bomb will be complete."

"What do we do until then?"

"Lie low and wait."

37

Sofia fidgeted.

Bob noticed. "Set a spell. Take your shoes off,'" he quipped, quoting the character Jed Clampett from the closing theme song of *The Beverly Hillbillies*. "We're going to be here awhile. Might as well relax."

Sofia studied him. Behind his jocular greeting resided an undertone of anger. Dressed in warm woolen winter clothing, he sat in a rocking chair on the wooden porch of a ranch-style house built on a rise looking across a vast expanse of snow-covered rolling prairie to distant peaks. Behind the house to the north, the ground swept up into a towering mountain. Set as it was with the sun rising to Bob's left and setting to his right, when the weather was clear, the house basked in sunlight the whole day. Halfway to the mountains outlined against the far southern horizon, the town of Livingston nestled in rolling hills, and a frozen lake glimmered off to the west. A long, cleared driveway with a few ice patches led from a secondary hardtop road up the gentle slope to the house.

"Nobody's getting in here that we don't know about," Bob went on. "We'll see 'em coming for miles, and if we miss 'em, we have sensors and monitors behind every bush, and local authorities are on the lookout." He took a sip of coffee from a mug in his hand while patting a Winchester rifle lying across his lap. "If Klaus sneaks in somehow, we'll deal with him." He brandished the firearm. "We've got plenty of ammo and lots more weapons."

Sofia pushed off from the rail she had been leaning against while she drank her coffee. She turned to look out over the vista.

"Ah, Bob," she said. "You know me too well. I can't help worrying about Atcho."

"Concentrate on feeling sorry for that Klaus guy," Bob said. "He's not going to get away again. Mark my words. Atcho is setting up an endgame."

"I have full faith in Atcho, but anything can happen."

Bob eyed her closely. "You're conjuring up something. I can see it in your eyes." He turned and leaned the rifle against the cabin wall, then picked up his coffee and stood, ambling over to Sofia. "Atcho figured you'd try to do something. He asked me to stop you."

Sofia chuckled. "And what did you tell him?"

Bob laughed. "That I might as well try to hog-tie a mountain lion. I said I wouldn't attempt to stop you because it would be useless."

Behind him, the front door opened, and Isabel emerged with the two children. They ran across the porch, squealing with excitement, and bounded down the stairs to play in the snow.

Isabel wrapped her arms around Bob and leaned her head against his shoulder. "What's up?"

Bob put an arm around her back, then gestured toward Sofia. "She's thinking she has to do something, and a plan is already forming in that head." He turned to Sofia. "Am I right?"

Sofia set her coffee cup down on the flat rail of the porch and rubbed her eyes. "Your family is here," she said. "You're safe. My husband—"

"Can take care of himself," Bob finished for her, striking a kind note. "And Jameson is here. He needs his mom."

"I know." Sofia's fatigue showed in her drawn face and sunken eyes. "He needs his dad too." She exhaled. "Atcho believes the government isn't taking the threat seriously. The FBI acknowledges the personal danger to us, but the larger threat seems beyond their comprehension. If someone doesn't do something, Klaus will blow that bomb."

"Why did Atcho go back to New York?" Isabel asked. "Why not DC?"

"Two reasons: Klaus wants Atcho, and he traced us to West Point; and

Burly got word through backchannels at the Mossad that the New York financial district is Klaus' target. By now, he must know the plan to hit us failed. He doesn't know where we are now, but he'll still go after his larger target."

"So again, sit back and relax. You can help me handle things here."

Sofia shook her head. "I can't, Bob. I'm a veteran analyst and operations officer. Klaus is after big targets. I can feel it. That's what he does. He tried to hit the embassy in Berlin and the oil wells in Kuwait. He's not after penny-ante stuff."

"I'll let you two hash this out," Isabel said. "Just know, Sofia, that Jameson is safe with us."

"You proved that," Sofia said warmly. "We're proud of you."

Isabel smiled appreciatively. Then she disentangled herself from Bob and headed toward the stairs while Sofia took a deep breath to regain control over moistening eyes and lips that had begun to quiver.

"I have to go," Sofia rasped to Bob.

"I know. But let me help you think through things. Do you have any idea what the target might be?"

Sofia gathered her composure. "I do, but it seems too outlandish to say out loud." She took in a deep breath. "Tell you what. I'll go over what I've been thinking, and you tell me your conclusions."

"All right. Try me."

Sofia dropped her head in deep thought. "Klaus was first spotted this time around in a video of the explosion at the Israeli Embassy in Buenos Aires." She paced the porch as she spoke. "Then he witnessed the one that took out the television station in Lima, and then the headquarters of the largest bank in Peru. Each explosion was larger than the previous one, and they're no longer striking just to make a political statement. That bomb in the Marine barracks in Beirut ten years ago was a huge strike, but it didn't do lasting injury to US capability. Now, they're hitting to inflict far-reaching economic damage beyond the carnage."

"I'm with you so far, but how does that lead us to now?"

Sofia spoke slowly, thinking out loud and choosing her words carefully. "The US has always been the target. Strikes in other places have been to train, try out new methods, and develop tactics. Now we're seeing evidence of collaboration between local terrorist groups with both Al-Qaeda and Hezbollah—and they're working together.

"The local groups unwittingly"—she arched an eyebrow—"or maybe wittingly, help spread fundamentalist Islam while they forward their own aims. That's what they think they're doing. And Burly says there's been a build-up of chatter about New York."

"That chatter has been going on for years."

"And the terrorists have been getting better for years. When do we start believing that they'll at least try to do those things they've chanted about for decades?"

"When do we start believing that we can't stop them? That's when the game is over." Bob caught the sharp glance that Sofia shot his way. He waved his hands above his head. "Hey, I'm just playing devil's advocate. I'm the last guy to pooh-pooh the idea that bad guys are coming our way. One came to my house two days ago, threatening my wife. But since we've got limited resources, we have to think through every possibility."

Sofia had stopped pacing. She glanced at her watch and then stood still, her eyes fixed on Bob.

"That's right," she said. "Rummage around with those thoughts for a while and see where they lead. I have to go. I have a plane to catch."

Startled, Bob jumped up from his chair. "You what?"

Sofia had already started down the stairs. "I packed early this morning," she called over her shoulder. "My luggage is in the car." With Bob trailing after her, she plodded rapidly through the snow to where the children played.

"Listen, sweetheart," she said, picking up Jameson and hugging him to her chest. "Mommy has to go away for a while."

"No-o-o," the little boy protested, tears welling in his eyes. "I want you to stay here. When is Daddy coming?"

"I'm sorry," Sofia replied, burying her head against his shoulder. "Your sister Isabel and Uncle Bob will take care of you, and you can play with Kattrina."

"No-o-o," Jameson wailed. "Don't go."

Isabel edged up to help comfort the child. Sofia handed him over, her face a mask of anguish. The little boy kicked and cried. Sofia's eyes reddened, and tears ran freely down her face.

"I'll be back soon," she whispered, kissing Jameson's cheek one last time.

Kattrina, who had continued building a snowman, now pulled at her mother's leg. "Mommy, where is Gigi Sofia going?"

Fighting back her tears, Sofia walked to her car. Bob followed at her shoulder.

"Don't do this, Sofia," he pleaded. "Everyone knows your instincts are good. Work through the analysis with me. We can feed whatever you come up with to the guys in New York and let them handle it."

Sofia swung the car door open and slid behind the wheel. "We don't have time to convince people and wade through red tape." Her tone was labored. "No more time to discuss. Think through what we talked about. If you come up with any conclusions, get them to Atcho."

"What do I tell him about you?"

"Tell him I love him, and I'll see him when this is all over. Tell him the target is obvious, but unthinkable. If I can confirm what I think, I'll get that to him." With that, she rolled up the window and, sliding over the ice patches, sped down the long driveway.

As she drove to the airport, Sofia reviewed her analysis. *Klaus is in New York, or at least in its vicinity. He's going after big targets that affect the economy. His weapons can take down any building. The last hit where he showed up was a skyscraper. There is no building more emblematic of US economic power than the Twin Towers. If he can lure Atcho there, he'll see it as a plus. That's where he's going.*

38

The next morning, Sofia dressed to draw attention. Strikingly beautiful with her fine features, green eyes, long dark hair, and elegant figure, she took care to look her best—to stand out in a crowd in such a way that anyone who knew her would surely recognize her.

As she sat in front of the hotel mirror primping her hair, she thought of the last time she had seen Klaus. That had happened only once, just over three years ago in Berlin, but she knew she would never forget his face, those burning eyes, and that voice that simultaneously commanded and mocked.

She recalled seeing Atcho disappear at Klaus' gunpoint into the hallway outside their hotel room, where a State Department security officer had lain unconscious. Across the hall, the rest of the security detail had been locked in their room and hit with pulverized tear gas, incapacitating them.

She hoped Klaus had equally vivid memories of her.

He had certainly succeeded in identifying and tracking her down fourteen months later, when he tried to have her detained in Little Istanbul, the Turkish enclave in Berlin. Months after that, he shot her in the leg across Lake Austin with a sniper rifle, though she doubted that he had actually made out her features. *He knows me, but he won't be expecting me to expose myself.*

As she rode a taxi into Lower Manhattan, she thought of Atcho. She had left a note in her room in Montana for Bob or Isabel to find, and she was sure that one of them had read it to Atcho by now.

"Stay focused and don't think about me," it read. "I'll call when I have something to tell. Klaus must be stopped. I love you."

Atcho would be angry, but despite the fact that all of his covert operations training had been gained on the job, and much of that by working alone, he was professional. He would weigh the risk she posed to herself against the danger to the nation if they did not succeed. He would proceed, stone-faced to be sure, but he would pursue the objective that must be met, and his thoughts would be on saving his family. They would work out their differences afterward.

She smiled. *Something to look forward to.* Then her expression became somber again. *If there is an afterward.*

The taxi arrived at her destination. She paid the driver, exited, and then looked up at the tall twin towers of the World Trade Center. Even on this overcast winter day, they gleamed in the cold light, their wide concrete expanse softened by trees, displays of art, and lower buildings. They stood proud, stately, evoking power and prosperity. *The very elements that the terrorists hate—when they belong to someone else.*

The cold February wind swirled around Sofia as she began her trek along the periphery of both buildings. She wore a white, heavy overcoat, styled for fashion as well as warmth, and she held her hair in place with a maroon scarf. On her feet, she wore knee-high leather boots with two-inch heels. *If they're still scoping out the place, they'll see me.* An image of Klaus' face formed in her mind. *I'll smoke you out, you bastard.*

After the third loop around the buildings, the cold whipped through her coat, especially on the Hudson River side. She ducked inside the North Tower and rode an escalator to one of the underground levels, where she found a coffee shop and warmed up.

When she felt sufficiently resuscitated, she took another loop around the Center and then rode the elevators in both buildings, stopping off for a drink in The Greatest Bar on Earth, one of the establishments that made up the Windows on the World complex at the top of the North Tower.

As she gazed across the cityscape and then over at the mighty structure of the South Tower, she wondered about the plausibility of bringing them down. *Maybe I'm crazy. It's unthinkable.* She shook off the thought and gazed again at the South Tower, magnificent in a now-waning sun, standing firm against the freezing winter wind that moaned against the glass. *Then again, building these towers was unthinkable in the first place. But someone conceived the idea.*

She returned to her hotel for the night feeling glum and alone. Calling Atcho would serve no purpose, so she went to bed early and slept fitfully.

The next day, she repeated her pattern, wearing the same overgarments. She moved quietly among busy New Yorkers on their various errands and visitors gawking at the sights. In some places, clumps of Asians grinned as their countrymen snapped away on cameras. She smiled. *Seems like everywhere you turn these days, people have cameras.*

On the third day, she did the same thing, alighting from her taxi and beginning her trek around the Twin Towers.

39

"She did what?" Atcho felt his normal self-control slipping away to dread.

Bob explained again what had transpired with Sofia. "She wouldn't tell me where she was going but made it plain that a good guess is New York City. That's where you are because you think Klaus is in the vicinity. That's as much as I know. She could be anywhere within the five boroughs."

"Why wouldn't she tell you where she was going?"

"You know why. You'd try to stop whatever she's doing. She aims to help and is dead set that you stay on mission until Klaus is neutralized. That's my word, not hers."

"But appropriate anyway." Atcho fought off despondency. "It might come to that."

"Hey, I'm not suggesting anything. I'm just saying that, regardless how it's done, Klaus has to be—"

"I get it," Atcho interrupted. "What else did Sofia say? Walk me through her analysis. Can you think of anything she said that would give a hint of what she's up to?"

The line was quiet as Bob put his thoughts together. "She was sure that you would stay focused and on the job."

"Great. What else?"

"She said that the target was obvious, but unthinkable."

Atcho felt his irritation grow. "Is she kidding? In New York City? It's all unthinkable. We've got the New York Stock Exchange, the Federal Reserve Bank, all of Wall Street. Klaus' bomb could take out a whole mile in diameter. If it's planted in the middle of Manhattan, he'll kill a lot of people and cut the US financial system off at the knees."

"That stacks up with what Sofia said about going for targets that cause long-term damage." Bob repeated her observation that the targets and the bombs had become larger and directed at destroying economic hubs.

"That's been my conclusion too." Atcho blew out a breath. "Finding and stopping him will take drastic action."

Atcho remained silent a moment, listening to the soft whirring of the telephone receiver. Then Bob asked, "What will you do?"

"I don't know, but if we don't stop him, let's hope the bomb is a dud."

40

"There's a woman circling the towers," Ramzi told Klaus. "She was spotted yesterday, and she's back today."

"You have people watching the towers?" Klaus asked. He had just come in from a workout at a local gym and was streaming sweat.

"Of course," Ramzi replied. "We keep several brothers posted around the center to notice changes in security."

"So, what's special about this woman?"

"Maybe nothing, but she walks around the buildings and inside them for no apparent reason. One of our men noticed her yesterday when she kept appearing. After the third sighting, he followed her. She's alone and doesn't seem to be waiting for anyone or have anything to do. She just walks around, sits for a while in various places, and continues on."

"Maybe she's a tourist."

"Could be, but she doesn't pay attention to the art pieces scattered around or take pictures. She just roams around the buildings. We didn't see how she arrived yesterday or today, but she left by taxi last evening."

"What's your concern?"

Ramzi sighed and raised an eyebrow. "Everything is my concern as we get closer. I mentioned the woman to you by way of thinking out loud. You have more experience." He closed his eyes and tossed his head back, surrendering a bit to stress. "Maybe I'm becoming paranoid."

Klaus studied Ramzi's face. "Allah the merciful, peace be upon him, put us together. He must mean for us to collaborate. If you think this woman could be an issue, we should consider her carefully. How are your other preparations coming along?"

Ramzi smiled, relieved that Klaus had not considered his angst to be ridiculous. "Everything is going according to plan." He sighed again. "However, our brothers are becoming too eager. I only hope no one talks too much. You know our security is not the best when it comes to that." His face took on a comical expression. "Then again, the Americans are so stupid. They underestimate us. They'll listen to our brothers talking on the phones to *jihadis* at home and think they're hearing the rantings of madmen, and they won't believe anything is happening until it does."

Klaus chuckled and put an arm across Ramzi's shoulder. "I pray that you are right, but anyway, disinformation is a tactic. Lots of repeated stories will camouflage our real plans." He glanced at his watch. "It's late. I'm going to clean up and go to bed."

He turned away, then added, as an afterthought, "What about the woman?"

Ramzi waved a dismissive hand. "That's probably nothing—just me being more anxious the closer we get to execution."

"Caution is a good thing," Klaus said. "If she shows up again tomorrow, have your man take a picture. We'll circulate it and have the other men watch out for her. If she's doing something that'll get in our way, we'll deal with her."

A distressed expression crossed Ramzi's face. "Ah, I almost forgot. One of the men took some pictures. Polaroid. They're grainy, but you can make out the woman's features."

He reached into his pocket, pulled out several photographs, and handed them to Klaus. "You can see that she is dressed for show. Scandalous. Walking around like that alone? We can only hope that she and all like her are taken down with the towers."

Klaus began flipping through them. The first two showed a tall woman at a distance away from the photographer. Klaus peered at them closely but saw nothing concerning. Then he turned to the third picture and gasped. There, in close relief, was Sofia Stahl-Xiquez.

"It's her," he exclaimed. "That woman."

Startled, Ramzi took the photo and held it for close examination. "You know her?"

"That's Sofia." Klaus' face shone with malicious excitement. "That's Atcho's wife."

Ramzi looked up from the photo. "What do you want to do?"

"If she shows up again tomorrow, take her," he replied in a raspy voice, his eyes gleaming. "Put a team together. Be ready. Make it a public spectacle."

Ramzi eyed him with concern. "Do you think that's a good idea? The police will search all over for her. With this mayor—"

"David Dinkins?" Klaus snorted. "We'll give him big crimes to worry about, and while he oversees a search for Sofia, we'll blast a gigantic pothole for him to fill in." He laughed again. "We'll even give him a new worry to think about—radioactive air."

He whirled on Ramzi. "Bring this infidel witch to me, and while the authorities search for her, we'll put our plans in motion." He clasped his hands together and rubbed them in exultation. "Before the bombing, we'll leave her mutilated body in a public place for the television cameras. Atcho will know I did this."

41

Atcho fretted. He hadn't known helplessness in many years. Isabel, Kattrina, and Jameson were safe in Montana, but the woman who had restored joy and meaning to his life had gone to places unknown. Meanwhile, Klaus threatened the huge population of New York City with a nuclear bomb.

"Can't crumble now," he muttered under his breath, while admitting to himself that crumbling was all he felt like doing. His other instinct was to wring Sofia's neck the next time he saw her.

He sat across the conference table from Jim Dude in the New York City FBI offices at the Javits Center. Burly sat next to him. A window on the opposite wall opened to a cityscape, the Twin Towers glistening in the late afternoon sun.

"Exactly what do you want me to do?" Dude asked. His voice remained businesslike, professional. "Your wife is a grown woman, free to come and go as she pleases. When did she leave?"

"A little less than forty-eight hours ago." He took a deep breath while collecting his thoughts. "My wife is a retired CIA operations officer," he told Dude pointedly. "She left a note to tell me that Klaus must be stopped. I think that clearly indicates her intent."

"And you think she came here, to New York City." Dude's tone was flat.

"That's what my son-in-law thinks based on the last conversation he had with her as she was leaving."

"Did you check the airlines?" As Dude spoke, he leaned back in his chair and picked at the end of a pencil in his hand, his expression indicating that he anticipated the answer.

Atcho nodded. "She must have used one of the many aliases she has stashed away. There's no record of her having flown."

"Now that, we could investigate."

Atcho bristled. Burly placed a calming hand on his forearm.

Dude reached across the conference table and picked up a telephone receiver. "Let me show you something," he said while tapping in a number. He spoke into the phone in a low voice and then hung up.

"You think we're not sensitive to threats against us," he said, "but that's not fair. Our charter is to investigate crimes already committed, not—"

"I got it," Atcho interrupted, his voice laden with disgust. "We know who the attacker is, the general area where he intends to strike, and the weapon. But you can't do anything about it." He leaned forward so that his eyes locked with Dude's. "Or won't."

Dude held his glare.

A secretary knocked on the door, carried a thick file to Dude, and left without saying a word.

"This," Dude said, holding the folder up for Atcho to see its thickness, "this is a fraction of the threats that we have on file." He opened the folder. "Here, I'll read you some snippets of conversation:

"'...we're going to bomb the George Washington Bridge. Watch for it, brothers.'

"'...we're going to bomb the White House.'

"'...two of our glorious *jihadis* will fly a plane into an office building. They will be martyrs...'"

He flipped through several pages. "Here's a doozy. '...we're going to bomb the Statue of Liberty.'" He looked up at Atcho. "This file is from two years ago. Shall I go on?"

Atcho sank back in his seat and shook his head. "I get the picture."

Dude's expression softened. "I'm sympathetic to your effort, Atcho, I really am. But how many agents do you think I have to chase all this down? If I assigned all of them to do that, we still wouldn't have sufficient coverage, and no crimes would be investigated. That includes rapes, murders, bank robberies, kidnappings..."

Atcho heaved a sigh and nodded.

Dude shifted his attention to Burly. "What is the CIA saying?"

"Pretty much the same things as you are. I'm retired from the CIA and on contract. I don't speak for it, but I can tell you that it is not perceiving an imminent threat."

"Even in light of the attack at Langley the other day?"

Burly nodded. "They see that as a lone wolf attack."

The three men sat in silence a few moments, and then Dude redirected his gaze to Atcho and raised an eyebrow. "Atcho, I have to ask another question. I wouldn't be doing my job if I didn't." His reluctance hung in the room.

Atcho regarded him with a stony look.

"How are you and Mrs. Xiquez getting along? Has it occurred to you that the pressure might be getting to her?"

Atcho's chair fell to the floor as he shoved it back and sprang to his feet. "You think my wife abandoned our son and granddaughter? You think she left me?" He whirled on Burly. "Let's go. This was another waste of time."

As Atcho and Burly walked into the freezing February air, a man followed them closely. When they reached the sidewalk, he called to them.

"Mr. Atcho, may I speak with you?" He called two more times before they heard him and turned to face him.

"Mr. Xiquez—uh, Atcho. My name is Sam Shook. Tom O'Brian in Chicago suggested I meet up with you. I saw you leave Jim Dude's office a minute ago."

Atcho studied the young man. He was lanky, in his late twenties, and had dark hair, sharp features, and an expression that dripped sincerity.

"Mr. O'Brian filled me in pretty thoroughly, including"—he glanced momentarily at Burly and then back at Atcho—"what's going on with your wife. Mr. Dude had briefed him."

"What are you supposed to do?"

Sam picked up on Atcho's impatient tenor. "I don't know that I'm supposed to do anything, or that I can, other than listen. I think O'Brian told you that he mentored me. That included keeping me at his side while he developed his sense of terror and counterterror. Meager as I am by myself, I'm the main counterterror effort here in New York. Sometimes I go undercover. I get into the mosques, and I listen."

He looked around at the passing crowd and blew into his cupped hands to warm them while shivering against the cold. "Can we go somewhere to talk? Maybe we can share ideas and spark some more."

Atcho looked him over and nodded. "I don't have much time. I need to find my wife."

"No one here would take O'Brian seriously," Sam said. The three men sat in a coffee shop on West Broadway. "He let me work closely with him because I speak Arabic fluently and can pass as a Middle Easterner."

"How did that happen?" Burly asked.

"I grew up in Lebanon, back when Beirut was still the Paris of the Mediterranean. My father was a construction superintendent. I ran the streets with the Arab kids."

"When did you return stateside?" Atcho asked.

"I came for good in my early teens. I'd been going back and forth for most of my life, but my parents decided I needed to finish my education here."

"How did you wind up in the FBI?"

"O'Brian recruited me. He'd known my father from a couple of cases he worked in Lebanon. He knew my academic record and that I was fluent in Arabic. I won a couple of athletic awards too, so he knew I could handle the physical requirements."

Atcho glanced at his watch. "This is all very nice, but how can you help us? I know the threat, but I really want to get Sofia away from here."

Sam gave him a tentative glance. "O'Brian routed her file to me. From where I stand, she can probably handle things on her end."

His face a mask, Atcho stared at Sam. "You checked out my wife's background?"

With rounded eyes and a taut jaw, Sam nodded. "I'm trying to help," he said. "Look, I'm the only FBI special agent in New York City who will give you more than lip-service support. We all know you're a national hero, so any of us will talk with you. But I'm the only one who knows fundamentalist Muslims. O'Brian tried to elevate attention on the questionable activities of some of them, and our superiors trotted him off to another city. If you want help, I'm it."

Atcho's eyes bored into Sam. He said nothing.

"Look," Sam went on, still sincere but flashing impatience, "something is going down here in New York City soon. I can feel it. When I go to the mosque, men clump together and talk in whispers. I've tried to break into inner circles and I'm making progress, but I'm still not trusted. I glean only what I hear when people talk in close proximity, but I can't appear to be trying to listen. The polite thing for me to do when they stare at me is to move away, and I do."

Burly leaned his heavy frame into the table. "What are you hearing?"

Sam exhaled, looked around the small coffee shop, and shifted toward Burly.

"Let me take a few steps back." He dropped his face into his hands and his shoulders drooped as if they carried a great weight. When he looked up again, his eyes revealed a haunted expression.

"A lot of Muslims hate us," he said, and glanced around again as if wary of unwanted listeners. "They hate our culture, our lifestyles, and mainly they hate us because we are infidels. They don't intend to assimilate into our culture. The aim of these extremists is either to change our culture or kill it—meaning, kill us."

Atcho looked at him skeptically. "Aren't you being a little extreme?"

Sam pulled back, startled. "You, of all people, say that?" He tossed his head back and forth in frustration. "You languished in a prison for seventeen years because a madman in Cuba wanted to play God. You took on a mission in Siberia because a lunatic wanted the Soviet nuclear arsenal. You were instrumental in liberating millions of people from behind the Iron Curtain and the Berlin Wall, and you stopped the disaster in Kuwait from becoming a global calamity, and you ask me if I'm being extreme?"

He blew out a breath. "You've seen what extreme people do, and they don't move quietly like I do. They don't live within the confines of a constitution and the laws promulgated under it, and they don't respect the rights of others. They kill and they burn, and they enslave by the millions, and that's what they want for our country. You've seen it, and I've seen it."

Atcho crossed his arms and studied Sam. The young man reminded him of himself at a younger age, roughly thirty years ago, in the jungles of Cuba when he had so passionately confronted Burly, the same man who now sat by his side and had participated with him in so many life-and-death situations.

"You've done your homework on me too," he said gently. "Sorry. I didn't mean to minimize what you have to say." He glanced at his watch. "But please get to the point about how you can help."

Sam pushed his chair back, leaned over, and rested his elbows on his knees. He looked up at Atcho, his air almost one of despair. "They're here," he said. "New York is going to get hit, hard. I feel it in my bones, and your wife might find herself in the middle of it."

"Explain."

Sam dropped his head and closed his eyes. "There's a man here in New York, a blind man his followers call Sheikh Omar. He preaches all the time at a local mosque. What comes out of his mouth is venomous. He hates the United States and rails against us. Frankly, I'm finding the line between the practice of free speech and advocating for the violent overthrow of our government to be incredibly thin. I think this guy crosses the line routinely. I've reported him. O'Brian tried to have our superiors investigate his activities, but we both got shunted aside like we're being ridiculous."

"The point," Atcho goaded Sam. "Get to the point."

Sam sighed. "Sorry. The sheikh is acting different now. He's more circumspect in what he says. The groups of men whispering to each other have grown tighter, and the chatter has fallen off. It's as if they're cautioning each other to silence. At the same time, you can see a zeal in their eyes, like they know something is about to happen but don't dare mention it outside of their own groups."

"And that's what you think Sofia might be wandering into?"

Sam drew himself back, closed his eyes, and inhaled deeply. "I don't know," he said. "I'm going on what I know of her disappearance. I think you told Jim Dude that she left a note suggesting she was going to head things off at the pass, so to speak."

Atcho nodded.

"Do you mind sharing what she said in her note?"

"She told me to stay focused and not to worry about her. She said the target was unthinkable."

"Aren't they all," Sam observed, a touch of irony in his voice. "Do you think she's identified the target, or thinks she has?"

Atcho put both hands against his forehead, clasped his fingers together, and dragged his hands through his hair, his concern manifest.

"That's what I think. And she doesn't want to raise alarms until she's sure. She won't want to divert resources and then find out she's wrong. But knowing her"—Atcho heaved out a breath—"she's probably nailed it."

The three men sat in silence for a spell. Atcho broke it.

"Do you know about Klaus and his bomb?"

"Only water-cooler talk. I know some believe he detonated a suitcase nuclear device in Afghanistan—a poor man's underground test. But that's never been confirmed. He supposedly tried to bomb three different facilities with similar devices, but you stopped him each time." He grinned tiredly. "You're a legend, Atcho."

Atcho shook his head. "Sure. One that no one listens to. One of those facilities he tried to bomb was my house. What do they say about his attempts?"

"That maybe his bombs are the problem. Maybe they just don't work."

Atcho folded his arms again and pursed his lips. Visions flashed through his mind of a huge cargo plane almost fatally landing in Moscow, of himself at the flight controls while Sofia applied a heat-generating device to the trigger mechanism of a suitcase bomb, hoping to melt it before it detonated.

He recalled ducking behind a heavy concrete wall inside the headquarters of the secret police in East Berlin when a rogue Russian general mashed the remote for one of the bombs. And only last year, Klaus had placed a similar bomb outside Atcho and Sofia's home in Austin.

"Maybe the critics are right," Atcho said. "Lucky for the terrorists, they only have to be right once. We have to be right every time. So, what do we do?"

"Tell me about your wife. Tell me how she thinks. She said the target was unthinkable, but you both thought it will probably be somewhere in New York City. Which target, in her mind, would be more unthinkable than any other one?"

Atcho regarded Sam with new respect. "I can see why O'Brian likes you." He glanced up to the ceiling while he thought. "There are so many possibilities. We thought we had seen a pattern." He paused. "Burly got information from the Israelis that narrows the field a bit. They think he intends to hit the financial district to cripple our economy. But we know that they also like to hit targets that are symbolic. They'll hit one that does the best of meeting both of those objectives."

He related his forays into Argentina and Lima. "The three times Klaus went there to observe, the bombs kept getting bigger and their economic effect more pronounced. These terrorists are not satisfied with thousands of small strikes that cause a little damage and then people forget. They want to make a statement that everyone will have to hear. They want to eviscerate the physical landscape and the economy. They want to strike a blow that will make the country reel and one they can then exploit for PR and further attacks on a similar scale. In short, they want to see our utter destruction."

"And which target in New York City gives them that opportunity more than any other?"

Atcho stared out the coffee shop window. The sun had begun its rapid descent, and gloom had already settled onto the long street. At its end, the Twin Towers rose above the dark outlines of the smaller buildings.

As Atcho ruminated, the sun glanced off the sides of the towers, imbuing them with a golden hue. A shaft of reflected light broke the gathering shadows.

Atcho stood, his face frozen in dread. "That's it," he rasped, pointing. "That's the greatest, most visible symbol of US financial wealth and economic power. It's the next step in hitting larger and taller buildings and doing it in the US. That's the target."

42

"Now that we think we know where Klaus is going to strike," Burly said, "what do we do?"

"We go there," Atcho replied. "If Sofia's come to the same conclusion, that's where we'll find her, and if we're right, that's where we'll find Klaus. Can you check with Eitan and see if he's come up with anything?"

"I can try," Burly said. "We've been trading phone messages." He turned to Sam. "Can you get me on a secure line?"

Sam nodded. "And I'll talk to the security director at the towers, not that he'll take any action. He shares our bosses' view of O'Brian and sees me in the same light." He paused as another thought surfaced. "The fact is, when the towers were built and the architects, developers, and owners discussed security, they decided against passive measures that would inhibit entry. So, for instance, they chose not to include obstacles and barriers that would slow down traffic into the parking areas. But you're thinking that the threat comes from a guy carrying a suitcase, right?"

Atcho nodded absently. "I'm not saying no one is going to try conventional explosives, but if we're talking about Klaus, that's a nuclear threat."

"All right. Let me see if I can get someone from building security on the phone at the towers. They don't like to talk to me, but they'll take my call because I'm from the FBI."

Sam left the table and walked across the room to a phone booth.

"Good kid," Burly observed in his absence.

"I can see why O'Brian puts so much stock in him," Atcho replied.

"What are you going to do about Sofia?"

"I'll leave a message for her with Bob. She lives for Jameson and Katt-rina and will call out there to see how they're doing. My message will say that we've reached the same conclusions she has regarding the Twin Towers, that security is informed, and that the FBI is cooperating. On that basis, I'll ask her to go back to Montana."

"Do you think she'll do that?"

Atcho sighed. "Only if she thinks the threat is neutralized."

"What do we do in the meantime?"

Atcho glanced at his watch. "She won't be there now. She has to sleep and she's smart enough to know it. We'll get there early in the morning and watch for her."

Sam returned to the table shaking his head. "I got the usual patronizing attitude from Twin Towers' security. They treat me like the boy who cried wolf." He rubbed his eyes tiredly. "They forget the end of that story—a real wolf showed up."

"Are they going to *do* anything?"

"They said they'll keep an eye out for Sofia and a guy with a briefcase—they were being sarcastic. Obviously, lots of guys with briefcases go there every day. I'll get photos of Klaus faxed over to them. I managed to set up a meeting for tomorrow morning. I figured if I bring you two along, they might take me more seriously. What do you think?"

"They should listen," Burly said. "We've had first-hand experience with Klaus and his bombs. Maybe that will make an impression. Meanwhile, get me to that secure line."

43

Early the next morning, Sofia sat up in bed, her eyes blurry from a restless night. Her head pounded, and her body ached. She sat contemplating a conversation she'd had with Bob and Isabel just before bed. Atcho had left a message for her, and she had understood it—he had reached the same conclusion on the probable target and wanted her to return to Montana to be with Jameson. Isabel had put Jameson on the phone for a few minutes, and his little voice begging Sofia to come and take him home had brought her near to tears.

"I'll be there soon," she had told him, her voice soothing. "Daddy too. We love you so much."

She analyzed the situation. *The Israelis tipped us that the financial area is the probable target, but they could be wrong. Even if we're right, that doesn't mean Klaus will hit the Twin Towers. But that is the tallest target with the greatest symbolic value. Regardless, Klaus must have at least considered it and probably has people scoping it out.* She took a deep breath, got out of bed, and crossed to the window.

Her room was on a low floor of a national chain, a good place to stay, but its view was limited to the buildings across the street. Already, people moved purposefully to work.

For a few moments, she thought of cancelling today's plan to roam the

World Trade Center again. The pull to return to a safe place and be with her baby son was almost overpowering, but then the pragmatism of a seasoned intelligence operations officer set in. *Klaus won't present himself. He won't be readily visible. We're going to have to draw him out.*

With dread in the pit of her stomach and a lump in her throat, she dressed, pulled on her heavy coat and boots, and once more made her way into the streets of New York City. She hailed a cab and watched without seeing as the rush-hour view passed by. Soon, the towers loomed ahead of her, their lower parts visible through the windshield.

The taxi pulled to the curb. Sofia mustered a positive countenance and stepped out onto the sidewalk. Then she began her trek.

The forecast had called for temperatures diving below twenty degrees with wind gusts up to thirty-three miles per hour. The biting cold caused her to tuck her chin into her collar. She turned her head as she walked to allow her own vapor to pass by—it impeded her view. Her fur-lined gloves barely seemed to break the icy breeze, and she thrust her hands into her side pockets for added warmth, pushing them against the inner lining to hug the coat closer around her.

The usual horde of pedestrians hurried through the plaza into the soaring buildings. Sofia moved with them, deciding that a hot cup of coffee and a bagel might help make her rounds more tolerable and allow for the sun to rise higher and do its work of warming the day.

As she sat in the coffee shop people-watching, her mind wandered through the events that had brought her to this moment. Despite challenges, she thought most of it had been happy. Tragedy had befallen her when her first husband had been killed in the Middle East.

An image of him formed in her head, young, strong-minded, handsome. After losing him, she had thought she could never love again. And then, five years later, Atcho entered her life, a filthy, brutalized political prisoner just released to the United States Interests section of the Swiss Embassy in Havana. Despite the obvious ravages he had endured, he carried himself with such nobility. His fellow ex-prisoners had treated him with high regard, and yet his overriding concern was for his daughter, Isabel, whom he had not seen in nineteen years.

Sofia did not see Atcho again until early 1988, when she received an invitation to a reception at a prominent hotel in downtown Washington, DC. Her CIA cover at the time was that of a senior intelligence supervisor for the US State Department, stationed at its headquarters.

The reception was to celebrate Atcho's recognition by Ronald Reagan at the State of the Union Address earlier that same evening. The organizers had invited all those who had been with Atcho in captivity or assisted with his release. The party was a surprise for him. By then, he had reunited with his daughter and forged a successful career as a real estate investor in Washington, DC. The attraction she had felt in Havana resurfaced.

Something about Atcho in the days and months after their reacquaintance had been enigmatic. Sofia noticed that he held friends away, and he ended their romance just as it had begun. Convinced that Atcho carried a burden thrust on him by outside forces, she had sought Burly's help. Her instincts had been vindicated when she learned that Atcho had resisted coercive efforts by a foreign power to be their secret agent. That power had threatened Isabel.

Together, Atcho, Burly, and Sofia had defeated the threat and then participated in subsequent clandestine operations in Siberia, Berlin, and Kuwait. In between the first two missions, she and Atcho had married, and between the second two, she had born Jameson.

Atcho had soothed Sofia's pain over losing her first husband, and together they had begun to live fully. *And now that could end abruptly.*

Sofia doused the thought. *No time to be maudlin.*

She left the coffee shop, rode the escalator back up to the main floor, and exited on West Street.

Klaus decided to oversee Sofia's capture personally. He arrived at the World Trade Center early and walked around to examine the complex from the point of view of each man stationed to watch for her. Satisfied that she could be spotted regardless of rush-hour crowds, he loitered between street vendors to wait.

Shortly after eight o'clock, a runner came to let him know that she had been seen emerging from a taxi, wearing the same white coat as the previous two days, and heading toward the North Tower's main door.

"Olek will pick her up there," the runner told him. "He'll wait for you. Amir is with him and will follow her when she goes by. He has a cell phone and will call back to Olek about her movements."

"Let's go." Klaus set off at a fast pace, shouldering past people who slowed him down. His mind raced as he anticipated bringing the wife of his arch-nemesis under his control. The last time Sofia and Klaus had seen each other face to face was in Berlin just before the Wall fell. He recalled her initial look of shock and then resolve as he forced Atcho at gunpoint to accompany him.

The only other time Klaus had seen her was through the reticles of a sniper scope as he pulled the trigger. She had fled across his field of view, leaving him no time for careful aim. The bullet had gone through her leg.

"You won't be treated so well this time," he muttered under his breath as he approached the building's revolving door. "Where is she?" he demanded upon seeing Olek. They spoke in Arabic.

"They took a down escalator. Amir just reported that she entered a coffee shop."

"Stay here and keep watch for her. I'll go down. We'll let you know if she comes this way."

Olek gave him the name of the establishment, and Klaus hurried to the escalator, still jammed with people making their way to work. Amir met him outside the coffee shop.

"She's in line," Amir said. "She doesn't seem in a hurry."

"We'll wait for her."

Amir pointed her out and they watched from a distance as Sofia took a seat at a table and sipped her coffee. Forty minutes later, she left and rode the escalator back up to the ground floor.

Klaus and Amir followed. When Sofia turned toward the West Street exit, Klaus ordered, "Get the car and the pickup team over there."

His heart beating faster, his breaths becoming shorter, he closed the distance. At the big rotating doors, Klaus stood back and waited for the next set of people to exit. Once outside, he spotted Sofia and hurried to catch up.

She turned north toward Fulton Street, ambling along against the wind, oblivious to the danger that approached from behind.

Klaus closed in on her right side, put his arm across her back, and clamped his left hand onto her left shoulder. With his right hand, he shoved a pistol into her side.

"Keep walking, Ms. Xiquez," he snarled. "You found me."

Sofia remained silent and kept walking.

"Veer to your left toward the corner of West and Fulton. With any luck, our car will arrive at the same time we do."

Sofia complied. If she felt anxious, her expression failed to reveal it.

Her composure amused Klaus. "You think you're tough," he said in broken English. "Listen to me. When the car comes, I'll open the door. Then, I want you to scream for help. Be loud, and then get in the car. If you don't do those two things, I'll shoot you on the spot and leave your body lying in a heap. Do you understand?"

"How's your bomb?" Sofia responded without emotion. "Have you got one to work yet?"

"How's your son?" Klaus retorted, his voice thick with brutality. "This is no game. I hope you gave Jameson—"

"Leave my son out of this," Sofia snapped angrily. "You attack children? Coward."

"He's an infidel, a combatant against *jihad*. I hope you gave him many kisses before you abandoned him. You won't see him again."

"Then I have nothing to lose."

"But you do. Atcho is still alive and might be able to save your son and himself, and maybe even you. You came here to draw me out. Now I'll use you to expose him."

"Which is why you want the drama as we get in the car."

"Exactly. One of our men will videotape the event and release the clip to the news agencies. Atcho will see it and come for you, I'm sure of that."

"Why not just kill me now?"

Klaus smirked. "I'm tempted, but I want Atcho to think he has a chance of saving you." He laughed without mirth. "He doesn't, but he'll try."

"You've got it all figured out," Sofia mocked. "Atcho's smarter than you. He beat you in Berlin, Kuwait, and Austin, and he'll beat you here."

"But you'll be dead." Klaus smirked. "I'll wave at you both from Paradise."

"Ooh, a martyr," Sofia derided. "How noble."

"Shut up," Klaus hissed. "There's the car."

Atcho hurried with Burly and Sam through the main doors of Building 7 at the World Trade Center. An escort waiting for them in the lobby whisked them through check-in and took them upstairs to the security operations center for the complex.

The head of security met them in the foyer of the office suite. "Mr. Xiquez," the man said, "I'm George Luciano. Jim Dude called to let me know you were on your way." He looked at Burly and tossed Sam a patronizing look. "I assure you that all is being done to locate and recover your wife. The police were informed immediately after the attack, and the FBI is already cooperating."

"Let me see the video," Atcho said tersely.

Luciano led them down a wide corridor to a conference room. "In addition to the clip that showed up on the news," he explained as they walked, "we also have surveillance video. Our technicians pulled it together. I'll show you what we've got so far."

Atcho only nodded as they entered the conference room, where a young man and woman worked over a VCR. They glanced up with grim faces as the group entered.

"We're ready," the woman said. "We've spliced together several views. The first footage is the news clip." She pressed a button on a remote control, and a television screen hanging from a corner wall lit up.

An image of a reporter appeared. "I'm at the corner of West and Fulton," he said, "where just a little while ago, a woman was abducted in broad daylight." He pivoted and held his palm out to indicate the location. "Just after rush hour, witnesses say they saw a woman struggling against an assailant who pushed her into a car. She yelled for help, but before anyone could react, it sped away. Fifteen minutes later, the video footage you are about to see was

delivered to our station with no attribution. Authorities are investigating."

As the group watched, the television screen flashed to a distant scene
showing a man and woman walking closely together across the World
Trade Center plaza. As they approached the street, the camera zoomed in
and focused on the woman's face.

Atcho sucked in his breath. Burly grimaced. Sam stared.

Sofia's face filled the screen. The video showed the man next to her with
one arm wrapped around her back, his hand clamping her shoulder. The
camera shifted to show the man's face.

"Klaus," Atcho growled.

"You know him?" Luciano asked.

"I killed his brother in a firefight. This is his fourth attempt at
revenge."

"So, this is personal," Luciano said flatly.

"This goes way beyond personal," Burly interjected. "That man is a
known terrorist. He's a threat not just to Atcho and his wife, but also to the
US, and specifically the World Trade Center. He intends to bomb it."

"Which explains why you're here," Luciano said, turning to Sam. "You
called last night to set up this meeting, and after that, Ms. Xiquez was
kidnapped. What did you want to see us about?"

Sam looked cornered. His eyes rounded. "To let you know what Burly
just said—that we believe this building is about to get hit with a bomb."

As he spoke, the conference room door swung open and Jim Dude
walked in. "That's a *personal* belief that my *very* young special agent
carries," Dude said sternly, his voice raised. "It's *not* the official position of
the FBI or the New York field office." He faced Sam. "It's a good thing one of
your more senior colleagues saw your phone traffic and clued me in. You're
walking on thin ice."

Atcho's eyes burned with anger. He stepped close to Dude. "Sam is the
only official in New York who takes the threat seriously." He pointed at the
television screen. "Look at the quality of that recording. Klaus pre-posi-
tioned his photographer. He wanted me to see this video."

"There's another thing," Burly interjected. He indicated for Dude to
step away a few paces with him so they could confer in private. "I spoke

with Mossad this morning. Their analysis also leads to the conclusion that the Twin Towers are targeted."

Dude regarded him sharply. "Is that a formal notice to our government?"

Burly shook his head. "It's wending its way through both bureaucracies. I got the information through backchannels."

Dude spun around and caught Atcho's furious gaze. "Does he know?"

"He does," Burly replied. "We think the attack is imminent. Like at any moment."

"Can you replay that recording?" Dude called to Luciano.

The security chief nodded to the female technician. She pointed the remote and started rewinding.

"Sir," she said as the VCR whirred, "while we compiled these recordings, we saw some things you should be aware of."

"What is being done to find my wife?" Atcho cut in, his attention directed pointedly at Dude.

The FBI agent exhaled. "The city police and our agents are combing the streets now." He turned to the young lady. "What did you see that was unusual?"

She glanced at Atcho worriedly and pressed the remote. The group watched again, mesmerized by the vivid details of Sofia's abduction. When it was finished, Dude turned to the technician. "Would you mind answering my question?"

She indicated the TV monitor. "We started looking for any footage that showed Mrs. Xiquez," she said. "We kept finding more and more of it. This is the third day in a row that she's been videoed all over the complex, always wearing that same overcoat, boots, and gloves." As she spoke, the technician let the video run. When the initial clip had finished, it continued on to other sequences of Sofia moving through the WTC complex. Footage toward the end showed Klaus in various places close to Sofia, apparently watching her. The technician stopped the machine, eyed Atcho, and said, "It was as if she was trying to be noticed."

"That's exactly what she was doing," Atcho responded. "She wanted Klaus to see her, to draw him out."

"Why would she do that?" Luciano asked.

"Because the FBI won't do its job, and neither will the CIA or the Department of Defense. They're more concerned with procedure than protection these days. That man planted a nuclear bomb outside our house, and they still don't take him seriously." He whirled on Dude. "We have a family to protect, and if you won't do your job, we'll do it for you. That's why she's sacrificing herself..."

He turned to Burly. "The president knows me. He backed our actions in Berlin and Kuwait. Why doesn't he back us now?"

Before Burly could answer, Atcho went on. "We know why—bad advice from his intelligence agencies and the Pentagon. And the FBI is cut off from information they need to make good decisions." His voice trailed away as he caught himself.

Then he poked a crooked finger at Luciano. "You're getting bad advice too. Klaus is part of an organization that's growing rapidly. It's got funding and technology, and it knows tactics. They've rehearsed in other countries." He faced Dude. "Have you bothered to connect the bombings in Buenos Aires and Lima? That man who kidnapped my wife is a recognized terrorist and was present at all three of those bombings."

Dude blanched, his eyes widening. He said nothing.

Atcho did not wait for a response. "They're coming for your Twin Towers," he told Luciano, "and the bureaucrats are wearing blinders."

The room descended into silence.

"I've reviewed Mr. Luciano's security arrangements," Dude said finally, almost apologetically. "They're robust and adequate. I can't second-guess our intelligence agencies. If the Pentagon and the CIA tell the president that our country is secure from a significant terror attack, I have to rely on that. My concentration at the moment is on finding your wife."

Atcho nodded, deadpan. "Find her, and you might find Klaus," he said. "But my best advice to Mr. Luciano is to start inspecting every briefcase, every purse, every bag that comes into this building." He leveled his gaze at the man. "If you had started yesterday, you might still be too late." His brow furrowed. "Would you mind if I stay in here for a while to review those tapes?"

Luciano assented with a nod. "Take your time. If you see something, let us know. Meanwhile, I'll do what I can to beef up security. How much time do we have?"

"I don't know, but I'd say an attack is imminent." Atcho sat down, leaned his elbows on the table, and buried his head in his hands. "Sofia deliberately baited Klaus. He knows it. He used her to lure me here. For all we know, the bomb is already somewhere in the complex. The stage is set."

"What's your plan?" Burly asked when everyone else had left the conference room.

Atcho shook his head. "I don't know. I'm going through the videos again. Maybe Sofia was able to leave a clue or a message. She'll try to learn Klaus' plan and communicate with us."

"Have you thought of what Klaus might do to her?"

Atcho closed his eyes and nodded. "I try not to think about it." He sniffed. "If she manages to free herself, I pity Klaus."

One particular detail in the video of Sofia's abduction haunted him. He re-ran the tape and watched again, his heart aching.

Just as Klaus had forced Sofia into the car, she struggled upright momentarily and faced back toward the building. As she did, she brought her right hand up, just for a second, to cover her heart.

Her gesture was one Atcho recognized, a message directly to him that said, "I love you. I always will."

On seeing the footage again, Atcho covered his face.

"Burly, please," he said in a broken voice. "I need to be alone for a few minutes."

44

Klaus studied his handiwork carefully, examining each connection and diode in minute detail. Yielding to impulse, he rubbed his hand over the lead sphere containing the plutonium. Satisfied, he rubbed his eyes and switched off the light over his workbench. He swung around on a swivel stool and observed Ramzi on the other side of the room, still bent over his own devices.

"I'm ready," Klaus called in Arabic. "We can go at any time."

Ramzi turned around and smiled. "I'll be finished in a few hours. We are already loading components onto the van. Is tomorrow soon enough?"

Klaus' eyes gleamed, and then he gave Ramzi a questioning look. "I'm curious about something. Why are we hitting the World Trade Center instead of the United Nations? The United States is not our only enemy, and we could hit several of them at one time if we bomb the UN headquarters."

"You're not the only person to come up with that idea," Ramzi replied while turning back to his work, soldering gun in hand. "You know that no target is sanctioned in the US without Sheikh Omar's approval—well, he doesn't give approval, but we all know that if he thinks something is a bad idea, that's a path we will not pursue."

"Why would hitting the UN be a bad idea?"

"I had the same question, but I understand the reasoning. A Muslim striking the United Nations would be bad for Muslims. Not only would we hurt some of our own countries, but also other nations who either support or tolerate us. That could make things hard for Muslims living in those countries, but even more importantly, we could find ourselves actively opposed there.

"There's a stronger reason, though. The UN headquarters isn't the head of the snake. It's the anus. It's where all the smelly waste pours out onto the world. No one means anything they say in all their meetings. It's just a place for people to pretend that they get along while scheming behind each other's backs.

"The US is the head of the snake, and the brain cavity is right here in New York City. We'll kill the snake by killing the financial system. If either bomb works as planned..." He blew over his hands to simulate an explosion, arched his eyebrows, and laughed. "Bye-bye America. We'll rip open its belly, leaving it easy prey for jackals and other filthy beasts that feast on carrion."

Klaus nodded his understanding. Ramzi continued working, the rancid smell of solder and strong chemicals filling the air. At the opposite end of the workshop, a van was parked with its rear doors open. Blue plastic barrels had already been arranged in its dim interior.

"I've had some experience with explosives, but your design is beyond anything I've worked with," Klaus said. "Can you explain what you've done?"

Ramzi looked up at him and smiled patiently. "The difference is that you've mainly used explosives intended for routine military missions or converted from civilian use, like for mining or road construction. We can't get a big enough blast out of those to do the kind of damage we need to topple at least one tower, and hopefully both. But knocking the second one down relies on putting enough force at the precise point on the first one. To do that, we had to identify the exact location against a foundation wall and enhance the explosives' power sufficiently to penetrate completely through the outer wall. That's where my powdered metals come in to expand the blast. Then gravity takes over. It's a simple combination of civil and chemical engineering, and physics." He chuckled. "If you like, you can help us load the nitroglycerine. We have four sealed buckets of it."

Klaus shook his head, laughing. "Never mind that. I have to make it to the target in one piece."

"How are you getting in? They'll be looking for men with briefcases."

"You know how stupid the Americans are. They barely check the people who keep their businesses and lives running. I'll go in through the employees' entrance. A brother who works in security there will let me in, and I already have a work uniform with ID. I'll carry a toolbox in with me. I reconfigured the bomb so that it's long and fits under a false bottom.

"All the parts interact the same way as in the original bomb. It was a matter of extending the wires and making sure the current to each component was the same. I've run all the tests dozens of times, and they check out. I'm ready."

Ramzi nodded his approval. "We're planning on striking just after noon. People will be going to lunch, and the restaurants near the parking garage will be packed. We'll kill a lot of people then. Which one of us detonates first?"

Klaus pursed his lips. "I'd say we detonate at the same time."

Ramzi shook his head. "We can't guarantee that we can do that. On my bomb, we're using detonation cords. There are four of them, and they feed into the nitroglycerine. We only need one. The other three are backups, and they burn at a rate that gives us time to get out. What about you? Have you provided sufficient time to escape?"

Klaus' eyes became somber. "I won't be staying around this time, brother. I'll be spending tomorrow night in Paradise."

Ramzi looked at him in wonder. "A martyr? You're going to blow up with your bomb?"

Klaus dropped his head and nodded. "I'm tired of them not working, for whatever reason. They're ruining my reputation. I can blame Atcho for that, but the fact is, nothing gets blown up. This time, I'm going to make sure the damn thing goes. I'll go up high enough in the building so that I won't be affected by your initial blast, and I'll set the timer to go off five minutes after your expected detonation. If mine doesn't go off then, I'll click the remote, and if that still doesn't work, I'll open the bomb. I set a failsafe."

The wonder in Ramzi's eyes had not receded. He crossed the room to Klaus and embraced him. "You have truly earned your way into Paradise with all the rewards of a martyr. I will make sure that no one forgets your sacrifice."

They discussed other details while Ramzi resumed his work. As time proceeded past midnight into early morning, he jutted his jaw toward a small door near the van.

"What about the woman?"

Klaus followed his glance. "She's yours. Do what you want with her. Give her to your men for sport, if you like. Just promise me one thing." He reached across and grasped Ramzi's shoulder. "Make sure she's dead before the day is out."

Ramzi held Klaus' gaze for an extended time and then dropped his head. "It shall be done, my brother, as you wish."

45

Sofia's eyes opened slowly; her mind felt dull. She tried to turn on her side, but her arms were bound at the wrist behind her back. Her ankles were also tied together. Finding herself constrained shocked her to full consciousness, and she struggled against the ropes momentarily as memory of her capture flooded back.

Fully awake in a dark room, she remembered walking to the car with Klaus.

Klaus. Her blood ran cold at the thought of him. She had played through his charade of making a public spectacle of her abduction—doing so served her own purpose of providing a positive identification of the terrorist to Atcho and authorities via the expected video.

She remembered her small gesture. Just before ducking her head to enter the car, she had brought her right hand over her heart in a circular movement. The motion was slight and would not be noticed by most people, but Sofia was sure that Atcho would see the video and understand.

The tiny action was one of intimacy between Atcho and Sofia. It had sprung spontaneously, a cute way of expressing their affection in public places when they caught each other's eye. They had used the signal in countless meetings, parties, even formal events, and it always served to warm their hearts when they found themselves separated by distance.

In this instance, Sofia had sent her love to Atcho as a last farewell. She did not expect to live through the events that were sure to follow. She only hoped that pulling Klaus out of the shadows would provide Atcho with an opportunity to trip him up, to save New York and the millions of people squeezed into a single square mile, the size of the blast area. And with Klaus eliminated, the direct threat against Jameson, Isabel, Kattrina, and the rest of her extended family would disappear.

Another man had been waiting in the back seat when Sofia fell into the car. He immediately clamped a wet cloth over her mouth and nose. She remembered nothing else.

Now, lying in the dark, her mind quickly turned to survival. She had no death wish. Having exposed Klaus and finding herself still alive with her mental acuity intact, she assessed her situation.

She still wore her heavy coat and boots. The only light entering the room came from under a door several feet away, and it was dim. Otherwise, she was in a pitch-black area of indeterminate size. The murmur of voices floated from the other side.

The surface on which she lay was cold and hard, and she guessed it to be the floor. She struggled onto her back, bent her knees, and shoved with her feet until she bumped her head against an upright surface. A wall.

She tilted her neck and shoved with her feet, repeating until the backs of her shoulders pressed against the wall. Her breaths came in short gasps as she watched the light for signs of approaching guards, but none came. She continued the action until she had propped herself up in a sitting position. Then, by rocking onto one side and then the other, she inched her wrists past her buttocks and up under her knees. *Thank God for all that ballet and martial arts training.*

Sofia's coat became an obstacle, its thick folds adding friction and bulk to overcome. Her eyes watered and her breathing became constricted as she curled her body into a tight knot and pushed her wrists over her feet, struggling unmercifully to pull the rope and her palms over the spike heels.

A sense of panic set in as she sensed that she had tied herself into a knot and could not slide the rope the remaining millimeters past the pointed toes of her boots. Then, holding back a scream, she scrunched her stomach, pushed her shoulders against her knees, and shoved her arms forward with her remaining strength. The rope slid forward, and her legs fell to the floor with a muffled thump.

Sofia stayed still and listened. The low murmur of voices beyond the door continued without interruption.

She rolled onto her stomach, pushed herself to a standing position, and hopped to the door. The voices on the other side continued in Arabic. Sofia distinguished two men, one of them Klaus.

She rotated her wrists by the faint light below the door as best she could until she could make out the ends of the rope and the shape of the knot. Then, using her teeth, she struggled with it until it came loose.

When her hands were finally free, she worked the cord around her feet until it fell loose. Then she felt her way around the bare room, judging it to be an empty storage room.

46

February 26, 1992

"It's time," Ramzi said. He shook Klaus for a second time. "If you're going in with the maintenance crew, you need to leave soon."

Klaus blinked. Ramzi had worked through the night, and Klaus had stayed with him until he fell asleep in a chair. As he woke up, he remembered the last thing Ramzi had told him.

"Don't detonate before noon," Ramzi had said, leering. "That's when we'll blow our bomb. Remember to get high enough that you won't be wiped out in the initial blast. When you feel the building rumble, you'll know my work is complete, and you can finish your task. If nothing has happened by twelve-fifteen, then, as the Americans say, bombs away."

"I'll go to the seventy-eighth floor," Klaus had replied, eyes gleaming with anticipation. "That's where the transfer lobby to reach the higher floors is located. It's low enough that, with the hole your bomb creates, we'll leave a massive crater in Manhattan, and it's high enough to generate a huge quantity of radioactive fallout. Mine will toss thirty-two floors full of infidels into the sky. With any luck, it'll shoot them into the jet streams and drop them in bloody clumps over the country all the way to California."

Klaus shook himself to wake up. "That's the wrong direction," he said flatly, almost in a growl. "The jet streams will blow everything out to sea."

Ramzi regarded him with a dreamy expression. "I know. I let my imagination run away with me for a moment." He scoffed. "Maybe some of it will land on Buckingham Palace in London."

Klaus stretched, yawned, and scratched the back of his neck. Then he went to the next room to clean up and dress.

"How will you get to the Trade Center?" Ramzi asked when Klaus emerged.

"I'll ride the bus. I scouted a stop used by a few of the center's employees, and I've ridden the line a few times, so I'll look familiar to them. I'll go in with them. Our brother on the inside will pass me through."

"He's doing a great service for our *jihad*. Do I know him?"

Klaus shrugged. "I don't know. My *hawaladar* in Tripoli directed him to me. He only knows to let me in, nothing more."

Ramzi nodded his approval and gestured to the small door of the storage room where Sofia was held. "Do you want to see the woman again?"

Klaus shook his head. "I don't want to be corrupted on this of all days. I'll just go. Be sure to deal with her as promised."

Ramzi gave him a somber look. "After the bombing, we'll celebrate with her, and then I'll take care of it. You can damn me to hell from Paradise if I fail. Do you want breakfast before you go?"

"I'll have several hours with nothing to do before you arrive. I'll put some fruit and bread in my toolbox to eat if I get hungry. That will make the contents look even more innocent."

They walked to the entrance of the workshop together, embraced, and kissed each other's cheeks.

"Live a long and happy life," Klaus said, "and then I'll see you in Paradise." He started to leave and then, on impulse, turned back. "Who's going to drive? Not Salameh, I hope."

Ramzi grunted. "Not Salameh. I have a friend who grew up in New York City. He was a limo driver here for many years and knows all the streets. He'll drive us to the target the smoothest way, without jarring the nitroglycerine."

Klaus stared, his doubt manifest in his expression. "Why have you tolerated Salameh?"

"He's my friend. He came here with me for *jihad*."

Klaus shook his head. Then he turned, waved over his shoulder, and started down the driveway carrying his toolbox.

After Klaus left, Ramzi went to the van and checked all the connections, then woke up Salameh and the limo driver.

"Time for final preparations," he said, his passive expression belying the tingling of excitement he felt.

Salameh turned over on his mattress on the floor, pulled his blanket back over his head, and groaned his objection to having his sleep interrupted. Then he yawned and reluctantly climbed out of bed.

Tariq, the limo driver, bounded to his feet. "Let's go." He prodded Salameh. "Who else will ever have an opportunity like this one?"

The two followed Ramzi back into the workshop. He opened a locker and gestured at four gray buckets made of heavy plastic with sealed lids. A very narrow tube protruded from the center of each one.

"These go in the van." He peered sternly at Salameh. "Do I need to remind you how carefully you have to carry them?"

Salameh regarded him with wild eyes and shook his head.

"If you drop them," Ramzi continued, "we'll leave a crater in New York City, but we won't hit our target and our rewards in Paradise will be greatly diminished. Do you understand?"

Salameh nodded and picked up one of the buckets.

"Arrange them in front of the blue plastic barrels," Yousef said.

Once the nitroglycerine was loaded, Ramzi demonstrated how to thread the detonation cords through the surgical tubing. "This will subdue the smoke, so people are less likely to notice it. In the parking garage, that probably won't be an issue, and we'll lock the van anyway. The tubing will also slow down the burning, giving us time to escape from the blast area."

"Do you mind telling me how it all works?" Tariq asked.

"Of course," Ramzi said with pride. "The blue plastic barrels are filled with several hundred pounds of urea nitrate crystals mixed with nitric acid. The yellow barrels behind them contain sulfuric acid. We'll insert the detonation cords through the tubes on top of the nitroglycerin in the gray buckets. They are the fuses that ignite the nitroglycerine. When it explodes, it will cause the other elements to explode. Above the barrels are pressurized canisters of compressed hydrogen. That's what will make the explosion reach high into the building."

"And above that will be Klaus and his bomb," Tariq breathed.

Ramzi nodded. "When we park in the garage, light the fuses—and run." He laughed.

They finished loading their cargo and inserting the fuses. Then Salameh glanced toward the storage room door.

"What about the woman?"

"She'll be here when we get back. Klaus gave her to me. You can have fun with her afterward."

Salameh looked at his watch. "We won't leave for another hour. Can't we play with her a little now?"

Ramzi glanced at the door and then back at Salameh's hopeful face. "All right, but just for a few minutes—if you can bring her here. She's tied up in there. Can you handle her by yourself?"

Salameh grinned, lascivious intent gleaming in his eyes. Without saying another word, he headed toward the room.

⸻

Sitting on the floor next to the door with one of the ropes in her hands, Sofia dozed intermittently. Not knowing when she might need agility more than warmth, she had taken off her heavy coat and draped it over her shoulders.

She heard the men in the other room moving about and talking, but she could make out none of the conversation. Then she heard approaching footsteps and the key turning in the door.

She leaped to her feet and crouched, the rope strung between both hands. Her coat fell to the floor.

The door opened. A man stepped in, silhouetted against the light.

Sofia sprang. Crossing her arms and tossing the rope around Salameh's neck, she yanked it tight.

Not being a true garrote, the rope tightened and pinched off Salameh's airway, but did not cut into his skin. He immediately tossed furiously from side to side, fighting to remove a demon from his back. As his breath constricted, he panicked and slammed Sofia back against a wall.

She held on, but Salameh slammed her again and again. The rope slipped through her hands, burning them.

In the other room, Ramzi and Tariq heard the commotion and came running. In the dim light that spilled into the closet, they saw that Salameh had fallen to his knees and was clutching at his neck while Sofia clung to his back, still holding the rope around his throat. They rushed to his side and beat their fists into Sofia's head and hands until she let go of the cord.

Salameh fell forward, supporting himself on his hands and catching his breath while Ramzi and Tariq pulled Sofia into the other room. Forced to the ground on her stomach, she was helpless to stave off the blows Tariq delivered to the back of her head while straddling her.

Moments later, Salameh reeled from the closet, lust for vengeance written on his face. He staggered toward Sofia and delivered a powerful kick to the side of her head.

Her mind reeled, her vision blurred, and she lost consciousness. Blood spilled to the floor from an open gash above her temple.

Salameh continued kicking until he had exhausted himself.

Panting and sweating, he looked up at Ramzi. "What should we do with her?"

"Throw her in the van. She'll be one more infidel the authorities will try to piece together in two hours."

47

"Atcho, get some rest," Burly urged. "Building management has a full staff and augmentation. If Klaus comes in, we'll get him."

Atcho shook his head. "He can set that bomb off any time. We have to get close to him before he knows we've spotted him. Let's hope he hasn't decided to go martyr on us. If he has, all bets are off. Have you distributed those NUKEXs?"

"We had some flown in last night, but we don't have enough for the entire staff. I gave them to Luciano and showed him how to use them. He'll distribute them as he sees fit. You got yours?"

Atcho patted his jacket and nodded wearily.

They were sitting at a desk in the middle of the World Trade Center security operations control room in Building 7 of the complex. From that vantage, they could see most of the plaza on the north side of both buildings. Arrayed on the walls around them were banks of monitors that officers were watching closely.

Atcho heaved a sigh. "Even with all these eyes looking for him, Klaus will be tough to spot. Is there any progress on setting up full inspections at the entries?"

Burly scoffed. "There are 'political considerations.'" He mimed quotation marks in the air, and his expression projected his disgust. "The building is governed by the port authority, which falls under city government, and the politicians don't want to upset the public." He shot Atcho a sympathetic glance. "Anything on Sofia?"

Atcho closed his eyes and shook his head. "The news stations broadcast the picture of her and Klaus everywhere, the police mounted a huge search, and the FBI is working with them. People are calling in by the hundreds, but no solid leads. The trouble is that law enforcement is viewing this as a vendetta kidnapping, and not what it really is—Klaus' deliberate diversion. He wanted me here in New York City for the big bang, and here I am."

"Then Sofia's effort was useless?"

Atcho pushed his chair back, dropped his hands between his knees, and lowered his head. "I don't want to think that. Her aim was to smoke Klaus out. She did that. We know for certain he's in the city, and he wouldn't have spotted her at the WTC if he wasn't scoping it out. She pinpointed the target. His freedom of movement will be restricted too, because more eyes will be searching for him."

He looked up suddenly and scanned the room. "We're looking at this the wrong way, Burly," he exclaimed. "He won't come in wearing a suit and carrying a briefcase. What time is it?"

"Nearly eleven o'clock. What are you thinking?"

"Remember in Berlin, Klaus and his brother came into the hotel dressed as maintenance men to kidnap me? They had inside help and breached State Department security."

He jumped to his feet and grabbed the nearest security officer, a shift supervisor, by the shoulder. "Do you monitor employees as they enter the building?"

The man nodded and pointed to a row of screens watched by only a light crew. "Over there. I can get them to pull up this morning's clips."

"Do it and have your crew check for anything irregular on employees coming in this morning." He handed the officer a photo of Klaus. "This is the face."

"We all have that, sir, but we've been focusing on the public entrances."

"Exactly. Get people to review videos of everyone coming in through the staff entries. Look for anybody carrying something, anything that appears bulky. Chances are, the guy we're looking for is already inside. If you spot him, track which building he goes to and let me know immediately." He paused a moment in thought. "Can you pull a one-hundred-percent accounting of where each employee is?"

The security officer nodded. "It'll take some time."

"How much?"

"Twenty, thirty minutes."

"Do it. Do you need to clear it with Luciano?"

"No. He told me to fully cooperate." The man hurried away to carry out Atcho's instructions.

Burly nudged him. "You really think he's here already?"

"He has Sofia, and he has me where he wants me. He's ready to pull the trigger."

Klaus remained in a men's restroom near the staff entrance for a time, and then moved to a coffee shop. He lingered there only long enough to appear to grab a cup of morning coffee before heading out to complete routine tasks. Then he went to another restroom, and finally made his way into a long underground tunnel that would take him to the North Tower. Arriving there, he looked at his watch with dismay. He still had three hours to kill.

Finding a broom closet, he deposited his toolbox in a dark corner and swept the floor outside, watching closely for anyone entering the storeroom.

Another hour passed. Retrieving his toolbox, he made his way to the Paths Concourse and sought out the coffee shop where he had observed Sofia yesterday, smiling at the memory of her forced composure when he had confronted her.

He looked at his watch again. Still two hours to go. *One hundred and twenty minutes—and then poof.* He smiled again, picturing flying, mutilated bodies disappearing in a cloud of smoke.

He sauntered back into the maintenance areas below ground and found a cargo elevator for the higher floors. His contact in WTC security had provided him with a pass, which he used with no difficulty. On arriving at the seventy-eighth floor, he took a few minutes to observe the breathtaking view of the city and the countryside beyond. He had read somewhere that, on a clear day, the Twin Towers were visible from Bear Mountain, a few miles south of West Point. He smirked at the thought. *We came so close to getting your family, Atcho, but we've got your wife, and we'll get you today.*

He made his way to the nearest maintenance room, found a dark corner to open his toolbox, and began munching on an apple.

Salameh held the garage doors to the workshop open while Tariq edged the van into the driveway, and then closed them. He hurried to enter the van through the rear, since the side doors were blocked by the collection of blue, gray, and yellow plastic barrels.

No one spoke. Ramzi sat in the front passenger seat. Sofia, bloodied, limp, and intermittently conscious, had been propped in the only unoccupied space on the floor. On entering and settling across from her, Salameh prodded her again with the bottom of his boot and then two more times for good measure. He grinned at Ramzi, who, eyes wide, signaled for him to stop and pointed at the nitroglycerine.

Salameh understood the message and fell into sullen silence.

Tariq guided the van with great care over the rough driveway and emerged onto Pamrapo Avenue, sliding into mid-morning traffic. He drove southeast and followed the main road, then turned north on Garfield Avenue. His route was carefully chosen for smooth driving with the fewest number of stops, the least traffic, and the best road surface. Tariq took care to keep a distance between the van and vehicles ahead, gliding to a halt when necessary, always mindful of the destructive cargo behind him.

Ramzi sat rigidly, allowing only his head and eyes to move, watching in all directions, including checking on Salameh to be sure he behaved himself.

Salameh continued to eye Sofia in sullen silence, nudging her with his boot whenever Ramzi was not looking.

They reached Interstate 78 and turned to traverse the Holland Tunnel. Tariq drove at a speed that kept traffic flowing past him on the left. On reaching the other side, they took the exit that wound around toward West Street and then turned south.

The tall spires of the Twin Towers loomed ahead of them. Ramzi viewed them with the detached attention of an engineer examining a project, reviewing in his mind the placement and magnitude of forces required to bring them down.

48

"There." Luciano pointed at the video screen in front of him. "Play that back," he instructed the officer working the controls.

As Atcho watched with Burly and Luciano, a man dressed in a maintenance uniform entered the field of view. He moved with a line of employees entering the World Trade Center through a staff portal.

"Look," Luciano exclaimed as the video rolled. "He has trouble with his ID card, then he's taken aside by a security guard, and watch this—he's allowed through." He turned to another officer. "Get that security guard and bring him to me."

"Have you tracked where the man went, the one who had trouble with the ID?" Atcho asked. "The video is too grainy to make him out. He looks like he's carrying something, a container of some sort."

"We're combing the files," Luciano said. "He went straight to a restroom and stayed there for an extended time, and then made his way to a coffee shop. We don't know yet where he went from there. We'll keep looking."

"I'll wait. Warn your people to look out for him, but if they see him, they need to keep a distance. That container could be the bomb."

"It's time to evacuate the building," Luciano said.

"If you do that, he'll know we're on to him, and he'll blow it," Burly interjected. "For whatever reason, he seems to be biding his time, like he's waiting for something. Instead of causing a panic that could alert him and trigger his action, let's use the time to get close to him."

Luciano hesitated, his face showing the weight of decision. He sighed. "All right."

An officer nudged his elbow and pointed to a screen. Luciano peered at it and turned to Atcho.

"We've got a clear shot of him. Is that your guy?"

Atcho moved closer to the screen and scrutinized the image in front of him. "That hat is hiding his full face, but the lower half of the face looks like him, and that's the right build. Where was that taken?"

"On the Paths Concourse. He appears to be headed to the North Tower."

A phone rang. The security officer at the control panel answered it. "Sir," he called to Luciano, "we've got him. He's on the seventy-eighth level Sky Lobby mopping the floor."

"Patch us in."

Atcho's heart thumped when the live image appeared on the screen. His face flushed red and sweat beaded on his forehead. His hands became clammy.

"That's him," he said, "and there's his bomb." He pointed to a toolbox sitting to one side of the screen, apparently against a wall. "Get me over there. Fast." He glanced at his watch. The digital readout blinked 11:50.

Luciano's face flushed with frustration. "I'm sending over a quick reaction force," he said. "We don't know when he'll blow that thing. I can get my men there faster than I can get you there."

"Fine." Atcho matched Luciano's tone. "But they have to keep control of Klaus' hands. I'm sure he has a remote, and he's willing to blow himself up. We've already seen that. Tell them to hold him until I get there. No one opens that container. And shut down those elevators."

"Agreed. I have some undercover men in suits I'll send up. They know what to do." He made the call.

Each of the passing minutes seemed like centuries to Atcho. He watched in fascination as Klaus mopped methodically back and forth. The flow of people entering and exiting the elevators slowed visibly. If Klaus noticed, he showed no indication.

Soon, only four men other than Klaus remained on the floor. Three had meandered into Klaus' vicinity and one had moved toward the container, which now could be clearly identified as a toolbox.

In a sudden flurry of action, the three men near Klaus lunged. One tackled his feet and the other two grabbed his arms. In an instant, they had him on his back. The fourth man walked over to the toolbox and took up a position next to it.

Atcho turned toward Luciano, who had just hung up a phone. "The subject is subdued, and our guys have the remote," the security chief told him.

"Get me over there," Atcho growled.

On West Street, Tariq maneuvered the van to the parking garage entrance they had already scouted. He coaxed the vehicle over the hump that led into the dim interior and then eased it down the long ramp. Continuing past the rows of parked cars, they made their way to parking level B-2.

Tariq slowed to a halt.

Ramzi stared in consternation.

Ahead of them, a concrete beam suspended from the ceiling. A sign posted on it warned of the maximum height that a vehicle could pass beneath it without scraping the beam. The van was two inches too tall.

Ramzi whirled toward Salameh and fixed furious eyes on him. "Didn't you check the height when you rented this van?"

Salameh shrugged. "It looked like the right height."

Ramzi closed his eyes and faced the front, containing his anger.

"What do we do?" Tariq asked.

Ramzi's mind flipped rapidly through alternatives. If they tried to ram or scrape under the beam, they ran the risk of detonating the bomb while they were still in the van. If they let air out of the tires, they risked being spotted, and the uneven wobble of the van driving on flattened tires could set off the nitroglycerine.

"Park over there," he told Tariq, pointing to an area reserved for delivery vehicles. Anger sparked in his eyes. "We won't be able to get to the outer wall. Pray for as much destruction as possible."

Tariq did as instructed.

"Hand me the fuses and get out," Ramzi ordered Salameh.

Gingerly, Salameh crouched and picked up the four fuses tied together and resting on one of the four buckets of nitroglycerine. The opposite end of each fuse led into a corresponding tube in the cylinders.

Ramzi took the ends of the fuses. "Go," he told Salameh. "You too," he said to Tariq. "I'll meet you outside."

Salameh clambered over Sofia, taking one last opportunity to kick her as he opened the rear door and hopped out. He closed it and ran. Tariq followed, their footsteps barely echoing in the cavernous parking garage.

Ramzi moved rapidly, holding the fuses together in one hand while pulling a cigarette lighter from his pocket with the other. The flame leaped when he flipped the lid on the lighter, and he watched it with fascination as he held it to the fuses.

The smell of flame and acrid smoke reached his nostrils. He coughed, and his eyes watered. He stayed only long enough to see the flame traveling along the surgical tube-coated fuses. Then he jumped from the van, locked it, and ran after his comrades' receding footsteps.

• • •

As Atcho rode the elevator up to the seventy-eighth floor of the North Tower with Luciano, he fought down overwhelming emotion. Worry about Sofia overrode all others, and his mind replayed the sequence of his interactions with Klaus: waking up in the Berlin Mövenpick Hotel to find the terrorist pointing a gun at Sofia's head and then forcing Atcho to crawl through the dark, smelly tunnels under that city; the firefight during which Atcho had killed Klaus' brother on the east side of the Wall; their confrontation inside the Stasi headquarters as the Wall crumbled; Klaus' orchestrated assault on Sofia there; his terrorist attack in Kuwait; and then his foray against Atcho's home in Austin.

The elevator halted and the doors slid open. There, sitting cross-legged against the opposite wall with his hands interlocked behind his head, was Klaus. He grinned when he saw Atcho.

Atcho strode across the foyer, and before anyone grasped his impulse, he seized Klaus by the throat and landed a fist square in his face.

Klaus sprawled across the floor onto his back and lay there, stunned.

"Where's my wife?" Atcho snarled. He took two steps toward Klaus and was about to grab him again when Luciano intervened.

"The bomb first," Luciano said.

His lungs heaving, Atcho caught himself. Blood slid from Klaus' nose and he wiped it with a thumb. "You can't save her anyway. She'll watch you die on TV with thousands of infidels—maybe millions. The news channels will replay the scene over and over for years."

Atcho looked across to the toolbox sitting against the wall. Klaus followed his glance and chortled. "The timer. Do you remember that it has a timer?" He laughed. "You can't stop what will happen now, and this afternoon your wife will die, but not before she entertains many men."

Atcho glared at Klaus, then reached into his jacket and pulled out a small cloth bag. He extracted a silvery device that was rounded on one side and flat on the other. The NUKEX.

He approached the toolbox cautiously, examining it from each side. As he did, a high-pitched tone sounded from inside.

Klaus, now sitting back against the wall under the watchful eyes of the undercover security men, laughed "It's over, Atcho," he called. "You have one minute to do whatever you think you can do. I set a short delay on the timer. I had no need of a long one."

The men looked at each other. Atcho froze momentarily and then squatted over the toolbox. Gingerly, he picked it up and turned it over.

Luciano ran to his side. "What are you doing?"

"The bomb has to be in a false bottom. Your people at the employee entrance would have done a physical inspection of the contents, right?"

Luciano nodded. "They didn't know to be on the lookout for a bomb when he entered, and they wouldn't be looking for a false bottom."

Atcho laid the NUKEX flat on one end of the bottom and pressed a button to activate it. "This thing takes thirty seconds to warm up," he yelled to Luciano, "and I don't know which end the bomb's trigger mechanism is on." Sweat already dripped from his brow and his heart beat rapidly. Gritting his teeth, he pressed the NUKEX to one end of the box and moved it along the center lengthwise. "If we have time, this should melt any electronic wires and components directly below it."

As seconds ticked away, Atcho knew he would fail. He should be feeling increasing heat from around the edge of the NUKEX. It was there, but not enough to accomplish its task. He needed at least another minute.

"Is anyone timing this?" he yelled.

"I am," Klaus called, indicating his watch with a mocking smile. "You have fifteen seconds."

Next to him, Luciano turned white and blew out his breath. He pulled up his wrist to see his own watch and inhaled sharply. "You're at five, four, three, two, one..."

49

Eighty floors below in the parking garage, the stench of burning plastic and det cord mixed with acid seeped out of the van. A pregnant woman walking by on her way to work noticed, but the smell was still only light, so she merely held her breath until she was past the unpleasantness and entered her place of work.

On the seventy-eighth floor, Atcho stared at the toolbox in disbelief. The timer had wound to zero, but he was still squatting over it. Nothing happened.

He stared over his shoulder at Klaus. "They won't be singing songs about you in Mecca." He coughed, surprised at the tautness of his voice. "Now we know. Your bombs don't work."

Klaus continued to grin, and Atcho stared at him in puzzlement.

"History is already written," the terrorist said. "You can't escape it."

Just then, a tremor vibrated through the floor and the huge plate-glass windows creaked. A roar sounded through the ventilation system. Moments later, smoke spilled through the air ducts.

Sitting against the wall, Klaus laughed uproariously. "You celebrated too soon."

Suddenly, he bounded to his feet. The security officers, distracted by the commotion, realized their immediate danger too late. Klaus connected a hard jab to the closest one's face and then, spinning around, brought his foot hard against the side of the second one's head. Both men went down.

Across the foyer, the third security officer reached for his gun. He was too late. In a flash, Klaus had crouched over his second victim, grabbed the man's pistol, and fired.

The security officer across the foyer dropped.

Klaus swung his weapon and fired again. Luciano fell to the floor.

"How things change," he called to Atcho. "I could have just let you die with me here, but I want to kill you myself. What a blessed day this is. Allah delivered you into my hands." Then, puzzled, he looked around for Atcho. "There's nowhere to hide," he said, and laughed.

Breathing heavily, Atcho crouched out of sight and considered his next move. When Klaus had turned to shoot Luciano, Atcho had scooped up the third security officer's weapon and dived behind a row of planters between the elevators and the Sky Lobby windows. He checked the magazine and then turned as the elevator doors from higher floors began to open, watching panicked people stream out and run to a second bank of elevators that would take them to lower levels. Many already held kerchiefs over their faces against increasing smoke. Atcho heard bits and pieces of their cries.

"An explosion in the basement..."

"They think a power junction blew..."

"Maybe a bomb?"

Then a cluster of people spotted the prone security officers and shouted for help to rescue them, then dragged them out of the crowd's path and tried to revive them. One of the rescuers screamed over the din upon discovering blood spilling from Luciano and the wounded security officer, adding to the pandemonium.

To Atcho's horror, there was a sharp *pop-pop-pop* as shots rang out. Klaus fired indiscriminately into the crowd in Atcho's direction to clear the field.

Atcho raised his head over the planters. Not able to spot Klaus, but seeing the wounded dropping, he understood Klaus' tactic. He leaped to a low crouch, aimed his weapon in Klaus' direction, and yelled at the crowd, "Get down. Get down. Get down."

Amid more screaming, the path in front of Atcho cleared, and he ran toward Klaus. The terrorist had stopped firing and was crouched against a wall, out of bullets.

He scanned the scene, defiance still plastered on his face as a crowd of angry people formed around him and closed in. Before Atcho could reach him, they bore down on him, fists flying and legs kicking. Klaus' pistol clattered across the floor.

Atcho waded in. When he broke through the crowd, the terrorist was lying in a pool of blood, battered but still conscious.

Atcho crouched beside him, grasped the front of his shirt, and leaned into the man's mangled face. "Where's my wife?"

Klaus opened his eyes, then gave Atcho a mocking grin and chuckled through blood bubbling between his teeth. "As you Americans love to say, the fat lady didn't sing yet." He raised his head and clutched Atcho's arm. "By now, your Sofia is on her way to hell. I hope she enjoys her farewell party."

Atcho cocked his fist back and plowed it into the center of Klaus' face. The back of the terrorist's head bounced off the marble floor and he lay still.

50

The long line of tenants, their employees, and clients plodded down the emergency stairs, descending into smoke-filled darkness. Two of the security officers manhandled a handcuffed Klaus between them. Behind them, gun in hand, Atcho followed, keeping close watch on Klaus as they descended.

Luciano had regained consciousness. Despite a wound to his chest just below the shoulder, he had insisted on staying in the Sky Lobby to assist and instruct people heading to the emergency exits. One of his men had applied first aid and stopped his bleeding.

The other wounded security officer had been less lucky, having sustained a shot to the head that had knocked him unconscious. So far, he was still out. Luciano had called for an emergency medical team and ordered his recovered men to join Atcho in escorting Klaus down to waiting authorities.

After reawakening, Klaus had at first been gleeful at the sight of throngs of infidels clambering down the poorly lit steps. Then, as minutes proceeded into hours and he realized that the North Tower would not topple, much less fall into its twin, he became morose. He mocked the rescue teams that passed them going up, laden with equipment, and brightened when, after two hours of descending stairs that sent pain shooting through even his very toned physique, he emerged with his captors to see the devastation wrought by Ramzi's bomb.

A squad of policemen closed around Atcho, the security officers, and Klaus as they followed the line of survivors through the dark and smoldering lobby at ground level and escorted them to a cordoned-off area.

A sedan and a dark van, both with flashing strobes, waited there. The front doors of the sedan opened. Burly stepped out on one side, Jim Dude on the other, and they came forward with solemn faces to meet Atcho.

"No news?" Atcho asked, anticipating the answer. Burly shook his head and put a hand on Atcho's shoulder.

"I'm sorry."

Klaus and his escorts continued past them. "What? No wife?" Klaus mocked.

Atcho ignored him.

Klaus suddenly and deliberately stopped. He turned and looked up at the Twin Towers looming above them. "Next time, we'll take them both down."

Jim Dude regarded him in disgust. With a nod of his head, five armed men emerged from the van and surrounded Klaus and his entourage. They wore jackets marked with "FBI" in big yellow letters. The police escort fell away, and the FBI agents hustled Klaus toward the van.

"I want a lawyer," Klaus jeered as he entered the vehicle. "Atcho assaulted me, and I was unarmed." He leaned back and guffawed as he was thrust into the interior. "I know my rights."

"Put him in a deep, dark hole," Atcho muttered to Dude.

Suddenly, a gunshot pierced the air. All eyes shifted to the van. Three of the agents lifted their hands in the air and backed away as Klaus appeared, wielding a pistol. He glanced about wildly, and his eyes met Atcho's.

A grin started to form across his face but ended abruptly as three more shots rang out and he was blown backwards by the force of bullets.

Atcho continued firing until his clip was empty. Then he walked over and looked down at Klaus while one of the FBI agents checked for a pulse. The agent looked up at Atcho and shook his head. "Lights out," he said.

Dude appeared at his shoulder. "Every agent and officer not involved here is out looking for your wife." His face fell. "I am so sorry..."

Atcho waved him away. "No time for that now." He looked around at the lines of ambulances, police cars, and fire engines, and then at the blackened base of the tower. "How many casualties?"

"Twenty-three dead so far, and scores wounded. We'll be searching for people through the night, maybe for days."

Atcho stared around again and started walking back toward the building. Burly followed him.

Atcho waved him away. "I need a few minutes alone."

Burly dropped back, and Atcho walked on, conscious of the thick coat of dust that covered everything; of the intermittent dark streaks of blood where people had lain, perhaps gasping out their last breaths; of the lethal glass shards strewn about; and of the flashing blue strobe lights all around him.

A stench invaded his senses: smoke, mixed with a sharp acidic odor and the smell of death. He heard the screaming of sirens, some waxing, some waning, as ambulances arrived and carried victims away.

Close to the building, rescue workers hurried in all directions, some bearing stretchers, others applying emergency care on the ground. Citizens helped citizens as more people emerged from the lobby, having labored down the staircases from the highest reaches.

Atcho continued walking toward the building, his mind and body weary. He stopped near the back end of an ambulance to see what was being done. Rescue workers carried a stretcher across the street, aided by dust-covered civilians. They struggled over the road surface made slippery by the thick dust.

Atcho sought to help but saw that the situation was handled and knew he would be in the way. He sat against a concrete planter on the side of the street and leaned his head back into the hedge, his mind descending into blankness.

A few feet away, the rescue volunteers continued to load the victim into the ambulance.

"Watch her hand," a female volunteer called to the others in a hoarse voice. "It's bleeding badly."

The volunteer's voice caught Atcho's attention. He raised his head and looked toward the ambulance. She was coated in dust, the color of her hair indistinguishable. Her clothes, too, were colorless, her shoulders hunched, and she moved as though in pain. She helped load the stretcher into the ambulance and then stepped back. When she did, she turned, and Atcho saw her face, her features obscured by matted dust and streaks of blood.

"We're good," she called to the drivers. "You can take her away."

That voice. Atcho marveled that the voice he knew so well came from this ghostly creature standing hunched in the street only a few yards from him.

He pushed himself upright and started toward her. "Sofia?" he called.

The woman did not hear him.

He tried again, still stumbling to close the few remaining feet. "Sofia?"

She turned and stood still, eyeing him as he continued toward her, ragged and dirty. Her lower jaw dropped, and her tired eyes widened and then filled with tears that streaked down her dust-covered cheeks. Then she flung her arms up and, ignoring the pain, hobbled over to meet him in an embrace.

EPILOGUE

"I'll always be haunted by the notion that I could have stopped the explosion," Sofia said. "I was right there. I could have pulled the fuses."

"You couldn't have known," Atcho replied gently. "You were beat up, you didn't know where you were, and you couldn't see through the smoke. If you had tried, you might have jostled one of those buckets of nitro and blown yourself up along with everyone else. Best to get that notion out of your head."

Sofia nodded absently and sipped her coffee.

"I'm just glad you made it," Atcho said.

Sofia nodded again, her mind still grappling with the surreal moments before the blast, now remembered only in bits and pieces. The acrid smoke had stirred her awake, and she sensed danger more than understood what it was. She was on the floor at the back of the van. Her survival instinct had kicked in, and she found the inside latch and grappled with it until it opened before she slid out onto the garage floor. Seeing an exit sign, she hobbled past it and then increased her speed as she remembered the nature of the danger. Reaching the street, she had just ducked down between some bushes and the outside wall when the explosion blew.

"I'll have survivor's guilt for years to come," she murmured.

They sat next to each other in a swing on the Montana ranch house's front porch, taking in the view. Two weeks had passed since the attack on the World Trade Center. Bob, Isabel, and Kattrina had stayed in Montana to be with the family while Sofia recovered.

"It's good the investigators found the van wreckage that first day," Atcho mused. "They managed to lift the VIN, and that led to the rental agency, so they caught one of the terrorists right away—a guy called Salameh. They must have been rough on him—he gave up information fast. Can you believe that idiot tried to get his rental deposit back? He claimed that the van had been stolen." Atcho gave a small laugh. "He needed the money to fly out of the country. I'd love to have seen his face when he walked out of the rental office and found himself surrounded by the FBI."

"He's the one who came after me in the workshop," Sofia growled. "He should be put away forever. If I ever get a chance at him..." She left the sentence unfinished. "At least they got enough information from him to catch the limo driver and stop the release of the bomb technician who was already in jail."

"How about the way that technician was able to help Ramzi?" Atcho said. "He would call one of Ramzi's men, who would conference Ramzi in and hang up. Then Ramzi could ask him whatever questions he wanted with no phone records tracing to him." He shook his head. "Unreal."

"And Ramzi got away," Sofia said glumly. "He was on an airplane out of New York City within a couple of hours." She snuggled Atcho. "I still can't believe I'm alive."

"I can't either." Atcho kissed her on the forehead. "You were in as bad of shape as the people you helped," he said reprovingly. "You should have gone to the hospital yourself."

"I'm resilient," Sofia replied with a small smile. "I heal fast. They needed the help more than I did." She sighed. "Any news on the wounded FBI agent?"

"I heard from Dude this morning," Atcho said. "The agent is back on his feet and expected to make a full recovery."

"What about the bomb? Any word on why it didn't detonate?"

Atcho chuckled. "Klaus modified the bomb to fit in the toolbox in order to get it through security. It was longer and narrower than the suitcase." He shook his head. "To do that required that he move some components closer to each other and others farther away. What he didn't know, because he wasn't a technician, is that amps required at each component would change. He sent enough electricity through the system for the test diodes to indicate positively, but not enough to set the reaction in motion. He outsmarted himself."

Sofia considered Atcho's words. "So otherwise, it would have been a viable bomb."

Atcho nodded. "We think so."

Sofia remained silent a moment. "What did they do with him?"

Atcho shook his head and pursed his lips. "A good guess is that he was dropped into a very deep ocean."

"And what about the remaining bombs? Do we know where they are?"

"No," Atcho said grimly. "At least two of them are out there loose somewhere."

Sofia gazed out across the serene landscape, then rose stiffly and limped to the front of the porch. There she watched Kattrina and Jameson making snowballs in the front yard.

Isabel emerged from the house and climbed down the stairs to play with the children. Atcho moved next to Sofia and put an arm around her waist while they both watched the peaceful scene.

"Maybe it's time we stopped this," Sofia said after a while.

"Stop what?" Atcho asked, genuinely puzzled. He took in his daughter at the bottom of the stairs, his granddaughter and son playing in the snow, and the mountains on the horizon far across the prairie. "I like what I'm seeing."

"You know what I mean," Sofia said with a slight edge to her voice. "You can't keep going out to save humanity. I need you at home. Your daughter needs peace of mind. Your granddaughter needs her grandfather, and Jameson needs his father."

"We all need you, too," Atcho groused. "Time for you to get serious about your gardening club." He was quiet for a moment. "Our kids can't grow up always believing in tooth fairies, and the bad guys won't quit because you and I are growing gray hair. When we're threatened, I'll meet it."

Sofia leaned her head against Atcho's shoulder and squeezed his arm.

Behind them, the front door closed, and Bob came to stand beside them. "Good speech," he told Atcho. "You're my hero." He laughed good-naturedly, slapped Atcho on the back, and headed down the porch stairs.

Sofia struggled down the stairs behind him. "You're right," she called over her shoulder to Atcho. "I'm with you."

"What do you mean?" Atcho called after her, a look of concern crossing his face.

Sofia waved him off.

"Bob, what did she mean?" Atcho called again.

Bob stopped on the stairs and turned toward Atcho.

"Think about it," he said, and chuckled. "She's your wife."

AFTER DUNKIRK
Book #1 in the After Dunkirk series

From the beaches of Dunkirk to the codebreakers of Bletchley Park, from Resistance bombings in the south of France to the machinations in the basements of MI-6.

Winston Churchill called it Britain's finest hour. The Royal Navy evacuated 330,000 soldiers from Dunkirk. But more than 200,000 were left behind.

On the beaches, Jeremy Littlefield hides for his life. His path home will draw him through the iron will and the unbreakable heart of the French Resistance.

Only a few miles away, his brother, Lance, rallies fellow soldiers to start a trek that will take them across Europe, sabotaging the Germans in a mission tantamount to suicide.

Back in England, their sister Claire works at Bletchley Park, cracking the codes that could save the lives of her brothers, and thousands of their comrades.

Finally, there is Paul, the cerebral eldest son, working for MI-6, who always knows more than he is able to tell his beloved siblings.

**Get your copy today at
severnriverbooks.com/series/after-dunkirk**

ACKNOWLEDGMENTS

I owe thanks to so many people who helped frame my books. In particular for this one, I must specifically express my gratitude to my stalwarts, John Shephard for keeping me on track, my sister Anita for reminding me to be sensitive, and my necessarily unnamed friend for paying attention to procedural and tactical detail. Beyond them are a host of people who contributed their insights. I am grateful to all of them.

ABOUT THE AUTHOR

Lee Jackson is the Wall Street Journal bestselling author of The Reluctant Assassin series and the After Dunkirk series. He graduated from West Point and is a former Infantry Officer of the US Army. Lee deployed to Iraq and Afghanistan, splitting 38 months between them as a senior intelligence supervisor for the Department of the Army. Lee lives and works with his wife in Texas, and his novels are enjoyed by readers around the world.

Sign up for Lee Jackson's newsletter at
severnriverbooks.com/authors/lee-jackson
LeeJackson@SevernRiverBooks.com

Printed in the United States
by Baker & Taylor Publisher Services